*So **this** was life on the edge.*

Rhys knew that a single call home could resolve their financial crisis, but logic wasn't governing his actions this evening. Looking at Trae, he held out their last coin. "This is it."

She smiled in approval. "Then we're in this together. How about showing this machine who's in charge?"

Rubbing the coin for good luck, Rhys dropped it in the slot. He didn't look at the symbols flash, focusing instead on Trae's hand on his arm until all at once, she released her grip with a squeal to the accompaniment of a million bells and whistles.

They turned toward each other, excitement overriding all other emotions. As she fell into his arms, Rhys understood that she merely meant to hug him, but between the thrill of winning—and her enticing scent—was it any wonder he wanted more than a simple embrace?

Dear Reader,

To this day I can't help but feel a certain thrill every time I hear the cry, "Road trip!" Maybe it's the challenge of it all, the setting off into the unknown, the call to adventure with its promise of fun and laughter. Caught up in the demands of our busy modern lives, when do we have time to escape so impulsively?

In *The Tycoon Meets His Match*, I'm offering the vicarious opportunity. Join Trae and Rhys as they set off on their cross-country journey. Along the way they'll hit snags, find surprises and experience how it feels to fall madly, deliriously, head over heels in love.

So buckle up and enjoy the ride.

Barbara Benedict

THE TYCOON MEETS HIS MATCH

BARBARA BENEDICT

SPECIAL EDITION

Published by Silhouette Books

America's Publisher of Contemporary Romance

SILHOUETTE BOOKS

ISBN-13: 978-0-373-24872-8
ISBN-10:   0-373-24872-5

THE TYCOON MEETS HIS MATCH

Books by Barbara Benedict

Silhouette Special Edition

Rings, Roses...and Romance #1104
Solution: Marriage #1392
The Tycoon Meets His Match #1872

BARBARA BENEDICT

Weaving a story has always been part of Barbara Benedict's life, from the days when her grandfather would gather the kids around his banjo to the nights of bedtime tales with her own children. For Barbara, starting a story should be like saying, "Come, enter a special new world with me."

Her 10 books and two novellas are set in varied places and time periods, but her heart is really in contemporary romance.

Prologue

It was a dark and stormy night…

Technically, it *was* a dark and stormy night, but if Teresa Andrelini hoped ever to be a published writer, she couldn't settle for such a cliché. Trae's professors, even her classmates, would insist she could come up with a better description.

The word *hokey* popped into her mind.

The "let's-make-a-vow" ceremony was Quinn's idea. Trae wouldn't put it past her drama-queen friend to have brokered a deal with the powers-that-be for the gale now howling outside their living-room window. Talk about atmosphere. Here they stood in this solemn circle, Trae and her three housemates, their faces shadowed behind flickering candles, trying not to flinch with each crash of thunder.

It was hard not to be impressed by everyone's grim determination. Well, by Quinn and Alana's determination, anyway. The way Lucie kept avoiding their gazes, Trae figured her poor roomie must be having trouble taking Quinn's oath.

Heiress Lucinda Beckwith believed in fairy-tale endings. If Lucie were the budding author, she'd write a romance and probably make oodles of money. Trae, though, had found that the guys who seemed to be the real-life charmers had a tendency to turn out to be jerks—the proverbial snake in Prince's clothing. Jo Kerrin's husband was a perfect example.

At the thought of their missing friend, Trae felt an uncomfortable pang. Jo would have loved the melodramatic hoopla of Quinn's ceremony, but she was now on her way to St. Louis to escape her so-called Prince Charming. Poor Jo had bought into the fairy-tale ending, and look what had happened to her.

"Earth to Trae."

Quinn's strained voice betrayed her impatience, but then they were all stretched tight after putting Jo on the bus that morning. Looking up to find Quinn frowning, Trae realized she'd been lost in her thoughts again, a habit that drove her roommate crazy.

"I said," Quinn tried again, "do you so swear?"

"Yes," Trae said in her loudest, clearest voice. "I won't get married until I've achieved my goal to be successfully published."

In actual truth, she'd already made the oath to herself years ago. Coming from an Italian father and five older brothers, she'd felt, early on, the need to establish her independence. Trae would *not* end up like her Cuban mama, an unpaid servant to the males in her life. If and when she hooked up with a man, *she'd* be the one in charge of her future. No male distraction was going to get in her way.

Satisfied with her answer, Quinn turned to Alana. "Do you, Alana Simms, swear not to wed until you've attained your goal of a successful career?"

Alana straightened her spine. "I swear," she said clearly, despite the soft purr of her Southern drawl. "No man will stop me from establishing my own modeling agency."

Trae didn't doubt her. With her black hair and classic beauty, Alana need only walk into a room to stop all male conversation, but she rarely dated. With her understated grace and her slender, gorgeous body, she could snag any modeling job she wanted, yet she was forever turning down lucrative offers to make modeling a full-time career. She only modeled the little bit that she did to pay the bills and learn the industry. She had every intention of putting the knowledge to use. Pity the fool who thought he could seduce Alana away from earning her business degree. Her features might have the delicate perfection of a Dresden figurine, but underneath that beautiful exterior was a core of pure steel.

"Okay, Lucie," Quinn announced, "that leaves you."

Seeing her friend's nervous expression, Trae offered an encouraging smile. Tiny, blond and seeming far younger than her twenty-two years, Lucie often relied on others to make up her mind. She'd become like the little sister Trae never had, and Trae often felt the need to protect her.

What Quinn didn't know—and what Trae had sworn not to reveal—was that Lucie was all but hitched to her parents' wealthy neighbor, Rhys Allen Paxton III, a man who, in Trae's opinion, acted more like Lucie's older brother than a lover. A strict, disapproving brother at that.

Talk about conflicted. Part of Trae felt a need to shield Lucie from Quinn's bullying, but a larger part, the one that knew Lucie's marrying Rhys Paxton would be a disastrous mistake, believed that if the oath should be mandatory for anyone, Lucie Beckwith was the gal.

"I swear," Lucie started hesitantly, letting the words trail off as she looked away.

"Swear what, Lucie?" Driven by her own ambitions, Quinn had little patience or understanding for anyone else's hesitation.

"I, uh, won't get married."

"Until?" Quinn prompted, tapping her foot. "What do you hope to accomplish?"

Good question. Lucie might have the funds and connections to achieve anything she wanted, yet here she was, nearing graduation, and she still had no idea what to do with the rest of her life.

Which made her doubly vulnerable to her Rhys Paxton arrangement.

"Well, I always wanted to be an actress," Lucie offered haltingly. "Remember, I got that A in drama class? How about I don't get married until I get my first movie role?"

Trae tried not to groan. Talk about reaching for the stars. As if Mitsy Beckwith would let her only child get anywhere near Hollywood. It was a miracle Lucie had even convinced her to let her go to college at Tulane—far away from their home in Connecticut.

Quinn didn't bat a lash. Either she accepted the answer as vintage Lucie, or she was too preoccupied with her own agenda to actually listen. "That leaves me," she said quickly. "And I won't marry until I've made partner in a law firm."

A loud clap of thunder rattled the walls, as if in answer to Quinn's pronouncement. Trae, Lucie and Alana shuddered, but Quinn faced them all squarely. "All those in agreement," she droned like a high priestess at some sacrificial offering, "shall now place their right hand in the circle."

With a solemn expression, Alana put her hand over Quinn's. Lucie gulped, then extended hers, forcing Trae, who still felt ridiculous chanting mumbo-jumbo in the dark, to stand alone outside the circle.

Reluctantly, she placed her hand on top of the others'.

As if they'd been struck by one of those accompanying lightning bolts, Trae could feel a current flowing between the women, filling her with warmth and a sense of belonging. Edifying her with a sense of commitment.

Never mind the melodramatic hoopla. This was what mattered. Them, here and now, joined in resolution, their grasp solid, their unity unbroken. Even with all the Beckwith money, you just couldn't buy a moment like this.

"When it comes to marriage," she chanted in unison with her friends, "just say no!"

Chapter One

Six years later...

They can't think I wanted to catch the bouquet, Trae thought with a frantic glance around her. The stupid thing had just landed in her lap. She wanted to toss the peach and white floral confection to the floor, but her Catholic upbringing wouldn't allow her to litter a church.

Not that anyone paid any attention to her. Each stunned face was focused on the door Lucie had just slammed behind her, the force of the sound still reverberating in the otherwise silent church.

She did it, Trae realized with a sudden sense of wonder. *Little Lucie Beckwith finally said no.*

No small feat, either, considering the three-ring circus her mother had assembled.

The picture-postcard chapel was filled to the brim with wealthy relatives, influential guests and a media army lining the walls. Clearly, Mitsy Beckwith had wanted her only child's wedding to be an event, *The Event,* talked about by everyone-who-has-ever-been-anyone for years to come.

Looked like Mitsy would get her wish. They'd be talking about this one forever.

Against her will, Trae's gaze went to the altar, where the groom still stood stiffly at attention. Rhys Allen Paxton III, owner of the Paxton Corporation, was accustomed to having everything go according to his plans. The epitome of tall, dark and handsome, his meticulously groomed appearance—as well as every other aspect of his life—was as well-ordered as a military parade.

Though if you asked Trae, he sure didn't seem so self-possessed at the moment. Maybe it was all that black—his hair, the tuxedo, the sleek Italian shoes—but all color seemed to have drained from his face.

As if sensing her gaze upon him, Rhys suddenly focused on Trae, his clear blue gaze probing her. Under his intense scrutiny, she felt like a butterfly pinned to the mat. "What?" she almost asked aloud, wondering if he was seeking her help.

But then she noticed the hostility animating his features. With a quick scowl, he sprang into action, leaping down the altar steps to go marching to the door.

It took Trae a few more beats to realize he was going after Lucie.

Sparing a quick "Be right back" for the still-speechless Quinn and Alana, Trae scrambled past her friends to the end of the pew. Lucie might have worked up some gumption at last, but she was a novice at this and she'd need support. No way was Trae giving Rhys any opportunity to bully her friend into a marriage she obviously didn't want.

As Trae hurried down the aisle, she saw that Hal and Mitsy Beckwith were close at her heels. If it was going to be three against one, Luce *really* needed her help.

Bursting out of the church, Trae squinted against the sudden bright sunlight as she searched for her friend, but the only remaining evidence of Lucie's exit was the blinking taillight on a sleek black limo, as it took a hard, fast left at the corner.

Mitsy Beckwith spoke the thought uppermost in everyone's mind. "She's gone." And then, as an afterthought, "I bet she's going home."

Luce, no, Trae thought. If her friend retreated to Mitsy's territory, she'd never get out alive.

Unfortunately, judging by Mitsy's pursed lips and narrowed eyes, Trae must have uttered the "no" aloud. "All her things are there," the woman articulated, as if dealing with an imbecile. "She'd never go anywhere without her ATM and credit cards."

She had a point there. Far too accustomed to the Beckwith resources, Lucie wouldn't know how to last five minutes without her money. As if recognizing this truth as well, both Hal and Rhys simultaneously dug in their pockets for car keys.

Watching the Beckwiths jump in their Lincoln and peel away, Trae felt a spurt of panic. She'd taken a taxi from the hotel and had no way to follow them. "I'm coming with you," she announced to Rhys. "To talk to her," she insisted, trailing behind as he strode to his black Mercedes. "Lucie will need someone to confide in."

"That would be me." Yanking open the door, he slid into his car.

Trae reached the passenger door just as he started the engine, but when she tugged on the handle, she found the door locked. Rhys, smiling grimly, seemed more than content to drive off without her.

"Let me in," she shouted through the window, giving him her "look." A girl didn't grow up in the Andrelini household without coming up with a way to let the males in her life know she meant business. Rhys merely narrowed his gaze as he shifted into Reverse.

Desperate, she dug in her purse and pulled out her cell phone. "She'll probably try to call me. If you leave me here, you'll never know what she said."

Though he said nothing, Trae heard the telltale click of the lock. Jamming her phone back in her purse, she yanked open the door and hopped inside. Rhys pulled away before she could completely close it.

Then again, he was smart to hurry. Everyone in the church had begun spilling out the doors, the press included.

Rhys didn't waste time with words, driving to the Beckwith house as if he were racing the Indy 500. Trae could have been invisible for all the attention he paid her, but watching him stomp on the clutch and jam the gearshift, she was just as happy to remain under his radar.

He did glance at her once—actually, he scowled at the bouquet clutched in her hands—but otherwise focused his gaze on the road ahead. Trae understood that she—not the peach-colored roses in her lap—prompted his irritation. Rhys never could disguise his disapproval of her.

"What did you say to Lucie?" he barked suddenly, downshifting adroitly as he rounded the corner.

"Me?"

He frowned, knowing she knew exactly who he meant, since there was no one else in the car to answer the question. Not willing to give an inch, Trae continued her pose of wounded confusion.

"You must have said something," he said curtly. "It's not like Lucie to be so impulsive."

"Oh, really? Have you forgotten Cancun?"

Apparently not, if his glare were anything to go by.

Cancun had been one of those spring break moments of insanity. Having had enough of the day-to-day grind at Tulane, they'd lit out for sun-drenched Mexico. Maybe it had been the wild college atmosphere, or maybe because Bobby Boudreaux, Lucie's on-again-off-again boyfriend, had joined them, but one minute Lucie had been quietly sipping margaritas and the next she was dancing on the table. Trae still didn't know how the fight had started, but in a blink, they were sitting in a Mexican prison, waiting for Rhys to bail them out.

"That wasn't my fault," she told him defiantly. "I didn't get us carted off to jail."

"And whose idea was it to go down there in the first place?"

"Why do you always…"

"With all the drinking and partying," he interrupted, "you didn't anticipate trouble?" Shaking his head in disgust, he skillfully rounded the corner on what seemed to be two wheels.

Trae felt compelled to protest. "Lucie is not a lost little lamb, you know. She's perfectly capable of making decisions for herself." She saw skepticism steal over his granitelike features, so she added, "When she's allowed to."

"And what's that supposed to mean?"

In Trae's opinion, the fact that Lucie had asked three distant relatives, and not her close friends, to be her bridesmaids made all the girl's choices suspect in the extreme. Including—no, *especially*—her decision to go against their Just-Say-No oath.

"You expect me to believe that this wedding was all her idea?" she asked.

The car jerked as he popped the clutch. "All I expect from you," he said tightly, regaining control of the vehicle, "is a little common courtesy. A true friend would back off and let us sort through what is so obviously a private matter."

The nerve of the guy. "On the contrary, a *true* friend would look out for Lucie's best interests. I've no intention of backing off until I'm certain she genuinely wants this marriage to take place."

He looked at her with disbelief. "We will be married, I assure you. There's nothing you can do to stop it."

"From the looks of it, Lucie stopped it just fine on her own," Trae ground out, unable to stop herself from making the dig. She was doubly determined to reach her friend first. She couldn't let Rhys turn sweet, fun-loving Lucie into the woman he thought he wanted—a perfect clone of her mother, a poised, self-possessed trophy wife he could trot out for public occasions.

It appeared he'd yet to grasp that every female has the will, skill and desire to make a scene and, given the right circumstances, even a control freak like Mitsy Beckwith was perfectly capable of coming apart at the seams.

The evidence of which greeted them as they pulled up the sloped, curving driveway of the Beckwith estate. Mitsy came charging at the car before Rhys could stop; her hands were pulling at her sculpted coiffure. Although her words were muffled, Trae was able to read her lips and make out, "She's not here. Do you hear me? She's not here. What do we do now?"

Judging by his continued silence, Trae had to assume Rhys had no ready answer.

Braking with caution, he took his time shutting off the ignition, and as he reached for the door handle, Trae could see a tiny tic beginning to spasm over his right eyebrow. For an instant, as he slowly emerged from the car, she almost felt sorry for him.

Until she got out of the Mercedes and found him as unflappable as ever, his hesitation vanishing as if it had never been. "We'll wait," he said firmly to the Beckwiths. "No doubt Lucie is driving around, gathering her thoughts. When she's ready to be logical again, she'll return with an explanation. Let's be calm when she arrives, okay?" Rhys looked from Hal to Mitsy, bypassing Trae entirely. "We don't want to do anything more to upset her."

"Upset *her?*" Misty exploded. "What about *me?* What am I supposed to do? The orchestra, the prime rib dinners, the melting ice sculptures…" She looked down the road with a horrified expression. "The guests! What if they come here? My God, the press!"

"Take it easy," Rhys said calmly. "It won't do any good to panic. Besides, I doubt the guests are going to come here for a wedding reception, considering there was no wedding."

He could have saved his breath.

"This is a nightmare," Mitsy barreled on, hysteria fueling her momentum. "People will talk. They'll snicker behind my back. I won't have it, do you hear me? Rhys," she said, grasping his arm with a wild look in her eyes, "you've got to do something."

"Do what?" He didn't raise his voice, but the words erupted out of him like a cannon blast. "Your daughter just left me stranded at the altar. What in the hell do you think *I* can do about anything?"

Mitsy blinked, visibly stunned. She was not alone in her shock. Clamping his jaw shut, Rhys acted as if his mouth had just betrayed him. It was the first time Trae had seen him even close to admitting he didn't have everything under control.

"I can call the police," Hal offered lamely.

Rhys shook his head. "Let's hold off calling the authorities. We don't want to get them or the press involved. Not yet, at least."

Typical, Trae thought. Poor Luce was out there wandering around helplessly, and he was worried about bad publicity? Disgusted with Rhys, with the lot of them, she thrust the bouquet in his hands. "Isn't there a phone in the limo?" she asked brusquely as she dug through her purse for her cell phone. "What's the number?"

Hal Beckwith searched his pockets, unearthing a business card with the company's information. It took two tries and several minutes on hold before Trae got the number for the phone in the limo. Dialing impatiently, she listened to it ring and ring.

After a few minutes of that, Rhys shook his head. Shoving the bouquet back in her hands, he grabbed her phone.

"Hey, gimme that." Trae reached for it, but Rhys held the phone against his ear, which, given their height difference, meant she had to jump like an overstimulated puppy to retrieve it.

Suddenly aware of how tall he was, how physically overwhelming, she instead waved the bouquet in his face. "You think you can do better?" she asked. "That Lucie will *sense* it's you calling and instantly pick up the phone?"

He eyed her as if she were a buzzing gnat—nothing to take seriously but incredibly annoying just the same. "I'm not phoning the limo," he announced curtly. "I'm dialing the dispatcher. All I need is their location."

Mitsy got a smug look on her face, as if she'd been the one to reach that particular conclusion. Trae endured her holier-than-thou attitude in silence, noting that the longer Rhys stayed on hold, the more Mitsy's smirk waned.

Then suddenly, Mitsy gasped. Following her panicked gaze down the road, Trae saw a car round the corner. With a burst of hope, she recognized the arriving vehicle as Quinn and Alana's rental. With their help, she still might get to Lucie first.

Yet even as she started toward them, Mitsy, who had the instincts of a bloodhound sniffing out trouble, cut across the lawn to reach her friends before her. Smiling graciously, Mitsy ushered Quinn and Alana into the house.

Hold on Luce, Trae mentally urged as she hurried behind them. *I'm on my way.*

Just remain calm, Rhys told himself firmly as he climbed the stairs to the family wing. *Go through the motions, act as if nothing is wrong. And never mind that half the world just watched you get publicly jilted.*

He should have put his foot down and insisted Mitsy limit the invitations. He'd wanted a quiet wedding, not a spectacle of five hundred-plus guests. Worse, Mitsy's need to dominate the social pages had drawn far too many media ghouls. Rhys suffered no illusions. The fact that he owned several publications wouldn't grant him immunity. This story would break in all the morning editions.

He glared at the cell phone in his hand. "Just give me something," he barked into it, despite still being on hold. Then he realized the battery had died. Frustrated, he bit his lip to keep himself under control. How like Trae not to keep her phone charged.

He knew it was useless to rant at dead air, but he hated the inaction, the not knowing. He had to get to Lucie, talk some sense into her. Hadn't they talked about this, both agreeing that their marriage was inevitable? Her parents expected it, everyone accepted it as a fait accompli. Today's ceremony should have been a mere formality, the punctuation point of a carefully constructed sentence—only Lucie had suddenly changed the words. Up until an hour ago, she'd agreed that this marriage would benefit them both immensely. What could have changed her mind?

But that was stupid; he knew what had happened. Her friends. More specifically, Trae Andrelini.

He'd seen Trae, of course, talking to Lucie at the back of the church. How could he miss her in that outfit? The sexy, lime suit, the patent leather stilettos, all that red hair. Of course she'd said something, he decided. Ever since the two friends had met at college, Trae had been the devil on Lucie's shoulder, forever coaxing her into trouble, yet never around when it came time to bail her out. That was *his* job—the mopping up, the covering over, all the king's men putting Lucie together again.

With a pang, Rhys pictured his fiancée, alone and frightened in some dingy bus depot, her rebellion running out of steam. He had to get to her. She'd expect it. Her family expected it. After all, when had Rhys Allen Paxton ever let her down?

Ah, Lucie, he thought in desperation. *Where the hell are you?*

"Rhys, you okay? I got here as fast as I could."

He turned to find his younger brother behind him, Jack's gold-blond hair and easy good looks so different from his own. "I'm fine," Rhys said more brusquely than he'd intended. To counteract this, he added a smile, but for once his brother didn't return it.

"Who am I kidding? This is useless," Rhys muttered, wanting to fling Trae's phone against the wall. "I'm wasting time. I don't suppose Lucie gave you any idea where she might be headed?"

"Me?" Jack shook his head. "I haven't a clue. Though, if you remember, I did try to warn you that you were making a mistake in pushing her into marriage."

Rhys bristled. "I didn't push her. And I don't make mistakes. I can't afford to."

"Whoa. Down, fella." Grinning, Jack held up his hands as if to ward off a charge. "You know how much you just sounded like the old man?"

An unfair comparison, Rhys thought irritably. If anything, he'd been the bridge between his father and brother. Jack had always called the man TA, as in Tight Ass, while their father maintained that Jack wouldn't know his head from a hole in the ground.

Which could be why Rhys, long accustomed to dismissing his brother's view of things, ignored Jack's vague warnings about Lucie.

Too, Rhys had been distracted by his latest acquisition, a company his father had tried for years to acquire. A major coup, but even were his father still alive to witness it, Rhys wouldn't get any pat on the back for his efforts. Not after the fiasco at the church. *Unacceptable,* was how the man would describe today's events. In the world according to Rhys II, once a goal was set, there was no excuse for not achieving it. In this situation, the goal had been marriage.

"So how do you plan to get her back?" Jack asked, as if Rhys needed the reminder that he didn't have a bride. "Not call the cops, I hope."

"No. This is something I need to deal with myself."

"Okay, then I'll hold down the fort while you're gone."

In truth, the thought of leaving his none-too-reliable brother in charge of the business filled Rhys with dread, which was why he'd asked Sam Beardsley, his father's right-hand man, to come out of retirement and oversee things while he was away on his honeymoon. Now it would be time away to win back his fiancée.

But the last thing Rhys wanted was for his brother to see his lack of faith in him, so, forcing a smile, he held out his hand. "Thanks, I'd appreciate that."

Jack beamed as they shook hands, until a sudden trill of female laughter from down the hall had him glancing over his shoulder. "I—I'd better go," he said, his attention obviously diverted. "Someone needs to calm down the Beckwiths—and anyone else who might have arrived."

Rhys knew Jack wasn't checking on the Beckwiths. His brother's ability to get distracted by the opposite sex was both legendary and inevitable, and a good reason why Rhys couldn't leave Paxton Corporation too long in his hands.

Shaking his head, he made his way to Lucie's bedroom. He wanted to change out of the tuxedo and his suitcases were there, since they'd planned to leave from the house for the airport. Then, too, he thought as he frowned down at the useless cell, Lucie had her own private phone line in her bedroom.

He went through the door, leaving it open, feeling claustrophobic amid all the pink. Thanks to Mitsy's decorating the room was a confection of chintz pillows, poofy curtains and fussy white lace, complete with an oversized, overdressed teddy bear perched on the canopied bed. All that was missing was the placard, *Rich Young Girl Sleeps Here.*

No wonder Lucie sometimes had a skewed grasp on reality. Even the phone was absurd, a plastic rendition of Cinderella's glass slipper. Who in their right mind talked into a shoe?

He did, apparently. Tossing Trae's dead cell phone on the bed, he reached for the slipper. He had calls to make, starting with his housekeeper in the Bahamas. Knowing how Rosa loved to pamper Lucie, he could picture the poor woman combing the grounds to find the gardenias Lucie adored. He could spare Rosa the extra work, if not the disappointment that Lucie wouldn't be coming.

"But Miss Lucie is on her way here," Rosa informed him. "She just called from the airport, telling us to expect her shortly."

He felt a surge of relief, knowing she was safe. Of course Lucie would go to the woman who acted more like a mother to her than her own mother did. Why rattle around on a bus when she could be spoiled rotten at his house in the islands?

At least now he knew she was within reach. With any luck, he might catch up with her at JFK and bring her back home before nightfall. At worst, even if she did fly off without him, he'd meet up with her on the island, where he could easily arrange a quiet ceremony in the local seaside chapel.

It didn't matter to Rhys where they got married, as long as they were wed by the end of the week. By then, of course, he'd need to be back in the office.

He smiled, happy to have a definite course of action. Within the next twenty-four hours, he would find his runaway bride and bring her back home as his wife.

Aware of the seconds ticking away, Trae raced down the hall, imagining Lucie's growing desperation. In Trae's mind, the fact that she hadn't come home, hadn't even *called* home, spoke volumes. Whatever might happen, Trae couldn't let Rhys get to her friend first.

Desperate to check her messages, she'd left Alana and Quinn with Mitsy to learn what they could while she went to retrieve her cell phone. Unable to find Rhys anywhere, she'd decided to use the private line in Lucie's bedroom, which meant no one else would pick up while she checked messages. *Let Luce have called,* she prayed silently as she approached the bedroom. *And make sure she says where she's going.*

Rounding the door, she came up short. To her shock, the room was already occupied.

His back to her, much too big, male and overpowering for his surroundings, Rhys began to bark into the phone. The receiver—the silly glass slipper Mitsy insisted went with the cotton-candy decor of the room—looked all the more fragile in his large, capable hands.

"…must follow her," he said briskly as he pulled at his tie. "I managed to change my booking to a four-thirty flight to Miami. Flight 213." He paused, shaking his head. "Yes,

I know she flew straight to the Bahamas, but there's not a single seat left on any flight tonight. Get my stuff to the Worldways terminal, at JFK, Bob Ledger's office. No, wait." He paused again, holding up his wrist as he checked his watch. "You won't have time. Just send everything to the boat. Bayside, slip 337. No seats out of Miami tonight, either. The boat's the quickest way."

He reached out to undo the cuffs of his shirt. "Make sure to send my briefcase. I've got papers to review before the meeting with Stanton, Inc. And I'll definitely need my BlackBerry. I've got to have a reliable phone."

He paused, scowling down at the cell phone on the bed. *My phone,* Trae thought, barely resisting the urge to barge in the room and snatch it up.

"Okay, yes," he continued impatiently. "Technically, I did promise Lucie I wouldn't work this week. But this isn't our honeymoon anymore, is it?"

Trae barely heard him, distracted by the man's ongoing striptease. At the moment, he was in the process of removing his shirt. Hard not to gawk at all that gleaming, taut and surprisingly tanned muscle. Who would have guessed the buttoned-up executive had been hiding such a magnificent body?

She wondered where a workaholic would achieve such a tan. And that physique. Even if Rhys did carve a niche into his schedule for the gym and tanning salon, surely the effort would require swim trunks and sweats. As far as Trae had seen, the man never wore anything but business attire.

Though it seemed she was about to get an eyeful of the real Rhys Paxton. As his hands went to his zipper, she backed away from the door, as appalled as she was embarrassed. Trae Andrelini was not a prude, but this was her best friend's almost-husband. She shouldn't be watching him undress, and she sure as hell shouldn't be getting turned on by him.

"Get started right away," Rhys finished abruptly. "I'm in a hurry. I've got to make that flight." He slammed down the phone with enough force to crack the slipper had it been made of glass instead of cleverly disguised acrylic.

Hurrying down the hall to find Quinn and Alana, Trae bristled with new determination. Damn Rhys Paxton and all his money and connections. Apparently, he knew exactly where Lucie had gone and he wasn't sharing.

Flight 213, he'd said, leaving at four-thirty for Miami. And after that, the Bayside Marina, slip 337.

Looked as though they were headed in the same direction.

"Trae?" Lucie Beckwith gripped the phone late that evening knowing she'd reached voice mail, but hoping her friend would somehow sense she was calling and miraculously pick up.

"You're probably busy cleaning up the mess but I'm sitting here on a stool watching these silly flamingos and I got to thinking that maybe I made a huge mistake."

No, that didn't come out right. "I mean, my mistake wasn't in saying no," she added promptly—or at least as promptly as three mai tais would allow. "I never should have come here to the Bahamas. Like Rhys wouldn't look for me here. He knows me so well. He'll guess in an instant I'd go right to Rosa to get her advice."

Twirling the little paper umbrella in her glass, Lucie frowned. Call her a coward but she wasn't ready to face Rhys yet. "He'll be so...so disappointed," she said, thinking aloud into the phone. "We made a deal."

At the time, it had seemed the perfect solution. Rhys

needed a Rhys IV and Lucie, well, as her mother constantly pointed out, having children would lend purpose to her otherwise aimless life. All evidence to the contrary, Lucie didn't enjoy being on the fast track to nowhere.

With her friends having careers and/or families to focus on, lately Lucie increasingly had to fight feeling left out. So when Rhys had suggested it might be time to tie the knot, she could see no reason to argue. Marriage was, after all, what she'd said she always wanted. Hadn't she always told him as much?

And she couldn't ask for a better friend, a more worthy champion. For every childhood problem, for every moment of teen angst, he'd been the shoulder she cried on. When she broke her arm falling off a horse her parents had forbidden her to ride, Rhys had gotten her to a doctor, made sure her parents never learned the true cause of her injury. When her date backed out of the senior prom at the last minute, Rhys had canceled his own important plans to escort her.

No doubt about it, Rhys was a wonderful man, a rock in the stormy seas she often made of her life, and lord knew any girl at the country club would take her place in a nanosecond. What more could she hope for when she had no real direction in her life? When she had no means of standing on her own, absolutely no experience in that arena? And when, sadly enough, no one had better claim to her affections….

And there stood Rhys, ready to provide everything a girl could ever dream of, promising the perpetuation of the pampered life her parents had laid out for her. All Lucie had to do was move out of one house and into another, the change of address entailing only one number.

All so easy. So perfect. So why was she sitting here on

a bar stool in the Bahamas, as far away from the groom as possible?

"I keep thinking about what you told me, Trae," she said into the bar's phone. "You know, about finding myself? You're right, I do deserve to know how it feels to be madly, deliriously, head-over-heels in love. I want that, Trae. I want it so much."

She had to stop, emotion bringing tears to her eyes and choking up her throat until she found it hard to speak. To remedy the condition, she took another sip of the mai tai.

As she did, she had a sudden mental picture of sitting on a similar bar stool in Cancun. Only then it had been margaritas and she hadn't been alone.

"Never mind," she said firmly into the receiver. "Forget I called. I just figured it out, all by myself, and I know what I have to do."

Draining the last of her drink, Lucie slid from the stool. "It's simple, really. I just have to go back in time to when life wasn't quite so complicated. Back to where I took my first wrong turn. And then I can figure out what the right direction is."

She sighed, feeling vastly relieved. "Wish me luck, Trae. I'm going to find B—"

Hearing a click, Lucie realized she must have used up the time Trae's cell phone allotted for messages.

Oh, well, no matter. Who had time for chatting, anyway? Life was waiting. Adventure was waiting.

Time to be moving on.

Chapter Two

Standing on the bridge of his yacht, Rhys struggled not to yawn. What a night. First, the snarl at the Throggs Neck Bridge, backing up traffic for over two hours then the thunderstorms, causing gate hold at JFK until after eleven. By the time he'd gotten out of Miami International airport and over to the marina, it had been the wee hours of the morning. No wonder he could barely keep his eyes open.

Yet as tiresome and frustrating as the night had been, he was now making good time. Barring any unforeseen difficulties, he should reach the island in a little over an hour, just as dawn was breaking. Quite symbolic, when he thought about it. What better time for him and Lucie to start their future together than the start of a fresh, new day.

Smiling, he pictured waking her gently. He'd give her all the time she needed, allay her fears, smooth away the doubts. And when he was done, he'd have them both headed in the same direction. The *right* direction—straight to St. Mary's Chapel.

All he had to do was remain positive. Envision success.

Feeling a sudden need for increased speed, he reached for the throttle. Turning dials and flipping switches, he set the course and put the controls on autopilot. He paused a moment, watching for problems, but the yacht plowed on, maintaining a steady course across the calm, placid ocean. Indeed, the only evidence of any disturbance was a sudden sharp growl from his stomach. In all the excitement, he now remembered, he hadn't eaten since yesterday's breakfast.

Maybe he'd head below, duck into the galley and make himself something to eat.

He made his way to the master cabin, carrying two suitcases he'd yet to take down, already planning his sandwich. Setting the luggage inside the cabin, he noticed that the closet doors stood slightly ajar. Orderly by nature, he went to close them. Might as well stow the bags inside while he was at it.

He strode to the closet with the bags, expecting a thud as he tossed them but instead heard a telltale "oomph." Flinging the doors wide, he discovered the source.

Trae Andrelini, clutching his carry-on, blinking the sleep from her startled eyes.

She'd removed her jacket, he noticed as she rose with surprising dignity to her feet. Large portions of her hair had tumbled free of its tightly wound knot, leaving the shiny dark-red strands to bounce on her nearly bare shoulders. Apparently, she was one of those women who were even more attractive in disarray.

"What the hell are you doing here?" he snapped, not liking his sudden strong urge to run his fingers through all that hair.

"You don't have to shout."

"Yes, I do. Otherwise, I'm liable to wring your neck."

She blushed, bringing a pleasant pink hue to her smoothly tanned features. "I'm sorry for stowing away. It's just that, well, I couldn't think of any other way to reach Lucie.".

She'd removed her shoes. Without her stiletto heels, her head barely reached his chin. Digging her painted red toenails into the deep pile of the carpet, she seemed so small, so vulnerable, so...

So devious, he reminded himself sternly. He should know better than to soften for an instant. He couldn't trust her. Hadn't he just caught her stowing away on his boat?

"Trespassing is a crime," he said, steeling himself against her wounded expression. "I should turn back to Miami right now and turn you into the authorities."

"Listen, I can explain."

"Please, do so." He stood back, crossing his arms at his chest as he frowned at her. "I can't wait to hear why you felt compelled to hide in my closet."

Frowning, she glanced around the cabin. "Do we have to do this here? This bedroom is hardly conducive to true confessions. Let's go up on deck."

His gut reaction was to refuse, to make sure he didn't concede anything to this woman, but following her gaze to the king-size bed, he had to agree that this was no place to conduct an interrogation.

She was blushing again, he saw when he turned back to her. Worse, he now noticed that the top two buttons of her blouse had come undone, revealing a froth of lace and incredible cleavage. Add that to the wild hair framing her heated face, and she could have just stepped out of the bed in question.

A prospect that caused a sudden, unwelcome spike in his pulse.

Sleep deprivation, he insisted to himself. The mind could do crazy things when exhausted, and nothing could be crazier than indulging in such a fantasy. He had to get them both out of this cabin. "Fine," he told her, marching to the door. "Let's talk in the galley then."

"But I don't want—"

"Frankly, I couldn't care less what you want." He paused in the doorway to glare at her. "I've had a long, trying day and my patience is virtually nonexistent. Either you come now and explain while I make a sandwich, or you can tell your tale to the authorities. Your choice."

Leaving her sputtering behind him, Rhys headed for the galley.

Trae would have loved to shout something defiant, had she been able to dream up anything worthy to say. The trouble was, she knew he had every right to be angry, and if the truth be known, a sandwich sounded pretty good to her right now. With a cold beer and maybe a dill pickle.

She could have told Rhys that her day had been no picnic, either. It hadn't been easy to convince Quinn and Alana that she should be the one to go after Lucie. They claimed she was too impulsive, too emotional and far too inclined to be unreasonable where Rhys Paxton was concerned. Only the fact that she had flight benefits—thanks to her brother's job at Worldways Airlines—tipped the scales in her favor. That and the fact that Vinny could get her on the 3:00 flight well ahead of Rhys's 4:20 departure.

In the end, Quinn and Alana had each chipped in a couple hundred to her travel fund, *after* Trae had promised to keep them informed of her progress every step of the way.

Which she might have done, since she had little else to do cramped in Rhys's dark, cedar-scented closet, but she no longer had her cell phone. All too vividly, she could picture it in Lucie's bedroom, a small, black stain on that cumulus cloud of a bed. In all the excitement of chasing after Lucie, she'd forgotten to go back for it.

If that weren't frustrating enough, she'd realized upon landing in Miami how hard it would be to actually locate Lucie. Thanks to Quinn and Alana—via Mitsy—she knew that Lucie had gone to the Paxton vacation home, but the Bahamas comprised hundreds of islands and she hadn't the slightest idea which one Lucie was on. Rhys could have no idea how much it galled her to rely on him to find her friend.

She shuddered, remembering his threat to call the police. She should have expected his cold, contained fury, she supposed, but then, she'd planned to sneak off the boat as surreptitiously as she'd slipped onto it. She'd never have guessed, on such a short trip, that Rhys would peek inside his closet.

Following him into the galley, she took in the khakis and dress shirt, rolled up to the sleeves, that he now wore. He had great forearms, tanned and powerful, tapering down to large, capable hands. You could tell a lot about a guy by his hands, she'd been told once, and ever since, she'd judged her dates by their grasp. Over the years, she'd found it an amazingly accurate gauge of character.

How would it feel to hold hands with this man? she couldn't help but wonder, watching Rhys duck his head as he entered the galley.

Not that she'd ever find out. Pointedly turning his back to her, Rhys stormed from cabinet to refrigerator and back to the table, opening and slamming doors in his search for sustenance. Trae knew she should be doubly intimidated by his display of temper, but the collection of meat, bread and fixings he'd amassed had her salivating. Her last "meal" had been the peanuts they'd served on the plane.

She nodded at the cold cuts. "Mind if I have some?"

He blinked at her, as if startled by her temerity. "Help yourself," he grumbled as he sat at the table and began constructing his sandwich. "Not like anyone can stop you from doing what you want, anyway."

Trae refrained from snapping back. The object was to get to Lucie, she told herself. Antagonizing the man would get her nowhere. Taking the chair opposite, she reached for the bread.

Unfortunately, Rhys, who had just finished slathering mustard on his two-inch creation, reached for his second slice at the same time.

They shared a startled glance at the unexpected contact, before retracting their hands simultaneously. The only difference being that Rhys came away with the bread. All Trae got was a vague impression of strength and warmth and a renewed—albeit unhealthy—curiosity about how it would feel to actually touch him.

Slapping the bread on top of his sandwich, he looked up with a scowl. "Okay, I'm in need of a good laugh. Let's hear your story."

Annoyed by her reaction to their contact—and his apparent indifference to it—she looked away, concentrating instead on building her own sandwich. "I have to find Lucie," she said as she slapped ham and cheese on her bread. "You and your boat happen to be my only hope."

Lifting his sandwich, he stopped halfway, his mouth open as he stared at her. "That's it? That's your explanation?"

"Would you prefer I made up something about being kidnapped by aliens?"

"What I'd prefer is that you answer my questions. For starters, how did you know I was coming to Miami? Or to the marina? Not to mention to this boat."

"I overheard you. When I went to Lucie's bedroom to use her phone." Hard not to cower as his sharp, blue gaze probed her. "Technically, it's your fault," she said with false bravado. "You stole my cell phone. What was I supposed to do?"

He shook his head in disbelief. "First you eavesdrop, then you trespass, and now you say I'm to blame for it all?"

"Not all of it. I admit I was wrong to hide on your boat." She bristled when he smiled in triumph, but she tamped down her temper, aware that any display of anger would only make matter worse. "I'm sorry, really I am, but how else could I hope to reach Lucie?"

Having taken a huge bite of his sandwich, he had to be content with glowering at her until he could swallow. "What makes you think you're *supposed* to reach Lucie?"

"We've been through this, Paxton." Even she could hear the irritation in her voice. "I have to find her," she added more calmly, leaning across the table. "I have to help her. It's the least I can do for my friend."

She watched his eyes widen. At first, she thought she'd impressed him with her resolve, until she realized his gaze was focused on her chest. Looking down, she saw her blouse had come unbuttoned.

Her cheeks now matching the color of her hair, she sat back and did her best to remedy the situation. "Lucie's my *best* friend," she continued vehemently as she buttoned. "I won't sit back and watch her get bullied."

"Bullied?"

"C'mon, Lucie obviously doesn't want to get married any more than I do. If you'd spend more time listening to her and less to her mother, you'd know that."

He bit off another chunk of the sandwich, chewing as he spoke. "And you've reached this conclusion how? Correct me if I'm wrong, but you two haven't spoken for six months."

Did the man know everything?

Before she could explain about busy lives and diverging paths, Rhys quickly added, "Except for your little tête-à-tête in the church. Just what did you say to her, anyway?"

"What makes you think it was something *I* said that made her run? Believe it or not, Lucie does have a mind of her own."

He shook his head firmly. "She might have her flighty moments, but she'd never run off like that. Not without encouragement, and certainly not there, in front of her parents and five hundred guests. I think even you would have to agree that it was an act that defied all logic and good sense."

"Not everything in life is determined by logic, you know," Trae countered angrily. "Sometimes, you have to go with your gut reaction. And in this case, Lucie's gut instincts told her to flee."

"Funny, though, how she didn't have any such instincts until you showed up."

How smug he seemed, calmly chewing his sandwich. How proprietary, as if he had sole knowledge of Lucie's inner emotions.

"Can you really be so sure you know what she's thinking, Paxton? Maybe she was just so afraid of how you'd react, she told you what she believed you wanted to hear."

That stopped him. But only for an instant. Narrowing

his gaze, he leaned closer. "Goes both ways, Trae. What makes you think you have the hotline to the real Lucie Beckwith? Don't tell me you knew she would bolt. I saw your face. You were as shocked as the rest of us when she raced out of that church."

He'd been watching *her?* "I was surprised, yes," she said primly, trying to control the flush now creeping up her neck. "But honestly, Rhys, it wasn't all that unexpected. It's not like she hasn't run out on you before."

He winced, and she suddenly wished she could take back the words. It was a low blow, bringing up the incident, but the man had a knack for getting her riled.

No doubt he blamed Trae for that defection, too, but Lucie swore to Trae that she'd come up with the idea on her own. She'd claimed she had a sudden urge to see London, but Trae knew how little she'd looked forward to her engagement party. "Rhys won't care," Lucie had told her blithely, suggesting Trae go to the party and see for herself. Sure enough, Rhys had smiled throughout, acting as if nothing were wrong, telling everyone that a bout with a minor virus had his fiancée confined to her bed.

But to this day, Trae regretted not flying off to England with her friend. The minute the party was over, Rhys had hopped the next flight to London, bringing Lucie back home a few days later with the huge rock still on her finger.

"The point is," Trae continued with a dismissive wave of her hand, "the poor girl is obviously confused. She needs to talk about this marriage. To someone other than yourself. The minute we reach that island…"

Cursing under his breath, Rhys glanced at his watch. "Damn, what am I doing?" Dropping what little remained of his sandwich, he rose and raced to the door.

"What's wrong?" Trae called out. "Where are you going?"

"The bridge. At this speed, we'll be slamming into the island in fifteen minutes."

Rhys stood at the wheel, watching the sky brighten above the approaching shoreline. Fortunately, he'd had ample time to slow the yacht down before they hit the island. Pulling the throttle again, he brought the engines to a crawl as they hit the harbor limits.

What had he been thinking, letting himself get so distracted? He must be more tired than he thought. How could he get so involved in Trae's incessant chatter that he'd put his boat—not to mention their lives—at risk?

Then again, had it merely been her chatter that had him so distracted?

Against his will, he recalled the sudden rush of desire as his hand had touched hers over the bread. He'd been caught off guard by how slender her hand had been, how soft and warm. Just like he'd been surprised by the unexpected view of her full white breasts, which had left him wondering if they were as soft and warm as her hands...

"Here."

Wheeling around, he found Trae behind him, holding two mugs. He hoped she didn't plan to make a habit of popping out at him from unexpected places while he was engrossed in his thoughts. Especially *those* thoughts.

Ignoring his frown, she smiled as she offered him one of the mugs. "I made coffee. I figured we both could use it."

He took the mug. As the rich, aromatic steam teased his nostrils, he could feel his anger dissipate. Trae was right, he decided after a long, reviving gulp. He did need it.

He did not, however, need her on his boat. Or interfering with Lucie. Studiously ignoring his unwanted passenger, he concentrated on bringing them into port.

"I thought of something while I was below," Trae said, oblivious to his displeasure. "In all the confusion, I had no time to grab my passport. Will there be trouble when we dock?"

"We'll be mooring at my place." Keeping one hand on the wheel, he gestured to the cove on the starboard side. "No one should question you there."

What he didn't bother to add was that while getting onto the island should be easy enough, getting off again might pose a problem. For her, anyway.

He had no intention of sticking around to find out. Once they docked, she was on her own.

Misinterpreting his smile, she returned it with one of her own. "This coffee sure hits the spot, doesn't it? I know I needed it. I took this pill for seasickness and it's got me feeling so groggy, I could have cotton balls jammed in my head. I guess it's made me a tad grumpy. I blurted out things I probably shouldn't have."

Man, the woman could talk. "Your point is?"

He saw the flash of anger, just for an instant, but she clamped down on it with an impressive exhibition of will. "My point is, I'm sorry. For getting in the way, for hiding in your closet, for everything."

"Everything?"

This time she wasn't quite as successful at hiding her temper. Green eyes flashing, she glared at him over the top of her coffee cup. "I'm not apologizing for wanting to help Lucie, if that's what you're asking."

"All I've ever asked is that you stop interfering in my life."

"I'm not…" Her hands tightened around the mug, but

with a sigh, she tried again. "Look, Paxton, I've said things and you've said things, some justified and some downright nasty. But right now, this is about Lucie. About her safety and future happiness. Can't we put aside our differences until we're sure she's all right?"

"Are you suggesting a truce?" he asked, incredulous. The woman barged in on his boat, berated and insulted him, and then expected his help in ruining his life?

"Yes," she said, beaming as she held out a hand.

Studiously ignoring it—as well as her question—he shut down the engines. "Hit that switch, will you?" he said, hoping to distract her. "We need to lower the anchor."

Gazing around them, hand still extended, she looked as if someone had just yanked the rug from beneath her feet. "We're stopping here? In the middle of the water? Not at the pier over there?"

"It's for smaller boats. If I take this yacht any closer to shore, she's likely to run aground. I generally use the skiff to get to the beach."

"Oh." Grinning sheepishly, she pulled the switch. "Don't mind me. I'm not very nautical."

No kidding, he thought, eyeing her fitted green skirt and bare feet. "It won't be easy climbing in and out of the skiff in that outfit," he told her. "Why don't you look through Lucie's bags? I took then down to the cabin earlier. Maybe you can find something more suitable. You can change down below while I finish docking."

"Good idea. Thanks."

He said nothing as she went below, knowing that in truth, he wasn't being helpful at all. While she was below, he planned to get the skiff in the water. If he hurried, he

could get to the island—and, more important, to Lucie—
before Trae realized he was gone.

It took less than five minutes to get the skiff in the water.
He was about to shove off when he heard Trae behind him.
"Oh, here you are. For a minute, I thought you'd left with-
out me."

Rhys saw no reason to grace that with an answer.

Besides, he was robbed of speech when he saw her new
outfit. Riding low on her hips and high on her thighs, the red
shorts showed off an alarming expanse of smooth, tanned
leg. The white T-shirt left even less to the imagination.

He didn't help her into the skiff, knowing better than to
risk coming in contact with all that exposed flesh. More to
the point, Trae didn't allow it. Dragging a suitcase behind
her, she stepped over the rail and dropped into the boat
before Rhys could recover his wits. "I figured Lucie might
want her things," she offered in explanation.

Cursing her soundly under his breath, he shoved off
and motored their way to the beach.

None too happily, either. Having Trae around changed
everything. How could he hope to talk Lucie out of what
was so clearly a case of cold feet with her so-called best
friend chattering in her other ear? That they'd eventually
get married wasn't in doubt—he and Lucie had talked
about and planned for this far too long—but Trae's inter-
ference could cause a lengthy and costly delay. Look at the
damage she'd done already.

Frowning, he thought about their engagement party.
Trust Trae to bring that up—he'd known for years that
she'd been behind Lucie's "impulsive whim" to visit
London. How like her to toss it in his face, as if he were
to blame for Lucie's erratic behavior. Mitsy Beckwith had

always maintained "that Andrelini person" was a bad influence on her daughter, and in this one thing, Rhys was in total agreement.

He had to get rid of her. For Lucie's sake, if not his own.

Trae sat on the other side of the skiff, also thinking about Lucie and how she was going to help her. That Rhys would do his best to stop her efforts, she didn't doubt for a second. Look at how he'd tried to sail off without her.

Not that she hadn't anticipated it. Figuring she had maybe five minutes while he moored the yacht, she'd grabbed the first clothes she could find. An unfortunate choice, it turned out, since she could scarcely breathe in Lucie's short shorts and T-shirt. There had been no time to change into something else, though, not if she hoped to get to the skiff first. Yet despite her rush, Rhys had still managed to get there before her.

Eyeing his house as they approached the shoreline, she felt her first misgivings. Rising up from the beach, the vast white colonial sprawled along the grassy knoll like a sleeping giant. A collection of structures in assorted pastels—each topped with a red–tiled roof—formed a maze around the main dwelling. So much for the simple vacation cottage she'd pictured. "Wow," she thought aloud. "It sure is…big."

"Some structures house the staff, but most are sheds and outbuildings."

Awed by the vastness of the place, Trae saw how it gave him a distinct advantage. It being his house and all, he'd know exactly where to find Lucie.

While Trae hadn't the slightest clue.

Hazarding a guess, she decided to try the main building.

To reach the wraparound porch ahead of him, though, she'd have to take off running the instant they reached the dock. With any luck she should have a step or two while Rhys had to stop and tie off the skiff.

Poised and ready to leap onto the dock, she was caught completely off guard when Rhys sped past the dock to run the boat up onto the beach. Yanking up the motor in a swift fluid motion, he leaped into the water and took off running.

"You just wrecked your five-hundred-dollar shoes," she called out as she scrambled after him.

Not that he seemed to care. With all his money, he probably had another hundred pairs waiting upstairs in a closet.

Watching Rhys reach the porch steps, she said goodbye to her last hope of outracing him to her friend. All she could do now was stand outside and yell. "Lucie," she shouted at the house, hoping her friend would hear her. "Lucie, come outside. We need to talk."

As if in answer, the door burst open, but it wasn't Lucie who collided with Rhys. A short, dark, middle-aged woman pulled up short, her alert gaze flashing between them. His housekeeper, Trae assumed, because of the black dress and white apron.

"I heard shouting," the woman said, looking from one to the other of them. "Is something the matter, Mr. Paxton?"

"No." His curt, clipped denial clearly surprised him as much as his housekeeper. "Everything's fine, Rosa. I'm just looking for Miss Beckwith. Is she upstairs?"

"She's not here, Mr. Paxton," Rosa said, a frown creasing her weathered features. "Didn't she call you? She left late last night."

Rhys turned back to glare at Trae, as if somehow this,

too, was her fault. Reining in his temper, he addressed his housekeeper again. "Did she say where she was going?"

Rosa shook her head. "All I know is she told my boy Raymond to take her to Miami in that old fishing boat of his."

"That's it? She said nothing else?"

Rosa shook her graying head. "Only that she was sorry. And that she left her wedding dress upstairs. She hoped you'd send it back to her mother."

Watching his shoulders sag, Trae might have felt sympathy had she not been struggling with her own disappointment. She hadn't realized how much she'd been counting on finding Lucie here, safe and sound.

Inhaling deeply, she approached the porch. "This changes things considerably," she told Rhys. "We can't waste time here. We need to hurry back to Miami and see if we can find her at the docks."

"You're right, of course," he said, running a harried hand through his hair. "Only, just so we're clear, there's no 'we' about this. I'm returning to Miami alone." Straightening, he started off for the skiff.

She grabbed his arm. "Whoa, wait a minute. You can't just leave me here."

"And why not? I'm under no obligation to transport a stowaway. Besides, you don't have a passport. You can't expect me to take the chance that I'll be stopped by the harbor patrol."

"That's low, Paxton. Even for you."

Shrugging, he removed her hand from his arm. "I've no doubt you'll manage to scheme your way off the island before too long. In the meantime, Rosa will make sure you have food and a place to sleep."

Watching him walk off, Trae felt the heat rise up in her

body. "What happened to working together? I thought we had a truce."

"Actually," he said over his shoulder, "if you'll remember, I never agreed to anything."

Thinking back, she realized he'd changed the subject by asking her to help drop the anchor. "Why, you…"

"Goodbye, Trae." He kept going, his long, steady strides getting him into the skiff well before she could reach the shore. Watching him motor off, she wanted to scream. She wanted to stomp and shake her fist in the air, but none of these things would help her one iota. "I thought you were a gentleman," she called out, anyway. "You didn't even leave me a change of clothing."

"Here." In answer, he tossed Lucie's suitcase in the water. "Only this time, try to find something that fits."

She could have told him that she was well aware of how ridiculous her outfit was. She could also flip him the gesture her brothers seemed so fond of, but knew she had better retrieve the suitcase before it sank.

"That man is the devil incarnate," she muttered under her breath as she dragged the bags to the porch.

"Oh, no, ma'am." Coming up behind her to take the suitcase, Rosa gently shook her head. "Here on the island, we consider Mr. Paxton a saint."

Inviting Trae inside while she made coffee, Rosa continued extolling the man's virtues. Her family would be homeless, she claimed, had Mr. Paxton not helped them after last year's hurricane. Not only had he provided them with cash, he'd come down there and helped rebuild their homes with his own bare hands.

Trae let her go on for a while because Rosa seemed sweet and it was only natural she'd feel compelled to defend her employer. Besides, Trae needed that second cup of coffee.

However, after fifteen minutes of listening to the woman drone on, not even the lure of caffeine could keep Trae in her chair. Actions spoke louder than words, after all, and that so-called saint had just stranded her on this island. Asking to use the phone, Trae decided it was high time she made her own plans to go after Lucie.

Upstairs, gazing at the huge four-poster bed, Trae realized she should have had the third cup of coffee, after all. Refusing to give in to the temptation to lie down, she made her calls.

Her first was to Quinn, who proved sympathetic after hearing about the night's events. Technically, a passport was required to get off the island, she said, but fishing boats made the trip from the Bahamas to the States every day. Her advice was to try to charter one and, if worse came to worst, to call her immediately. She had a connection in customs who owed her a favor.

Hanging up, wishing for the hundredth time that she still had her cell phone, Trae decided to check to see if Lucie had tried to call her.

She had four messages. The first had come in late last night—Quinn, demanding to know what was happening. Next was Alana, wishing her luck. Then her mother, reminding her not to miss next Sunday's family dinner. Rolling her eyes, she wondered how she could ever forget when the woman called twice each week with the same reminder.

On the fourth, she heard Lucie's soft, breathy voice. Clutching the phone as she tried to decipher the garbled message, Trae felt the first, faint stirring of hope. Surely it was a good thing that Lucie wasn't heading back to Rhys with her tail between her legs. That she was setting off on her own, determined to find a man she could madly, deliriously, head-over-heels love. The fact that said man wasn't Rhys, that Lucie was still running *away* from him, reinforced Trae's decision to help her.

When she replayed the message, though, her euphoria faded. What did Lucie mean, going back to where she had taken her first wrong turn? When had her life seemed less complicated?

And then with a sudden, sinking feeling, Trae knew Lucie was referring to her college days. And more specifically, to Bobby Boudreaux.

The ultimate bad boy, with his blond, surfer looks and slow, sexy drawl, Bobby was a far cry from the staid and proper Rhys Paxton. To a parent, Bobby might represent the ultimate nightmare, but for a young, sheltered coed like Lucie Beckwith, he'd been walking, talking excitement. For all Trae knew, Lucie might have stayed with him forever, if not for their brief stint in the Mexican jail.

Rhys had meant to leave Bobby there, Trae later learned. It wasn't until Lucie had promised never to see him again that Rhys secured his release. Lucie had kept their agreement, insisting Rhys knew what was best for her, but she'd never stopped regretting it. She'd been asking herself *what if?* ever since.

Faced with the prospect of Lucie's hooking up with Bobby Boudreaux again, Trae raced down the stairs two at a time. She had to get off this island immediately. Alone, vulnerable and naturally impetuous, her poor friend could land herself in a real fix this time.

Trae had to find Lucie before it was too late.

Chapter Three

Rhys glanced at his watch, then up at the gate sign, as if the departure time would miraculously change. Flight Delayed, it continued to flash, the same as the last hundred times he'd checked it. Apparently, they had gate hold at JFK again. Thunderstorms, the scourge of summer travel.

He counted slowly to ten, trying to control his frustration. This, after wasting two-and-a-half days in Miami searching—no, combing—the area near the docks and finding no sign of Lucie. Nor was she registered at any hotel, staying with friends, or, to his relief, making an unscheduled stop at any local hospital. She might as well have vanished off the face of the earth.

As his brother pointed out, Rhys was accomplishing nothing in Miami. He might as well return home to take care of business. Lucie was bound to run out of cash sooner or later, and she'd eventually call for help. Just like she always did.

Jack had carefully omitted all mention of the looming crisis at their Dallas subsidiary, another encouragement to race home. Rhys might have panicked, but, having had the foresight to ship his laptop to Miami, he was able to detect and correct the problem quickly by remote. He'd been working on his laptop while waiting for his flight, but due to his recent lack of sleep, his eyes were now dry and scratchy. Rubbing them briskly, he nearly missed the blur of dark-red hair dashing past.

He blinked hard, certain his weary eyes had to be deceiving him.

But no, it *was* Trae. Her hips were now adequately covered by a snug pair of black jeans, with a sedate green silk blouse draping her upper torso. She nonetheless managed to exude a sultry sexiness as she raced to the gate across the way.

Sitting up straight, Rhys checked the board for her destination. New Orleans. Departing at ten-fifty-five. Alert now, he watched Trae thrust a boarding pass at the waiting attendant, who ushered her into the tunnel before promptly shutting the door behind her.

Determined not to let her get the advantage, he jumped up and raced to the counter. Too late to get on that flight, but he meant to be on the next plane to New Orleans.

"Bobby? Nah, he ain't here."

Stifling a groan, Trae stared at Bobby's cousin, Beau Boudreaux. From his greasy brown hair and unshaven face, to the questionable stains on his jeans and gray sleeveless sweatshirt, he could be the poster child for Skid Row Inter-

national. At two in the morning, she found it no easy task
to decipher his soft, slurred speech from six feet away—
the minimum distance required to prevent his pawing her.
"Okay," she tried again. "Are you expecting him back any
time soon?"

Swaying slightly, Beau stared blankly, as if her words
couldn't quite penetrate his fog. "Who?"

"Bobby. Remember, I asked if I could see him?"

"Yeah. Yeah, right. Nah, you can't."

"What do you mean, I can't?"

"I mean he ain't here. And he ain't coming home for a
while. Went off to Hollywood. Back in May. No, April.
May. Yeah, May." He scratched his head, obviously con-
tinuing to debate, in his thoughts, the actual month of
Bobby's departure.

"Bobby's in California?"

"Yeah, making movies." He grinned, blatantly happy to
move on to a new topic. "Ain't that a hoot and a half? With
his looks and all, most folk hereabouts always thought
he'd be starring in pictures one day. Nobody guessed he'd
be making them instead."

He leaned forward, as if to impart an important secret.
Trae instinctively took a step backward.

"Film production, that's his thing now. My little cousin
has himself a backer, some guy with more money than he
knows what to do with, willing to bank money on his
genius. Out there on the coast, that's where y'all find
Bobby. Living the good life, mooching off some rich dude
up in Beverly Hills."

"I don't suppose you have an address?"

"Matter of fact, I sure do." Reaching behind his apartment door, Beau grinned as he pulled a ragged piece of

paper from a drawer. "Wrote it down to give to Aunt Livie. Says she wants to mail Bobby a birthday present, but 'tween you and me, I'm betting she's out to snoop. You know Aunt Livie."

Trae didn't, but saw no reason to prolong their conversation. Snatching the paper from Beau's none-too-steady hand, she stuffed it in her pocket. "I don't suppose he took anyone with him?" she asked, to distract him from noticing that she'd taken his paper.

Beau shook his head, the grin sliding into a leer. "Plenty of chicks wanted to go, though. Especially that blond that came looking for him a day or so back. Pretty little thing. Man, wouldn't I love to get a…"

"You said blond?"

With visible effort, Beau did his best to focus. "You… her…hey, y'all used to hang around with Bobby years ago. I remember you."

His leer deepened. Trae edged back another few steps.

"Hey, where ya going? Got a six-pack I'm willing to share. We can, uh, hash over old times."

"It's been a blast seeing you again, Beau, but I've got to run. Places to go, people to see. Flight to catch." This last was uttered over her shoulder as she hurried down the street. Behind her, she could hear Beau calling, first pleading then turning increasingly nasty as she rounded the corner and ducked out of sight.

Did he honestly think she'd step one foot inside that dive he and Bobby called an apartment? Hadn't her quest to find Lucie already been enough of an ordeal?

It had taken her over two days to get here from Rhys's estate. She'd been forced to wait for Rosa's grandson, Raymond, to return with his boat. Convincing him to turn around and go back to Florida had taken considerable patience and tact, not to mention a serious depletion of her funds. And then, once she got to Miami, she'd spent the rest of the time in bureaucratic hell while Quinn and her government contact straightened out the mess of her missing passport.

And now she had to grab a flight to California.

Hailing a cab, Trae fought off a growing uneasiness. Her funds—even with Quinn and Alana's supplement—were rapidly dwindling. She eyed the backpack she'd stuffed with Lucie's loosest clothes and necessary toiletries, and the three hundred dollars she'd found jammed in a pocket. She'd brought it along, figuring her friend would need the cash, but unless she found Lucie soon, Trae might have to use the money herself.

It would be a loan, used only in an emergency, but it wouldn't hurt to be prepared. Bad enough to imagine Lucie in New Orleans, a place they knew from their days at Tulane, but the prospect of her friend wandering around the streets of Hollywood was even worse.

And what about once she did find Lucie? Back when she'd started this search, Trae hadn't thought past the moment they would connect. How there would be two mouths to feed, two bodies needing shelter, two fares for the long journey home…

Then again, Rhys had been in the picture, she realized as the taxi sped to the airport. Rhys, who always took care of everything.

Entering the airport and walking to the gate, she found herself thinking about him, wondering where he was, what he was doing. Probably still spinning his wheels back in Miami, she thought with a grin. His stubbornness would never allow him to admit defeat. She wondered if he'd figured out yet what a mistake it had been to leave her behind, to underestimate her abilities. He would eventually, when she was the first to reach Lucie.

See how you like it then, Paxton, she thought. *Not fun, is it, being left in the dust?*

Watching her from the other side of the concourse, Rhys felt anything but dusty. On the contrary, he felt at the top of his game. All things considered, he could be pleased with his progress. Okay, maybe it had been sheer luck, spotting Trae on Bourbon Street last night, but the difference between success and failure lay in how a man played out his hand. With skill and decisiveness, he'd tailed her. Undetected, he might add, to the dingy apartment on Esplanade that somehow seemed familiar.

Granted, he'd heard little while she'd grilled the drunk at the door, but he'd been in the perfect position to overhear her instructions to the cab driver when she left. From there, it had been a snap to follow her to the airport, where he'd found her flopped in a seat, waiting on standby for a flight to Los Angeles.

Which still wouldn't take off for at least another hour.

A full hour in which he could be working, he thought in frustration. Hoping to maintain a low profile, knowing even a carry-on would slow him down, he'd opted to check his laptop with his luggage. All he had left was his BlackBerry. And the Times Picayune, which he held up to shield his face.

Peering over the top of the newspaper, he had to marvel at Trae's stamina. Most women he knew would have given up long ago, or gotten someone else to do the job for them.

But there Trae sat, in her tired green blouse and rumpled black jeans, her posture betraying her exhaustion as she continued to gut it out.

He was suddenly reminded of Mexico, when he'd escorted Lucie and her friends back to college. Refusing to be anywhere near him, Trae had sat across the concourse then, too. She'd claimed she didn't want any more lectures, but he suspected it had had more to do with her pride. She'd hated that she couldn't afford to pay the fine, that she had to rely on Rhys instead—as evidenced by the check he received five months later. Certainly Lucie had never repaid him, or that bum of a boyfriend, either.

And all at once, Rhys remembered how he knew the Esplanade address, having paid a small fortune to get Boudreaux out of jail.

Sitting up straight, he began to put it together. This changed everything. Clearly, Trae knew Lucie's whereabouts.

The question was, what to do next?

It wasn't as if *he* could become *her* stowaway. Most likely, he couldn't even follow Trae. With all the freeways branching out from LAX, all she had to do was hop in a cab. And there would go his only link to Lucie.

Not good.

Rhys resettled himself in the chair, thinking hard. Managing his father's company had taught him that the key to success often lay in an ability to recognize change, to adapt to it. When you hit a snag, sometimes you had to forge new partnerships. Not permanent ones, necessarily. Make it a brief alliance, make it last only long enough to get what you wanted. And what he wanted—no, needed—was to find Lucie and make sure she was okay.

Eyeing her over the paper, he decided that he and Trae would have a little chat.

Hours later, Trae shifted in her aisle seat, stirred from the strangest dream. She'd been in the jungle, with a bare-chested Rhys Paxton carrying her over a wide, swollen stream. It had been hot, August-in-Miami hot, and not just from the humidity. A considerable amount of the heat had been generated between them.

Half-awake, she could still feel the rush, the anticipation, the excitement as they'd gazed into each other's eyes. *"Trae,"* she could still imagine him whispering, his breath warm and soft on her cheek and the subtle scent of his aftershave lingering in the air. With a strange reluctance, she opened her eyes.

And there, mere inches from her face, was Rhys Paxton.

She popped up so quickly, she nearly clipped him on the chin. Seeming as startled as she felt, he straightened and took a step backward. "Sorry, didn't mean to wake you," he said stiffly. "But it's imperative that you and I talk."

Talk? Trying to shake off the effects of the dream, she stared at him. Nothing could be further from jungle attire than the charcoal-gray suit he now wore, with a cobalt-blue shirt and what was, for him, a rather dashing burgundy striped tie. With his freshly shaven face, he looked ready for the office. While she…

With what precious little sleep she'd gotten lately, she probably looked like death warmed over. "What are you doing here?" she snapped.

He wore a self-satisfied smirk as he took the vacant seat across the aisle. "Actually, I was about to ask you the same thing."

Trae struggled to regroup, her thoughts chasing themselves through her head. Clearly, he'd been following her but how…when…where…

"Miami," she thought aloud. "You must have been lying in wait for me there."

He seemed taken aback for a moment—no doubt astounded by her cleverness—but he recovered with a quick shake of the head. He leaned over the armrest. "All that should concern you is that I'm here and not about to go away. We have—" he paused to consult his watch "—approximately one hour and fifty minutes until we land. So, for the time being, you're not going anywhere, either."

The last vestiges of the dream evaporated with his brusque words. No matter how he'd gotten there, Rhys Paxton was planted a mere two feet away and she had to deal with him. "Okay, so what do you want?"

He ignored her less than gracious tone. "I've been thinking about what you said. A truce might be a good idea, after all."

"Ah, so *now* the man wants to make nice. This have anything to do with the fact that I have a viable lead and you've got nothing?"

That wiped the smirk off his face. "Keeping score isn't going to help either of us find Lucie. We can continue to fight, but if we really want to find her, we can increase our chances considerably if we pool our resources."

Trae shook her head. "No, thank you. I'm trying to save the girl, not deliver her to the Inquisition."

"And your idea of salvation is to leave her in the clutches of a lowlife like Boudreaux?"

Not good, Trae thought uneasily. Not good at all if Rhys knew about Bobby.

She clung to the hope that he wouldn't bother talking to her if he had all the pieces to the puzzle, or even any hope of collecting them in the near future. He thought he was so clever, but Trae could see right through him. He planned to use her, then spit her back out once he had what he wanted. "Here's my problem, Paxton. You're asking me to trust someone who just left me stranded in a foreign country without a passport."

"Okay, I admit that was low. But I'd had a rough day and wasn't thinking clearly. Now, however…"

"The only difference now is that I've got something you want."

He stared at her, frowning. She imagined he wasn't accustomed to people sassing him back.

"You're right," he said finally with a solemn nod.

She hadn't expected the admission. Oddly enough, it disarmed her.

Until he added, "But keep in mind that I have the funds and connections to prolong my search indefinitely. I think we both know that I'm not about to give up. I will find her, with or without your help."

"Is that a threat?"

With a shrug, he leaned back in his seat. "No, ma'am. Just a statement of fact. I can guarantee that I'll bring her home eventually. Can you say the same?"

"My, my, my. Aren't we cocky?"

"Not at all. I'm being realistic. We both know you'll run out of funds long before I do."

She thought of the three hundred dollars in the backpack. A comfortable cushion in the short term, but if this dragged on…

No, she'd worry about that when she had to. "Forget it.

Your proposal is all win-win for you, and lose-lose for me. Not to mention poor Lucie. I'm not offering up my best friend to a loveless marriage."

"Lucie and I have a steady, caring relationship," he protested, appearing insulted by her words. "You've always refused to acknowledge that, but you know it's true. I've been there for Lucie just as much as you have and if you don't believe me, you can ask her yourself once we find her. I'm confident you'll find she wants this marriage as much as I do."

"Yeah, and that's why she fled from the altar."

"She panicked. Who can blame her? All those strangers in the church, her mother nagging, her friends stuffing her head with pointless advice."

"Okay, Paxton," Trae said, having no wish to confess the part she may have played in Lucie's bolting. "Say I buy into your theory that Lucie panicked. It's been days. Isn't that enough time to come to her senses and head back home?"

"Mitsy just blew a damn fortune on that wedding. Would you want to face her any time soon?"

Good point. "Okay, but why hasn't she contacted *you?* You two having this steady, caring relationship and all."

His jaw was clenched so tight, it was a wonder he got the words out. "It's complicated. You wouldn't understand."

This time, Trae leaned across the aisle. "Try me."

He stared at her face for what seemed an aeon, as if taking her measure. "I know you want to paint me as the bad guy here, but I swear to you, all I want is to make sure she's okay. Once I can see that she's fine, you can talk to her all you want. Say whatever you want."

"Even if I talk her out of marrying you?"

He shrugged. "You're welcome to try. But right now,

you need me as much as I need you. It's vital we find Lucie before she ends up in serious trouble."

Gazing back at him, Trae found it hard to doubt his sincerity. Against her better judgment, she could feel herself soften. "This promise of yours. I want more than simply being allowed to talk to Lucie. I need to speak to her *first*."

"And why would I agree to this?"

"Because you're confident she wants this marriage as much as you. Really, Paxton, what do you have to lose by letting me talk to her first?"

He narrowed his gaze as if suspecting a trick, but nonetheless nodded and held out his hand. "Fine. Then we have a deal?"

She didn't know that she could trust him, but the more she thought about it, the more joining forces seemed the most practical solution. He had all the money, why not let him pay for the rental car, make him drive into the hills? All she'd have to do was go along for the ride, then whisk Lucie off to safety once they found her. "You don't go anywhere near Lucie until I've had my say?"

"You have my word."

She still wanted to argue, but really, what was the point? Reaching across the aisle, she clasped the hand he offered.

How could she have forgotten the jolt she got from touching this man?

No, not quite accurate to call it a jolt—more like a readjustment, her trying to get around the awareness that his grip could be rock solid, yet tender and warm and sincere at the same time.

If Trae truly believed she could judge a man's character by his hands, she had to believe in a man who could hold hers like that.

Even if the man was Rhys Paxton.

Disconcerted, she looked up to meet his eyes, and for an instant got lost in his gaze. She'd never realized how blue his eyes were, how honest and direct. Gazing into them, she flashed back to her dream and found herself feeling heated inside, almost breathless, almost…

Was she out of her mind? This was Rhys Paxton, the most arrogant man she had ever known and, none too co-incidentally, her best friend's fiancé.

That damned dream, she thought, yanking her hand out of his grasp and sitting back in her seat.

She made a shooing motion with her hands, anxious to have him gone. Watching him make his way to the front of the plane, she sighed in exasperation. Figured he'd be in first class.

Okay, he'd gained the advantage in this round, but she hoped, for his sake, he wasn't assuming he'd always get the best of her. Trae was taking nothing for granted, especially not his so-called word. He might not be as selfish and ruthless as she wanted to believe, but the Rhys Paxtons of this world almost always had their own agendas, and they rarely included standing aside for the Trae Andrelinis. She might have to work with the guy, but it didn't mean she had to trust him.

Stretched out in the plush leather seat, Rhys knew he should be resting but he felt too unsettled to sleep. He was worried about Lucie—where she was, what she was doing, what kind of mischief Boudreaux could get her into this time.

Contrary to what Trae implied, he *did* care about Lucie. How could Trae call it a loveless marriage? She'd made it sound like another business acquisition. Granted, maybe their relationship didn't have all the sizzle of a paperback romance, but he'd been looking out for her for years and couldn't imagine ever doing otherwise. Everyone knew Lucie couldn't ask for a more dependable or more devoted husband.

Yet…

The instant he'd touched Trae's soft, warm skin, something shifted in chest. Holding her hand in his, staring into her deep, emerald eyes, his sense of obligation moved ever so slightly away from Lucie and onto…

He shook his head. He owed Trae nothing more than his promise that she'd get to speak to Lucie first. So why, then, did he suddenly feel guilty about leaving her scrunched up in economy while he luxuriated in first?

This wasn't about anyone's comfort—he was here to find Lucie. And if he expected to do so, he had to concentrate on what lay ahead. The wise man—the winning man—always came prepared.

He'd arranged the rental car, convinced Trae—albeit reluctantly—to lead him to Lucie and had two seats reserved for the red-eye to JFK this evening. As long as the Worldways baggage handlers didn't go out on their threatened strike, he and Lucie would be home and back to business as usual by early tomorrow morning.

Smiling, he sat back in his seat. The ball was in his court again, just where he liked it.

Consulting the map in the glove compartment, Trae stifled a grin at Paxton's grumbling as she guided them out of the airport. Apparently there had been a mix-up and all the agency could offer was this tiny, well-used Neon. Bad enough not to travel in the style to which he as accustomed, but to make matters worse for him, the baggage handlers had misplaced his luggage.

Clearly poetic justice. Yes, Rhys might find it hard to survive without the abundance of suits and ties, but he had no right to complain about his laptop and PDA when he'd promised Lucie he wouldn't bring them. So much for his new bride being his first priority.

Luckily, Trae was good with directions, and once he'd stopped snapping at her long enough to listen, she had them speeding up the 405 to the Santa Monica Freeway. Looking out the window at the palm trees, she sighed. Nothing like a summer afternoon in Southern California. All that was missing was the Beach Boys wailing on the radio.

They followed Beau's directions up into the hills, pulling to a stop in front of an ultramodern collection of stucco and glass. Trae had to admit Beau was right. This time, Bobby had found himself a mega-wealthy benefactor to glom on to. Taking the long walk up to the mammoth double oak doors, she felt like poor Dorothy approaching the Great and Powerful Oz.

No fearsome wizard greeted them, though, just a young and very inebriated blonde in a skimpy yellow bikini. Giggling when they asked for Bobby, the girl shook her head. He wasn't there, she informed them, but they were more than welcome to join the party.

They heard someone shout, "Yo, Gigi," from out back, and with a squeal, the girl dashed off, a telltale splash sounding moments later.

Staring at the door she'd left open behind her, Rhys shook his head.

"Let's go." Trae stepped forward, only to realize Rhys was heading back to the car. "No, I mean, let's go join them."

"For crying out loud, do you ever think of anything *but* partying?"

Annoyed, she faced him with hands planted on her hips. "And do you ever look past the tip of your holier-than-thou nose?"

"I don't think…"

Trae was not about to be derailed. "For your information, I'm in no mood for partying, either, but a little mingling won't hurt us. Want to bet somebody in there knows where Bobby went, and whether or not he went there with Lucie?"

He frowned at the house, as if pained by the prospect of entering it.

"Well, if you've got anything better to try, you're welcome to get to it," she told him. "Me, I'm going inside to find Lucie."

Chapter Four

Shaking his head, Rhys watched Trae disappear into the house. Like it or not, she had a valid point. Their only real lead was Boudreaux, and their best bet at finding out where he went could be inside. With a little finesse, they just might gain valuable information.

Correction, *he* might. Rhys was not only experienced in negotiation, he'd honed the skill into an art form. Smiling grimly, he marched into the house after Trae, determined to show her how this should be done.

Inside, however, he suffered his first misgivings. Skillful negotiation required finding a common ground, but how was he going to find anything in common with these nouveau riche Hollywood types? From the ornate crystal in the huge chandelier, to the miles of polished chrome and glistening black marble, the house made a statement about its owner. *I just made a ton of money,* it all but screamed, *and I don't know what to do with it.*

And then there was…the backyard. Wrought-iron fences enclosed the tennis and basketball courts, their packed clay surfaces so perfect, they were either newly laid or rarely used. Surrounded by shrubbery, stone and splashing waterfalls, the pool looked like something out of a Tarzan movie, and the top-of-the-line outdoor kitchen was equally ostentatious. Any hope Rhys might have had of connecting with the owner disappeared once he saw the ten-foot naked statue of Adonis plopped in the middle of the lawn, with a dozen stone maidens gazing up at him adoringly.

In keeping with the theme, most of the guests were female, the average age being twenty. Barely clad, drinking Cristal Champagne from the bottle, they'd be at home at any party at the Playboy mansion.

Rhys made the rounds anyway, trying to strike up a productive conversation, feeling out of place in his sedate dark-gray suit. The women—no, girls—giggled at his questions, and the males stopped him before he could complete a sentence. They were here to "chill, man," not to talk business.

The more Rhys tried to picture Lucie in this place, the more he hoped she hadn't come here in the first place. If he felt out of his element, he could just imagine how lost she'd be among these champagne-guzzling groupies.

Trae, on the other hand, seemed quite at home. She had a crowd gathered around her, he noticed resentfully, all listening avidly as she made broad, sweeping gestures with her hands.

As the group erupted into laughter, he remembered Lucie telling him why she liked her former roommate so much. Trae was just plain fun, she'd said. Not in a who-cares-about-tomorrow way, but more as an everything-now-feels-better way. When Trae smiled, it was like the sun coming out after a long hibernation. Her laughter called to you, and you knew it was time to go outside and play.

Watching Trae charm her audience, he had to admit she had a certain Pied Piper ability. She sure seemed to be leading that horny young surfer by the nose. Was she joking? The kid had to be young enough to be…well, her younger brother.

Rhys wondered if she noticed the lust in the boy's eyes as he handed her a glass of champagne. Apparently not, for the next thing Rhys knew, Trae was tugging his hand, leading him out to a makeshift dance floor. The kid was pathetic, but Trae swayed with the sinuous grace of a serpent led by the snake charmer's flute. Holding her glass with one hand, resting the other on her hip as she undulated in perfect harmony to the Latin beat, she had her poor partner mesmerized.

Rhys as well, apparently. Realizing that he was gaping, he snapped out of his trance and stepped up to her. "That's enough," he said, taking the glass from her hand and dumping its contents on the ground.

"Someone sure woke up on the wrong side of the bed today." Still dancing, she leaned closer to the kid. "I think he might need a nap, Josh. He's getting kinda cranky."

"Forget him, Red. You keep dancing and I'll get you another glass."

Watching Josh scramble off, Rhys couldn't contain his irritation. "I thought the object was to find Lucie. Not get wasted."

"I had one glass. Maybe it's no big deal to you, but sipping Cristal Champagne happens to be a real treat for me. Know how often I get to drink that stuff on my budget?"

"And how can you resist the temptation when you have your boy toy to run and fetch it for you?"

She didn't seem to appreciate his sarcasm. "Jealous, Paxton?"

"No, I'm fed up. Stop playing spring break, and let's get out of here."

"Oh, really? And who died and left you boss?"

"You're making a scene," he told her, conscious of the many heads turning their way. "Let's go."

He reached for her arm, hoping to minimize any further unpleasantness, but before Trae could acquiesce—or, more likely, argue—they heard a shout from behind.

"Back off, dude," Josh cried out. "The lady's with me."

Coming up from behind, he shoved Rhys as if to move him out of the way, not realizing how close to the pool he was standing. Rhys had time to register this fact, and feel the ground disappear beneath him, before he landed in the water with a loud, painful *thwack*.

As he surfaced, gasping for breath, he heard a vigorous chorus of, "Banzai!" Within seconds, bodies began flying, flailing, hitting the pool like boulders from the sky.

Treading water in the resulting waves, Rhys glanced up to find Trae grinning down at him. "Sorry," she said, not looking contrite in the least safe and dry on the deck. "Here, let me help."

She leaned over and extended her hand. Rhys could have taken her offer of help and that would have been the end of it, but for some unknown reason, he had an inexplicable urge to give her hand a tug. He had an instant to acknowledge her stunned expression before she, too, dropped in the pool beside him with a resounding splash.

A little surprised himself by his action, Rhys reached

down to pull her up, treading water for both of them. As she broke the surface, he expected her to sputter and spit out every bad name in the book, but trust Trae to remain unpredictable. "Touché," she said, laughing as she flipped the hair off her face. "You know, Paxton, there might just be hope for you yet."

Her eyes actually twinkle, he thought in bemusement as he gazed down at her. Her entire face seemed to sparkle with laughter. How happy she seemed, how alive. He had a sudden strange urge to pull her closer yet.

"It's cold," she said suddenly, breaking away to swim to the side.

Funny, he thought as he watched Trae climb out of the pool—that was the warmest he'd felt in years.

Not that it lasted. By the time he reached the top step of the ladder, he could feel the chill in the afternoon breeze. He'd have to get out of his jacket, and he'd definitely have to lose the shoes. Second ruined pair this week, courtesy of that woman.

Trae was standing at a nearby table, holding out a towel. "Look at you." He took the towel from her and she reached for another. "You look like a drowned rat."

"And what do you suggest I do about it? I can't change. As you'll remember, my stuff is somewhere between here and Kansas."

"Oh, yeah, right."

Her gaze went to the pool, brightening when it settled on Josh. The way the girls around him were squealing, lord only knew what the kid's hands were doing under the water.

"Hey, Josh," Trae snapped her fingers in his direction. "Get up here. I need your help."

And just like that, Josh gave up playing lecher to hop

out of the pool. "Hey, doll," he said with a beaming grin as he sidled up to Trae, hormones surging, wet skin and all. "What's up?"

"I need you to help Rhys."

Josh's grin died at her request.

She looked from one to the other of them. "Okay, I guess you two have had a bit of a rocky start. Let's remedy that by starting all over. Josh Carino, I'd like you to meet Rhys Paxton. Rhys is from Connecticut. He owns and runs the Paxton Corporation. Josh is a student, Rhys. He'll be starting out as an art major at the University of Arizona this fall."

"Yeah, but me and my buds are all majoring in surfing this summer."

Josh chuckled at his own joke, but Trae was not to be sidetracked. "Rhys needs something dry to wear," she explained patiently. "C'mon, be a sport," she coaxed when Josh showed no signs of budging. "It's the least you can do after pushing him in."

Rhys watched the kid struggle with indecision until the need for Trae's approval won out. "For you, Red, only for you. Come upstairs, man, and we'll see what we can find you."

"You own this house?" Rhys asked, unable to believe this could be the "rich dude" they'd been looking for.

Josh made a face. "I'm in high school, man. Where would I get the money for a house like this? It's my old man's place."

His old man? Even better. Finally, someone who could provide useful information. "Where is your father?" Rhys asked brusquely. "I need to talk to him."

"What for?" Every freckle on Josh's face paled as he vehemently shook his head. "No way, dude, I'm not giving you his number. He'll freak if he hears I'm having a party while he's away. I'll get grounded for a month."

So much for appealing to a sane, responsible adult.

"Look, I'm sorry I pushed you in." The kid was reduced to pleading. "Forget my old man and I swear, you can have anything in my closet."

Rhys shuddered as he considered the probable wardrobe choices. Still, Trae was right, he couldn't go traipsing around looking like a drowned rat. "Fine, lead on," he told Josh, sparing a backward glance at Trae as they headed toward the house.

She was grinning. "Pick out something sexy," she called after them.

Rhys didn't bother to grace that one with an answer.

Not exactly sexy, Trae thought when Rhys later returned in baggy board shorts, a pale-blue Surfrider T-shirt and flip-flops, but somehow, the casual clothes seemed to soften him, make him more approachable. As if they could sit down and talk, and maybe even find something on which they could finally agree.

She flashed back to the moment he'd held her in the pool. He'd surprised her by pulling her in, then caught her doubly off guard by the strength with which he'd not only yanked her out of the water but kept them both afloat. Gazing into his intense blue eyes, she'd been struck by the uncomfortable possibility that there could be a good deal more to this man than she'd ever suspected.

Staring at him now as he walked up to her, she found herself wondering if the guy might indeed have some potential.

Until he opened his mouth.

"I feel ridiculous," he muttered under his breath. "Hook

me up with a surfboard and a Twinkie, and I, too, can get grounded for a month."

"Careful, he'll hear you." Dimpling at his words, she nodded behind her to where Josh was turning on the charm for a bevy of lovely young ladies. "Want him taking back his clothes?"

He scowled at Lucie's pink running suit. "You certainly look warm enough. How many outfits do you have stuffed in that backpack?"

Ignoring him, she held up the black plastic trash bag Josh had given her. "Here, put your damp stuff in this."

He started to put his suit in the bag, then hesitated.

"If you're reluctant to mix your stuff with mine, it's too late. I already put your jacket and shoes in first."

"No, that's not it," he said distractedly as he dug through the pockets of his pants. "I wanted to pay your pal for his clothes but I can't find my wallet." He dug in the bag, pulling out the jacket and searching it as well. "It's not in here."

"It has to be." *Men.* If she had a nickel for every time her brothers couldn't find something that was staring them in the face, she could die a rich woman. "Here, let me check," she said, grabbing the clothes from him.

But after turning every pocket inside out, she had to agree. "It's not here."

"Didn't I just say that?"

"Don't get smart. Go back upstairs and look around the room where you changed. It must be there. And just in case it's not, I'll check the pool."

"Who died and left *you* boss?"

Hearing him use her own taunt against her, she had a sudden, infantile urge to stick out her tongue. "Fine, *I'll* go upstairs then."

"I'm on it, okay?" he snapped, heading back into the house.

How like Paxton, she thought as she watched him head back to the house. Everything always had to be *his* decision.

"Hey, Red, wanna dance?"

Trae forced a smile as Josh ambled over to her. He was a cute kid, but too young, and way too blatantly on the prowl. "I'm busy looking for Rhys's wallet," she explained. "He lost it."

"So? Let *him* look for it." He hooked an arm around her shoulders. "C'mon, you and me should go have some fun. I don't get what you see in that guy, anyway."

"I don't see anything in him," she snapped, dodging free of his grasp. "I told you. We're working together to find my friend and until we do, I'm stuck with him. That's all there is to it."

"Yeah? So if I can tell you where she is, you'll ditch him and hook up with me?"

Trae felt a spurt of excitement. "You know where Lucie went?"

"Me? Nah, I just got home this morning. But my old man has these guys, Rico and Johnny. They look out for the place. They're cool. Never rat me out about my parties, as long as I slip them a hundred and clean up after. They see everything, if you know what I mean. Bet they'd know where your friend went."

"Let's go talk to them then."

Josh shook his head. "They won't talk to the guests. Not allowed."

Following his gaze to the back of the yard, Trae understood his hesitation. Two supersized gentlemen stood at attention, legs akimbo, watching the proceedings with stony expressions. At first glance, you might think they were Secret Service agents, but Trae knew they were a far cry from government issue. You didn't grow up in the neighborhoods of Brooklyn without recognizing the slick designer suits, the telltale bulges under the silk jacket lining. These guys were muscle, with a capital *M*.

All at once, Josh's last name took on new significance. "By any chance, is your father's name Lou? Did he move here from Brooklyn?"

"Yeah." He tilted his head, surprised by the question. "Why?"

She shrugged, half to appear nonchalant, half to shake off her growing uneasiness. "I once knew a guy who worked for him back in New York."

Ray DeLucca had not been one of her finer moments. In a spurt of independence, she'd tried to prove her family wrong by dating the neighborhood "wiseguy." Three months was all it had taken to recognize that her parents were right, that she had better ways to ruin her life. Last she heard, Ray was doing serious time up in Attica.

And now here was Lucie, hanging out with the same, dangerous people. How on earth had she ended up getting involved with the mob?

But that was obvious. Bobby, the mooch, who apparently saw only the ultimate cash cow, not the price you'd pay once you milked it.

"Your dad, where did he go?" she asked, silently hoping it wasn't Las Vegas. Lou had a casino there, she remembered from Ray, a place called the Snake Pit. She didn't enjoy imagining sweet, innocent Lucie anywhere near it.

"Dunno," Josh said with a shrug. "S'ppose I could ask Johnny and Rico."

"Do that. Please."

As Josh wandered off, she decided she had better look for the wallet before Rhys came back. Walking over to the pool, she peered into the shimmering blue water but could see nothing. She even asked two girls to dive down and double-check, but they merely confirmed her suspicion—the wallet was not in the pool.

She was searching the yard with less and less hope when Rhys stormed out of the house and marched right past her. "Any luck?" she asked as she fell into step beside him.

His dark expression said it all. "It's not in the house. It's not anywhere. Someone must have stolen it."

"Sure, Rhys. Because the people here clearly need the money," she said sarcastically.

He ignored her, grabbing the plastic bag with their clothing and reaching inside. He whipped out his Black-Berry with a grim expression. "I'm calling the police."

Conscious of the two thugs watching every movement in the yard, Trae put a hand on his arm. "Don't. Let's just get out of here."

Busy punching buttons, he looked at her, incredulous. "Now, you're suddenly in a hurry to leave?"

Glancing over her shoulder, Trae saw Josh headed back their way. Once he arrived with the information, they could go. Had to go, before Rhys said or did something to make a scene.

"This is useless," Rhys said angrily, tossing the cell phone into the bag. "The water must have shorted the circuits. I'm going inside to find a phone that doesn't leak."

"No," she said when he turned to go. "Let's just find a pay phone on the way."

He eyed her as if she'd just suggested standing on their heads. "Forget it. I'm not going anywhere without my wallet. I've got five major credit cards inside it. Not to mention my identification."

"You can replace credit cards. Your license, too."

He tilted his head to study her. "What's going on, Trae? Why this sudden urgency to leave?"

Uneasily, she looked back at the bodyguards, glaring like a pair of pit bulls from the rear corner of the yard. "I know about Josh's father from my old neighborhood. Let's just say he doesn't act like the polite folks you hang with in Connecticut."

"If you're trying to protect that kid so he doesn't get punished…"

"No, it's you I'm worried about. Trust me, you don't want to make a fuss here. Unless you want to replace your fancy wing tips with cement shoes."

"You can't be referring to the mob?" At her nod, he looked incredulous. "You're serious, aren't you? Jeez, Trae, we're all adults here. Well, most of us," he added, looking behind them at the girls still giggling in the pool. "I'm sure if I talk to this guy like a civilized…"

"No." Trae shuddered at the thought of Rhys pontificating at Lou, or worse, at Rico and Johnny. "You have no idea what you're dealing with. Unless I miss my guess, those two are packing."

He glanced over at Josh's bodyguards, his expression going taut.

"Besides," she went on, "if you bring the police here, Lou Carino won't be the only one facing public scrutiny. After the debacle at the church, do you really want to leave yourself open to more adverse publicity?"

"Lucie's more important than…"

"Yes, she is. So think about this. While you're busy pursuing justice, she's out there somewhere with Bobby. And given the mob connection, lord knows who else."

His jaw tightened. "Fine, you made your point. We'll go, but we stop at the first pay phone we come across."

Just then, Josh strolled up to join them. "Got it," he said to Trae, holding up a piece of paper. "Figured I'd forget what they said, so I wrote it all down for you."

Taking the paper from his hand, Trae stuffed it into her pocket. "Josh, you're an absolute prince."

He beamed, looking really pleased with himself. "So, this mean we can go now and have some fun?"

Trae shook her head. She wished she'd made this clear to him earlier. "I've got to go find Lucie, remember?"

"But you promised." Frowning, Josh reached for her arm.

Rhys stepped between them, glaring down at the boy with a menacing expression. "You heard the lady. We have to leave now. If we didn't, you and I would be sitting down and having a serious conversation about what might have happened to my wallet."

"I don't know what…"

"Funny thing, Josh, how it came up missing somewhere between when you pushed me in the pool and I changed in your room."

Eyeing Rico and Johnny, poised and ready to pounce, Trae sucked in a breath. Wasn't Rhys paying attention?

Josh looked equally incredulous. "You saying I stole your wallet?"

"He isn't accusing you of anything, Josh," Trae intervened. "He's just upset about not being able to find it."

"I'm standing right here, Trae. I'm more than capable

of explaining my own words, and I bet Josh is equally adept at understanding every single syllable."

"Uh, yeah. Whatever."

"If it turns up, call me at this number." Reaching into the bag, Rhys pulled a damp business card from his jacket pocket. It dangled limply in his hand as he held it out to the boy. "If I don't hear from you soon, I'll be calling your father to ask if *he* ever found it."

Going pale, Josh hastily took the card from his hand. "Hey, no need to drag Dad into this. I'll tear the house apart, if I have to. Okay?"

"Thank you." Nodding grimly, Rhys took Trae by the elbow. "Now if you'll excuse us, Red and I have to go."

Trae yanked free of his grasp, not at all pleased with the way Rhys was treating the boy. *Bully,* she wanted to shout at him as he marched off without her. And to think she'd been afraid of what these people would do to him.

"Sorry about that, Josh," she offered, turning back to their host. "It's no excuse, I know, but things haven't been going particularly well for Rhys lately."

"You know, Red, he doesn't deserve you."

"He doesn't have me."

"You sure about that?" He fixed her with a leveling gaze, surprisingly mature all of a sudden. "The way you guys look at each other, the way you fight…" He shrugged, then shook his head. "I don't know, you remind me of my parents."

Trae's gaze went to Rhys, now disappearing back through the mansion. Were they really behaving as if they were a couple?

Heaven forbid.

Shaking her head, Trae thanked Josh again before hurrying through the house to the waiting Neon. As she slid into her seat, she found Rhys drumming his fingers on the wheel. "I thought you were in a hurry," he growled as he ground the ignition.

"I thought it only fair to thank Josh for all his help. Especially after you accused him of stealing your wallet."

Yanking the gearshift, he jerked the convertible out into the street. "If the shoe fits…"

"We live in America, remember? Here a person has to be *proven* guilty. Ever stop to consider that maybe you just misplaced it?"

He glared at her. Glaring back, Trae realized they were doing it again, spatting like an old, married couple. Appalled, she turned to stare out the window.

This was ridiculous. Rhys was ridiculous. How could she expect this partnership to work?

"I'm sorry, okay?" he said suddenly. "I went off on the kid and I probably shouldn't have. Not without proof. It's just, well, it's been quite a week and I'm worried sick about Lucie. Now how the hell are we supposed to find her?"

Taking out the paper Josh had given her, she waved it before his face. "It's all right here. Thanks to Josh. And, of course, me."

"What is that?"

She yanked it back before he could grab it. Smoothing the paper on her lap, she tried to decipher Josh's scratchings. "I think it's directions," she told him. "To some film set. Hmm, maybe Bobby really is making a movie. Looks to be just outside of…"

She paused, staring at the map with growing consternation. "Uh-oh, it's Vegas."

"Okay, it's not my favorite place, either, but what's wrong with Las Vegas?"

"From what Josh said, there's a good chance his father went there. Knowing Bobby, he and Lucie are probably staying at Lou Carino's place. Trust me, even in that town, the Snake Pit Casino has a bad reputation."

He gave her a curt nod of agreement. "Yeah, I've heard of the place. You're right, we've got to hurry."

Eyes narrowing, he gripped the wheel with intense concentration as he fed the car more gas. Watching him weave through traffic like he was driving the autobahn, concern etched onto his face. Trae had to concede that he must really care about Lucie. Hard to fault the guy for that.

Which made it doubly hard to impart the next bit of bad news. "Uh, Rhys, you might want to pull over."

"What now? You leave something behind at that house?"

"No, worse. There's a cop behind us flashing his lights."

Chapter Five

"Great." Scowling, Rhys watched the policeman hop on his motorcycle and drive away. "This day just keeps getting better and better."

"Should you be driving?" Trae asked as he started up the car. "After all, you did just get a ticket for driving without a license."

As well as one for going over thirty miles over the limit. "Do I have a choice? We need to get back to the airport to see if my luggage has arrived."

"And you're the only driver? News flash, Paxton. I'm all grown up with my own license and everything. Let me drive the car and maybe you can avoid yet another ticket."

He must have made a face, given the speed with which she pounced. "What?" Are you afraid to ride with a woman behind the wheel?"

"Not at all."

"Good, then let's switch places," she said, popping out of the car and giving him no chance to argue.

He knew her offer made sense but he found the prospect alarming. Wasn't the battered Neon bad enough without Trae behind its wheel? But there she was, jiggling the driver's-side handle, and he knew he really couldn't afford getting another ticket.

It was only until they reached LAX, he tried to tell himself, though sitting quietly while Trae negotiated the congested L.A. traffic was difficult at best.

Especially when she insisted on thinking aloud. "You know, your losing your wallet changes everything. You can't fly without your license. To get to Vegas, we'll have to drive."

Six hours with Trae Andrelini in this cramped compact? "Stop at that gas station," he told her abruptly. "I need to use the pay phone."

"What now, Paxton? You need a booth so you can change into your tights and cape?"

"I wish. I have to call the office."

She shook her head, visibly annoyed. "Do you ever think of anything besides your precious business?"

"Actually, I'm calling my secretary to overnight my passport. Mary can also cancel any cards and arrange replacements. She can book us some rooms in Vegas while she's at it. I figure we can run a tab there until we locate Lucie, after which Mary can arrange our flights home."

"Yeah, don't want to leave anything to chance."

Though he bristled at her obvious sarcasm, he refused to rise to the bait. "Maybe you can get some food while I make my call. I'll meet you at the car in say…a half hour?"

"Shouldn't we synchronize our watches?"

From habit, he glanced at his wrist, finding only condensation on the face of his watch. "Yet another item to thank Josh for. A six-thousand-dollar timepiece that no longer works."

"Ask your secretary to overnight another one," she suggested oh-so-sweetly. "I bet you have a dozen more sitting in a drawer somewhere."

"Just go get the food, Trae. At the rate we're going, we won't get to Vegas before midnight."

"You haven't seen me drive," she said with a grin as she strolled off.

She was enjoying this, he thought with resentment as he watched her. While here he was, dressed like a bum and considerably poorer, dragging his wet, meager belongings around in a black plastic bag.

Shaking his head, he strode to the phone and dialed the operator, feeling ridiculous at reversing the charges. Nobody picked up. Concerned—what the hell was going on at his office?—he called his brother at home.

After his initial shock at getting a collect call, Jack gently pointed out the three-hour time difference between the West and East Coast. As Rhys explained his predicament, he heard giggles in the background. He should have known his brother would be entertaining. Stressing the urgency of his request, he got Jack to promise he'd call Mary the instant he hung up. To be safe, he made Jack write down—and repeat back to him—each task he'd needed done.

"Okay, big bro, I've got it. Report cards, book pads and overnight cash." The giggling sounded closer to the phone now, more breathless. "You go find Lucie and I'll take care of things on this end."

"Speaking of which, how are things at the office?"

Too late, Rhys realized he was talking to dead air, Jack

having rung off before Rhys could finish the question. He thought about calling him back, but that would mean calling collect again. And Jack being Jack, he probably wouldn't answer, being preoccupied with his guest.

Knowing there was little else he could do now, Rhys strode back to the car and waited for Trae.

She sashayed up nearly fifteen minutes later, carrying a single bag. Handing it to him without a word, she climbed into the driver's side and started the car.

"Where have you been?" he asked angrily, sliding into the passenger seat. "You've been gone all this time and this is all you have to show for it?"

She shrugged. "I don't have a lot of cash. I had to choose wisely."

Looking down at the collection of fruit and granola bars, it was all he could do not to roll his eyes. "And that took a half hour?"

She made a face. "Actually, it took twenty minutes. The rest of the time was spent watching television. According to the news, the baggage handlers went on strike, after all. Looks like you won't be getting your luggage any time soon."

Rhys groaned. "And there goes any hope of flying to Las Vegas."

"So we drive there. Relax, make yourself comfortable. How bad can it be?"

"How bad? I can't stretch my legs without making a dent in the dashboard or having my knees become permanently embedded in my chin."

"Okay, it's a touch short on leg room," she agreed. "And yeah, it shakes a bit over sixty-five and maybe the emergency brake seems iffy…"

"The emergency brake doesn't work?"

"…and the spare tire takes up most of the trunk. But look on the bright side. You don't have any luggage to put in there, anyway."

One look at his face must have convinced her to drop this train of thought. Pulling out of the gas station, she got them back on the freeway.

"Do you know where you're going?" Rhys finally felt compelled to ask. He could not, however, keep the doubt out of his tone.

She nodded. "I checked the map and from what I can see, the trick to getting around Southern California is a simple matter of following numbers. I take the 105 to the 605 to the 10. Then I hop on the 15 all the way to Vegas."

Rhys repeated the numbers to himself, committing them to memory. All well and good to know the route but knowing when to change freeways was more important. No offense, but he didn't trust Trae's concentration. He'd be watching to make sure she didn't get lost.

She looked over briefly, frowning as if she'd overheard his thoughts. "Really, Paxton, I've got everything under control. If you're tired, just slide the seat back and go to sleep."

"Fine." Turning away, Rhys decided he was just as happy not to speak. In fact, he'd prefer to pretend he was driving alone to Las Vegas.

Yet as the miles whizzed by, he couldn't quite manage to ignore her. Something about Trae's scent teased his senses. He kept trying to figure out what it was. Fruit or flowers, or something more woodsy? It drove him crazy. Worse, it kept drawing his gaze her way.

He noticed how her hair curled about her face like a soft, burgundy cloud. Every now and then, she'd reach up to tuck a strand behind her ear, giving him an uncluttered view of her profile. Surprised by how soft and smooth her skin was, how flawless, he kept fighting the urge to reach out and touch her face.

He could probably get away with it; she'd never see his hand coming. She kept her gaze on the road, concentrating hard, as if driving wasn't something that came naturally to her. He noticed she had a funny little habit of nibbling at her lips when she got tense, like every time she had to pass another car, or switch to a different freeway.

To his amazement, she made every turn correctly. By the time they reached the 15 freeway, he had to accept that she might be right. That she really did have a handle on this and he should relax.

Until he glanced at the speedometer and saw that they were cruising along at close to a hundred. "Think maybe you should slow down?"

She didn't bother looking at him. "This, from the king of highway safety. Just how many tickets did that cop give you?"

"No need to get snippy. I was just trying to help. If you'll notice, this vehicle is starting to shake. We don't want it coming apart at the seams."

"As I remember, the object was to get to Lucie as soon as we can."

"Yes, but the hope here is that we can do so in one piece."

Pursing her lips, she slowed the car down to ninety.

As the rattling subsided, Trae just about had it with his smug superiority. If Rhys made one more crack to her, she was liable to haul off and smack him upside the head.

"I don't get you, Paxton." Biting her lip, she realized she'd voiced her confusion aloud. He looked far from pleased, but, hey, might as well get all her beefs out in the open. "What exactly is your problem?"

"*My* problem?"

"Yeah. The way you march around looking down your nose at us lesser mortals. The way you treat every adversity as a personal affront and anyone in your way as a useless obstacle. So, yes, I repeat, what is your problem?"

He sat up straight. "Maybe *you* are. Ever since you started interfering in my life, it's been one disaster after another."

Oh, so now everything was her fault. "Disaster, Paxton? Aren't we melodramatic. Help me out here, just so I get this straight. Are you blaming *me* for your lost wallet? Or the ticket—excuse me, *tickets*—for speeding?"

He sat back, arms linked belligerently across his chest. "You know full well that I wouldn't be here right now if you'd minded your own business and left Lucie alone. Everything was proceeding according to plan until you came along."

"According to plan? Do you hear yourself? I bet that's why Lucie took off. Not because of anything I might have said."

"Oh, really. Care to enlighten me about that deduction?" He was doing it again, acting all cool and superior, making her feel like she should be squirming in her seat.

She decided to make him squirm instead. "Maybe Lucie doesn't want you meticulously plotting out every moment of her life. If you bothered to listen to her at all, you'd know she hates following schedules. She prefers spontaneity."

"Is that what you call your slapdash approach to life? Being spontaneous?"

"It's not slapdash." Not liking the defensive tone creeping into her voice, she sat up straighter. No squirming.

"You've had, what, three different jobs in the past six years?" Rhys went on, pressing his advantage. "Lucie insists your heart isn't really in teaching, that you dream of being a writer instead. If that's the case, why aren't you writing?"

"I am!"

"Oh, really? Where is your novel?"

Trae thought of the unfinished manuscripts saved on her laptop. As she often told her friends, it was a snap to start a book, but quite another story when it came to finishing one. What at first seemed like such a brilliant idea inevitably ran out of steam before the third chapter.

Not that she'd ever admit this to Rhys, though. "I'm on hiatus," she said primly.

He snorted. "I bet. All that hard work, how can you bear it?"

"What is that supposed to mean?"

He shrugged. "Maybe you're not cut out for it. Writing requires spending hours at a time alone in a chair. Let's face it, Trae. You don't have the self-discipline."

"I've got plenty of self-discipline," she protested, secretly acknowledging it wasn't her strongest suit. "Besides, even if I didn't, I more than make up for it with creativity."

"Really?" He couldn't sound more condescending. "If you ask me, I think you should fire your muse. She certainly isn't helping you get your book written."

She pursed her lips, angry enough to spit. "Who do you think you are, making cracks about my work habits? Nobody knows better than me how much hard work and dogged determination it takes to write a book. I get it done my own way, in my own time. If I had to plot my life to death like you do, it would kill any spark inside me."

"I don't plot my life to death."

"Yeah, right. Who couldn't even start off for Vegas without calling ahead? You had to call your 'people' and arrange for a hotel room."

"All necessary precautions. You expect me to fly by the seat of my pants?"

If she wasn't so angry, the thought of Paxton trying to "wing it" might make her laugh. "You wouldn't know how to improvise. You inherited a kazillion dollars. You've never had to get by on your wits alone."

"Trust me, I'd do just fine." He now had an edge of steel in his tone. "I didn't get where I am by being afraid of adversity."

"Of course not. Anything goes wrong, your daddy's money always bails you out."

"Money doesn't make the difference, planning does. Case in point, your own life. I bet many of your troubles could have been prevented had you exercised a little foresight."

Exercised foresight? Did anyone really talk that way? He sounded so self-satisfied, Trae wanted to sock him, square in the jaw.

But then she'd have to let go of the wheel, and besides, she wanted to be as calm and unruffled as he was. "I can see how planning can have its advantages," she said slowly. "And okay, maybe I could use more discipline in my life. But you, Mr. Happy Face, need to lighten up."

"I laugh. When there's anything the least bit humorous to laugh at."

Having seen little evidence of this, she ignored him. "You go ballistic at minor setbacks, like missing bags and traffic tickets. I can only imagine how you'd react if a real disaster struck. I bet you couldn't last five minutes without a meltdown."

"And I bet that once again, you don't know what you're talking about. I've proven capable of improvisation. I don't need my father's money to make a success of my life."

There he sat, so pleased to be left king of the universe. She wanted to prick that bubble of supreme self-confidence and make it blow up in his face. "Yeah, so how about putting your money where your mouth is?"

He paused, visibly backtracking. "Excuse me?"

"Back up your boast with a little cash. I bet you can't last until we find Lucie without your resources."

"Don't be ridiculous."

"Yeah, I can see why you'd hesitate. It's a daunting prospect to be cut off from your safety net. No more Paxton money, no more family and business connections. All you'd have is you and your wits. No wonder you're sitting there, quaking in your boots."

"For your information, they're flip-flops. And I'm hardly quaking."

"Then, in that case, you won't mind a little wager. Say we make it, I don't know, a hundred dollars?"

"A bit steep for a silly bet, isn't it?"

Of course it was, but she wanted to force him into backing down and conceding her point. "Pinching pennies now, Paxton?" she taunted. "Or are you chicken?" She turned to him, clucking.

"You're on," he said through gritted teeth. "Only make it double or nothing."

It was Trae's turn to pause. She'd been stretching her limits already; two hundred would just about break the bank.

Then, too, she had her friend to consider. If their finances ran out before they found Lucie, Trae couldn't risk her safety. She had to do everything in her power to win this bet quickly.

Especially considering the way Rhys now smirked, which left her no choice. "Fine," she told him, holding out her right hand. "Wanna shake on it?"

Though he seemed far from pleased about it, he clasped hands anyway.

Once again, his grasp was a solid one, startling her for a second time.

"Okay, then," she said, pulling her hand away, focusing once again on driving—and ignoring the goose bumps his touch gave her. Though she'd never admit it to Rhys, that was the trouble with being spontaneous. It sometimes led you places you should never go.

She risked another quick glance at him, sitting so stiff and straight on his side of the car. Probably plotting and planning how to make sure that he'd win the bet.

Poor boy, didn't he see that here, at least, she had the advantage? Of course she could outlast him. She'd lived her entire life on a limited budget. Rhys, on the other hand, had already shown he was lost without his money.

"So, just how much cash do you have on you?" she asked, rubbing it in.

He made a great show out of emptying his pockets. "Counting the change that I managed not to lose in the pay phone, I've got a grand total of four cents."

It was all she could do not to smile in triumph. A man like Rhys Paxton would hate taking money from her. She'd play her hand for all it was worth.

Although she wouldn't be playing for long, she realized uneasily. Her own financial situation teetered on the brink of ruin. She had a mere two hundred fifty for gas, food and their rooms for the night.

Looked like she'd have to hurry up and win that bet.

Rhys fumed silently on his side of the car. Watching her shapely foot—her shapely *lead* foot—on the gas pedal, he scoffed at Trae's accusations. Was she serious, calling him a spoiled brat, a stick-in-the-mud, an automaton with no heart and even less imagination? Couldn't she understand that someone in his position rarely had the luxury of spontaneity, most aspects of his life being governed by responsibility and duty?

Like his courtship with Lucie.

He felt another spurt of anger at Trae for putting such doubts in his head. Then again, maybe Lucie deserved some resentment for putting this whole crazy chase in motion. He'd been going along fine, his life comfortable and perfectly predictable, and now, thanks to his runaway bride, here he was in a world spinning out of control.

Trae seemed convinced that he was out of his element, unable to handle it. He had to show her that nothing could be further from the truth. Granted, he was unaccustomed to going without his money and resources, but he had maybe twenty-four more hours, at most, before they found Lucie and this ridiculous quest was over. He'd deserve Trae's scorn if he couldn't prove he could survive—no, prosper—without the advantages his wealth gave him.

And just why was it suddenly so important to prove himself to his woman?

It had nothing to do with Trae, he insisted to himself. She'd thrown down the gauntlet and what could he do? A Paxton never backed down from a challenge. Pride demanded he win the bet; it was as simple as that.

Up ahead, the glittering neon of Las Vegas lit up the dark desert sky. *Showtime,* he thought wryly. Trae wanted creativity? Well, maybe he could get inventive with their hotel reservation. Convince the desk clerk to find some nasty, little cubicle for Trae to sleep in. Something close to the elevator or right over the casino.

And she said he couldn't improvise.

Pleased with himself, he stole a glance at her. He found her concentrating fiercely on her driving, biting her lip again, seeming distracted, even worried. And just like that, aware that he'd caught her in a rare, openly vulnerable moment, his anger melted.

And suddenly when he looked at Trae, he saw a fiercely loyal friend, a complex flesh-and-blood person, a woman he couldn't help but admire.

Dangerous thoughts. Sitting up straight, leaning against the passenger door, he put as much space as possible between them in the tiny, cramped vehicle. Far more comfortable, far safer for his future plans, if he continued to brand her the enemy.

Note to self, he vowed silently, make sure to get her a room on the far opposite side of the building.

Chapter Six

"What do you mean, you can't find my reservation?"

Trae took in the mob behind them, lined up for their turn to register at the front desk. The place was a zoo. It had taken three swings around the parking garage to find a spot, and then they'd had to muscle their way up here to the lobby.

Shifting her backpack to her other shoulder, she waited for Rhys to lose it. Better yet, maybe he'd use his connections to get them a room. Not even a full hour, and she'd already win their bet.

"Fine," he said instead, forcing a tight smile. "Then give me two rooms in the tower, as near to the ground floor as possible."

The desk clerk, a cute brunette straight out of high school, stared at him blankly.

Trae felt compelled to intervene. "I'm thinking they

don't have any rooms in the tower. In fact, looking at this crowd, they probably don't have any rooms at all."

The desk clerk nodded solemnly.

"Maybe you can call around for us?" Rhys persisted. "There must be something in one of the other hotels."

"I've tried, sir. The Fourth of July weekend is coming up and a lot of people are in your situation. Those hotels that still have rooms post a three-night minimum. I don't suppose you'd be willing to stay an extra two days?"

Rhys turned to Trae, a question in his eyes. She didn't even bother to do the arithmetic. Even with what was left of Lucie's "loan," there was no way they could stretch their remaining cash to cover three nights. "We could always sleep in the car," she suggested, picturing him tucked in the fetal position in the rental.

She watched the tic start above his eyebrow, and waited for the explosion.

Again, he surprised her. "The thing is…" he paused, looking at the clerk's name tag "…Lisa. It's been a hell of a day. The airline lost my luggage, and then someone stole my wallet. I've had to drive all the way here from Los Angeles in borrowed clothes that don't fit, and now I'm told that someone's misplaced my reservation."

"I'm sorry, sir, but…"

"I'm not blaming you, Lisa." He flashed her the most charming smile Trae had ever seen. "None of this is your fault. But I have a crucial business meeting in the morning, and I need to shop for clothes before I can attend it. It wouldn't hurt to shower and shave, and I sure wouldn't mind getting some sleep. Isn't there *something* you can do for me?"

Trae noticed how he kept speaking in the singular, as if she weren't there. As if he thought his poor-little-me routine would spur more sympathy in Lisa if he were a single man traveling alone.

Then again, maybe he was right. With a sympathetic sigh, Lisa again consulted her computer.

"I really appreciate this," Rhys continued as she typed.

Nodding, Lisa pursed her lips, as if girding herself for action. "If you'll excuse me a minute." Opening the solid pine door behind her, she disappeared into the office.

"Slick, Paxton," Trae said grudgingly. "If it works."

"You were a big help. We can *sleep in the car?*"

She grinned up at him. "Thought that would get you. Which proves I *was* helpful. Look how I spurred you on."

To her surprise, he laughed. It did something nice for his face, she thought. He should try it more often.

"Let me guess," he said, shaking his head. "That was your creativity at work."

"Don't knock it until you try it."

"If you'll notice, I was both practical *and* inventive. I happen to think the crucial business meeting was a nice touch."

"Not bad."

"Thank you. And by the way, I never once mentioned that I'm on a first-name basis with the manager of this hotel."

Apparently, he didn't have to. Charging through the door with Lisa cowering at his heels, a man wearing a manager pin leaned over the desk to offer his hand. "Mr. Paxton," he said smoothly. "So nice to have you back with us."

With a what-can-you-do shrug for Trae, Rhys leaned forward to clasp the man's hand. "Chad, you're looking good."

And didn't Chad know it, preening as if he were the Don Juan of Nevada in his black Armani suit. His jet-black hair was designer styled, too, and he had one of those megawatt smiles you saw in Hollywood, teeth artistically capped and perfectly whitened. A smile, Trae suspected, he generally saved for the ladies.

Watching the man show off his dental work while Rhys engaged him in small talk, Trae couldn't help but compare the two. Chad might have a movie-star face, but if you asked her, Rhys was far more attractive.

As she realized where her thoughts were straying, she reined them back in. Rhys *was* attractive, no denying that, but the acknowledgment shouldn't cause a warm glow inside her. All other considerations aside, the man positively loathed her.

"But enough about me," Chad was saying in a conciliatory tone. "Lisa tells me we have a problem here. I can't imagine how this happened."

"Yes, well, I've been wondering about that myself."

Rhys eyed him like a stern parent, while Chad stared at the computer screen, hoping it would provide a much needed answer.

Or maybe he was hoping Rhys would give up and go away.

If so, Chad couldn't know him very well. Even in the short time they'd spent together, Trae recognized the tight jaw, the intensity in those steel-blue eyes. Outwardly, Rhys might seem cool and calm, but every last cell in his body was focused on getting what he wanted. And if she had to pick a winner between them, then *sorry, Chad, you don't stand a chance.*

As if recognizing this as well, Chad spoke in a subdued tone. "I'm sorry, Mr. Paxton, but someone else has your usual suite for the week."

"I don't need a suite. Just find me a room. And one for Ms. Andrelini, too."

Chad looked up—perked right up—the instant he realized Rhys was with a woman. "I heard you were getting married." Though he spoke to Rhys, he focused his attention on Trae. "Is this your fiancée?"

Trae felt intensely awkward, but Rhys acted as if showing up at a hotel with another female was the most natural thing in the world. "Didn't I introduce you? I'm sorry. Guess that just shows how beat I am. Chad Ryan, this is Trae Andrelini. Not my fiancée, by the way. She's a…a business associate."

Chad's smile turned smarmy, making Trae feel like she should be wearing a big, red *A* on her chest. She could see two choices here. She could make a stand, let Chad know what he could do with his insinuating glances, or she could play along and let him think whatever he wanted. The latter, she knew, had a better chance of getting them rooms for the night, not to mention making her two hundred dollars richer. Accustomed to special treatment, Rhys might not recognize the fact, but he was about to use one of his connections. Once Chad handed the room keys over to him, Trae would win their bet.

"Nice to meet you, Chad," she told him with her own megawatt smile. "I so-o-o appreciate your help. I can't tell you how badly I need a place to sleep."

The way Chad looked at her, you'd think they were alone on a desert island. "For you, ma'am, I'll definitely find something."

Next to her, Rhys smiled broadly. At first she thought he was pleased with her efforts, but then she realized he could be hoping to twist this into a personal victory, claiming *she'd* gotten the rooms—not him, using his connections.

Chad began punching buttons. "I'm afraid we're booked solid. All I have to offer is one room. A standard queen, out in the back building."

It took several beats before Trae, still preoccupied with who would really win the bet, realized the implications. The two of them, caged in a room together? The way they argued, they'd never survive the night.

Turning to Rhys to express this opinion, she had a sudden, vivid mental picture of climbing into that single queen bed with him.

"I don't…" she started to say, but Rhys, speaking at the same time, cut her off. "Can we at least get a cot?"

"Certainly." Chad's oily tone implied that he didn't believe for a second that they'd actually use it. Looking from the unruffled Rhys to Trae's heated face, Chad grinned broadly. "So you'll be wanting the room, then?"

Rhys turned to Trae. "What do you think?"

In truth, she couldn't think at all. Not with him staring at her like that and her mind spinning around the fact that she'd be alone with him all night. Absurd to get so rattled by it, especially after spending hours in a car in far closer proximity, but the prospect of falling asleep with this man not ten feet away made her insides turn to jelly.

"Thanks, we'll take it," Rhys said at last, turning to Chad and Lisa. "Just tell me where to sign."

"Lisa, why don't you help Mr. Paxton get registered while I make sure the room is ready for check-in. It will only be a few minutes."

Watching him fill out the form, Trae noticed he knew the license number of the rental. Had a head for facts, that Rhys Paxton. In some ways, he might actually be handy to have around.

Not that she wanted him around, she quickly amended.

When he was done, he reached into his back pocket. "That's right," he said distractedly. "No wallet."

"It's okay," Lisa said brightly. "We can bill your office."

Yes! Trae thought with a spurt of excitement. Then there would be no doubt that she'd won the bet.

"Uh, no, thanks. I'll pay cash."

Lisa wore a puzzled expression, as if wondering where he'd get the money if his wallet was stolen. Answering her unspoken question, Rhys turned to Trae, impatiently holding out his hand.

So much for her theory that he'd be too proud to take money from a woman. "How much?" she asked, not bothering to mask her irritation.

"Two twenty-one."

It was all Trae could do to keep her eyes from bugging out of her head. Carefully counting out the bills, she wondered how on earth they were going to eat.

Leading her off with a grim smile, Rhys took the backpack off Trae's shoulders and carried it for her. Weaving through the maze of the casino, he found a door to the back of the property. Once outside, though, they became hopelessly lost. He knew his way around the tower, Rhys admitted after they'd gone in and out of the casino twice, but until tonight, he hadn't even guessed that a back building existed.

Asking directions, they discovered why they couldn't find their room. The back building stood off by itself, hidden behind the pool area, fronting the alley. Normally, the hotel didn't rent the room, they were told. The manager used it for nights he worked late.

Icing on the cake, Trae thought. Stuck for the night in

Chad's cozy little love nest with Rhys Paxton. How was she ever going to get through this night?

When they finally located the room, they found the maid hadn't left yet. From the sound of her voice, mumbling fiercely in Spanish, the "preparing for guests" involved a good deal more than changing the sheets.

"Let's wait by the pool," Rhys said, gesturing to some tables just inside the gate. "It should be more comfortable than hanging out here."

Inside the gate, Trae went straight for the first table, but before she could sit, Rhys stepped up to pull out the chair for her. Again, he did it so effortlessly, so seamlessly, she could tell that this was how he acted with every female, yet somehow he still managed to make her feel special.

As she sat, he grabbed the arms of her chair and slid it into the table. Momentarily held captive, Trae was intensely aware of his warmth behind her, the controlled power in the arms surrounding her own. She kept seeing him as he'd been in Lucie's bedroom, slowly stripping off his shirt, and she had the sudden, inexplicable urge to lean back into the solid warmth of his chest.

"While we're waiting," he said into her ear, "we can work out our strategy for finding Lucie."

Appalled to be caught fantasizing while he was formulating their daily schedule, she couldn't keep the irritation out of her tone. "Give it a rest, Paxton. It's got to be after twelve and we're both dead tired. Besides, nobody will be on location this late."

"I know." Moving away, he sat in the chair next to hers. "I meant tomorrow. We should get to the site by daybreak. We don't want to take the chance of missing them again." Leaning forward, he was a daunting few inches away from her face. "Here, let me look at those directions," he said, holding out his hand.

And there it was, the excuse she needed to slide back her chair. "Yeah, right, I hand them over now, and when I wake in the morning, bingo! No more Rhys Paxton."

"Where would I go?" Sitting straight, he looked surprised, maybe even hurt. "You're the one with the car keys. Not to mention the money."

"Which reminds me. Where's my two hundred dollars?"

He looked at her as if she'd just spoken in Russian.

"The bet, Paxton. You lost. You used your connections to get us a room."

He shook his head as if he were disappointed in her. "No, I was careful about that. If you'll remember, Chad offered me nothing until I introduced you."

"Oh, come on. You can't seriously expect me to believe you set it up that way."

"Didn't have to. *'For you, ma'am, I'll definitely find something,'*" Rhys mimicked, sounding eerily like Chad. "Let's face it, Trae. Your flirting got us the room. Poor Chad never could resist a pretty face."

"So, you're content to skate by on a mere technicality?"

He shrugged, looking far too pleased with himself. "Whatever it takes to win. Trust me, if I'd used my influence, we wouldn't be out two-hundred-plus dollars. We wouldn't have paid a cent at all."

Glancing back over his shoulder, he shook his head with a rueful grin. "Besides, let's not credit anyone with a victory yet. We haven't seen this room."

Good point, and even more valid when they finally entered it fifteen minutes later. Trae gaped as her suspicions about Chad's use for it were confirmed. From the red satin quilt to the subdued lighting and half-dozen mirrors strategically placed on the ceiling and walls, the place screamed out male fantasy. All that was missing was the low, seductive music. Not that she'd put it past Chad to have a stereo socked away somewhere.

"Ouch," Rhys said as he eyed the bed. "Almost makes me grateful I'll be spending the night on a cot."

She knew he was trying to be the gentleman again. "Don't be ridiculous, you won't fit. I'll take the rollaway. If they ever deliver it."

He shook his head. "You did all the driving. You paid for the room. It's only fair you get the bed."

Annoyed by his stubbornness, Trae crossed the room and flopped down to stretch out on the soft, red satin. "Hmm, not bad. I could curl up and go to sleep right now."

She glanced up, her smile meant to taunt, but the intensity of his gaze caused the teasing words to stick in her throat.

Disconcerted, she looked away, but everywhere she turned she found another mirror. There she was, her flushed face staring back at her, just as she must appear to him. Hair spilling around her shoulders as she luxuriated on the satin, she could as easily have been saying, "Here, come and get it."

Horrified, she scrambled to her feet. Unfortunately, her impetus landed her in front of Rhys. Still watching her every move, he dominated the tight space between them, taller and more in command than ever. She felt paralyzed, unable to look away, trapped like some wild creature snared by unexpected headlights. She wished he'd stop staring at her like that. She wished...

Quite frankly, overwhelmed by the strange longing now welling up in her chest, Trae no longer knew what she wanted.

It's this room, she thought frantically. Chad's tacky ode-to-lust hideaway was putting silly ideas in her head.

Rhys stepped closer, gently brushing at her hair. "A leaf," he said hoarsely, never taking his gaze off her face. "Must've gotten stuck there out by the pool." Mere inches away, he continued to stare down at her with a perplexed, almost hungry expression.

Trae felt a funny fluttering in her chest. "I need air," she blurted out. "Let's go out for a while."

Brushing past him to the door, she heard his quick intake of air behind her. "Wait, where are you going?"

"We should look for Lucie," she said, grasping for straws. "For all we know, she might be staying at the Snake Pit."

"But what's the sudden hurry? I thought we decided to wait until morning."

She ignored him, racing out the door. She knew she'd startled him and no doubt he deserved an explanation, but really, how could she admit the reason for her panicked flight?

That would mean having to admit the real cause of it to herself.

Following Trae to the lobby, Rhys knew he, too, should be in a rush to find Lucie, but he could no longer summon up the same sense of urgency. Yes, he was eager to make sure she was safe and sound, but the rest of it, the happily-ever-after part, suddenly seemed to require more careful consideration.

Not that he suffered any doubts about his upcoming marriage. Lucie had formed such a large part of his future for as long as he could remember, a major cog in his Grand Plan, and it was hard to imagine a life without her in it.

But do you love her?

As if she'd mouthed the words, he again heard Trae asking the question. Up until now, his response would have been an automatic "of course," but for the first time since he'd known Lucie, he felt the doubts slipping in. There was no disputing that he cared about her, wanted the best for her and would protect her with his life.

But do you love her?

He felt confused and didn't like it. It was all Trae's fault, putting these questions into his head. He'd made a promise to Lucie. Whatever else, he couldn't go back on his word. Misgivings or not, he was going to marry the girl, and that was the end of it.

So why these sudden, unexpected urges to touch Trae?

Blame that moment in the car, he decided firmly, when he imagined he saw her vulnerability. Obviously, he was so tired he could no longer think straight. Must be exhaustion. An overload of the senses. Those mirrors, all the red satin, her soft, enticing scent. No wonder he'd fantasized about snuggling up with Trae on what Chad had so optimistically labeled a queen-size bed.

Before they went looking for Lucie, he suddenly decided, he had to make sure housekeeping delivered that cot.

Catching up with Trae in the lobby, he asked her to give him a minute while he went to the desk. Strolling over to have a chat with Lisa, he was somewhat mollified by the horrified look on her face. Apologizing profusely, she got on the phone immediately, chewing out some poor soul named Juan, before assuring Rhys that the rollaway would be in the room shortly.

That should take care of it, he thought with satisfaction as he found Trae and ushered her out the door.

Saying nothing, Trae walked briskly beside him, her

wide-eyed gaze taking in the sights around them. He came to Vegas often, but seeing it through her eyes, he decided it was like going to the circus. In ring one you could watch dancing fountains, a squealing roller coaster, a laser beam reaching for the sky. In ring two you found mumbling panhandlers and fast-talking pitchmen handing out cards for adult entertainment. But in the center ring, the main attraction, were the thousands of hapless tourists, milling from one casino to the other in a desperate quest to blow all their money.

Having seen it all countless times, Rhys found himself focusing on the woman beside him. Her hair blew in the warm desert breeze, taunting him and making him want to run his fingers through it. It was all he could do not to lean down and touch the strands.

"You're quiet all of a sudden," she said as they neared their destination. "A penny for your thoughts?"

As if he'd divulge what he'd been thinking for a mere penny. "Don't mind me, I feel like a fish out of water here. Can't say I'm much of a fan."

"What's not to like? All the lights. The action." She gestured at the flashing signs, the hordes scrambling across the multilane highway from one casino to the next. "The fun."

"Gambling, fun? Me, I don't get it. Can't these people see the odds are against them? That they stand to lose far more than they can ever win?"

She shook her head. "Not everybody bets the farm, Paxton. Most come prepared to wager a set amount, the same money you'd put aside for the ballet, or opera, or any other form of entertainment. For them, that's all it is. Entertainment."

"Losing money is hardly a hoot."

"Yeah, and I bet you still have the first dime you inherited."

He was getting fed up with her cracks about his wealth. "I take my profits and invest them wisely. Which is why I have the resources to find Lucie."

"What resources? Last time I checked, *I'm* the one funding our little expedition."

And she missed no chance to toss it in his face. "Until tomorrow when we find her," he reminded her, doubly annoyed. "And let's face it, you can't have much money left. After the hotel bill, I bet you don't have enough left to pay up once I win our wager."

"*Another* bet, Paxton?" She came to a halt, placing her hands on her hips as she faced him. "Hypocrite. If you're so dead set against gambling, how can you be so eager to challenge me?"

"That isn't gambling. Gambling implies risk. I know full well I'll win."

She pursed her lips. "Okay, then let's make it triple or nothing."

He had to school his features to hide his surprise. Had to hand it to her, she didn't back down from a challenge. "Fine. You're on," he said, offering his hand to shake on it. "But do you have the cash to cover it?"

The color drained from her features. "Don't worry about me," she told him tightly, clasping his hand.

"Good. Then this should prove interesting."

He held her hand a trifle longer than necessary. He tried to tell himself it was to keep her flustered, but deep inside, he wondered if he was merely indulging himself. He liked the feel of her grasp, he realized. It made him feel warm. Connected.

She yanked free, nodding behind her. "Here we are, the Snake Pit Casino."

Looking up, Rhys saw the bright pink-and-orange neon depicting a writhing serpent. Certainly made the place distinctive. That, and the suggestive pictures of the scantily dressed dealers inside.

"We should split up," Trae added quickly, as if hoping to forestall his objections. "You check the front desk while I case the casino."

Rhys looked up, uncertain. The Snake Pit was even seedier than he remembered, with its darkly lit lobby and aggressive hawkers luring customers—mostly men—inside. "I don't know," he started, only to realize she'd left him no choice. Already at the door, Trae was fast disappearing with the crowd into the casino.

So much for being connected.

Funny, she could drive him up the wall with her outrageous ideas and incessant chatter, but take her out of his line of vision for one minute and all of a sudden, he felt at a loss.

Fighting a strong need to go after her, he strode briskly into the hotel. At the front desk, he learned there was no Lucie Beckwith registered there, and no Robert Boudreaux, either. As for Mr. Carino, he just missed him. The boss had left for home late this evening.

And wasn't Lou in for a big surprise, Rhys thought as he pictured Josh trying to get the house cleaned—and all the girls out—before his father arrived on the scene.

Anxious to tell Trae what he'd learned—which, in essence, was nothing—Rhys hurried into the casino. They needed to compare notes, he told himself. It had nothing to do with a sudden, unexpected need to see the woman herself.

Caught in a hell of deafening noise, flashing lights and a haze of cigarette smoke, he combed the casino with the logical side of his mind on hold. The other side, the heretofore less explored emotional part, kept insisting that he'd been crazy to let Trae out of his sight.

All these conventioneers on the prowl, chugging down drinks and saying "see-ya-bye" to their inhibitions. Trae, alone and oblivious, would be too busy searching for Lucie to watch out for herself. As he imagined beefy hands pawing her in some dark corner, he quickened his pace.

But if he'd entertained any visions of slaying a dragon on her behalf, he was doomed to disappointment. The only evil-doer threatening Trae was of the one-armed variety. Coming up behind her, he found her stuffing coins into a rather large and noisy slot machine. So fierce and total was her concentration, she didn't notice he was there.

"You don't seem to be doing so well," he said, startling her so badly she actually jumped. "Maybe it's time to call it a night."

"Not now," she hissed, not bothering to glance at him.

"You have limited funds, Trae," he advised gently. "Don't you want to save what's left for emergencies?"

This time she looked back, giving him a glare that could have frozen a rock. "If you have to be such a buzz-kill, can you kindly do it somewhere else?"

Rhys held up his hands in mock surrender. Not that she noticed. She was too busy donating her cash to the casino.

Stepping up beside her, Rhys watched as she rapidly went through the bucket of quarters, her enthusiasm waning with each lost coin. He missed seeing her dimples, he realized, that cute, little upturn of her lips, the gleam in her eyes. When Trae was laughing, she had spark enough to light all the neon in Vegas.

All at once, it became vitally important to put the smile back on her face.

He took the bucket from her hands. To his surprise, she didn't argue, or even try to regain it. "Maybe you were right," she said, shoulders slumping. "Looks like all I've done is make everything worse."

"Sorry, I must have the wrong person. I thought I was talking to Trae 'I'll-never-give-up' Andrelini."

She shrugged. "Now that it's too late, I might as well admit that all I had left was thirty dollars, which will barely buy breakfast in this town. I figured, what the heck, maybe I can put the money to better use. As you can see," she added with a heavy sigh, nodding at the pitiful pile in the bucket, "my plan failed miserably."

Snatching up the bucket, Rhys walked to another machine. "What are you doing?" she asked, grabbing his arm. "That's all the money we have left."

He grinned. "If you're going be a buzz-kill, can you kindly get lost?"

"I'm serious. After that's gone, we're dead broke."

"Then we really have nothing to lose, do we? I say, let's go for it."

And there it was, the reappearance of her dimples. Lucie was right, Rhys decided. It *was* like the sun had come out and now it was time to play.

"And here we thought *I* was the impetuous one," she said with a grin. "All right, Paxton, let's see what you can do."

Rhys shook his head, holding out a quarter. "Ladies first."

"Okay, but we take turns," she insisted as she took the coin from him. Crossing the fingers of one hand, she stuffed the quarter in the slot with the other. After a great deal of clanging, during which Rhys discovered he was holding his breath, all the machine had to offer was a shamrock a cherry, and a better-luck-next-time.

"You try," she said, nudging closer. "You've got to be luckier than me."

Apparently not. Yet as they took turns dropping coins into the various machines, losing quarter after quarter, Rhys realized he was enjoying himself immensely. So this was life on the edge.

Logically, he might know that a single call home could resolve their financial crisis, but logic wasn't governing his actions this evening. He was running on sheer emotion and he was amazed—no, enthralled—by the rush of exhilaration it gave him. In fact, he wished it could go on all night.

Unfortunately, they reached the end of their quarters all too soon. Looking down at Trae, he held out their last coin to her. "Okay, this is it."

She nodded solemnly. "Just do it. Get it over with."

He was stunned by a sudden strong urge to kiss the concern off her features. "If we lose, don't worry," he reassured her. "I'll make sure you get home safe and sound."

"Even if it means losing our bet?"

"Even if."

She tilted her head, as if taking his measure, before smiling with what seemed like approval. "Okay then, we're in this together. How about showing this machine who's in charge?"

Rubbing the coin with his thumb for good luck, Rhys dropped it in the slot. He didn't look at the symbols as he yanked the lever, focusing instead on Trae's pale hand, digging deep into his arm, making marks that would still be there in the morning.

She squeezed, increasing the pressure for an interminable moment, until all at once, she released her grip with a squeal. "I don't believe it," she cried out to the accompaniment of a million bells and whistles. "Paxton, you lucky devil. You did it!"

They turned toward each other at the same moment, excitement overriding all other emotions. As she fell into his arms, Rhys might understand that she merely meant to hug him, but between the thrill of winning and her enticing scent, was it any wonder he wanted more than a simple embrace?

And what should have been a brief kiss of celebration swiftly accelerated into desire as his body touched hers. He could feel the heat of her, the very pulse of her, as his lips covered her own. Parting them with his tongue, he could taste peppermint in her mouth, and maybe cherry cola. Whatever it was, he couldn't get enough.

He wanted—needed—craved to taste all of her. To touch all of her. Yet when he pulled her closer, she groaned deep inside her throat and gently pushed him away.

"Whoa," he heard her say in a daze. "Talk about unexpected."

Chapter Seven

Unexpected? Trae thought later as she towel-dried her hair. Of all the words to choose, why had she picked that understatement? Unexpected was when someone from your past dropped by for a visit, or you found a stray bill in your pocket. Being kissed by Rhys Paxton in the Snake Pit—and enjoying every second of it—was one of those blow-your-mind-and-you-might-never-recover experiences. Really, who in the world could have seen that one coming?

Not even Nostradamus could have predicted that buttoned-up Rhys Paxton would turn out to be such a dynamite kisser. Lucie sure as hell had never mentioned it before.

She had to stop dwelling on it, stop playing it over and over in her mind. And while she was at it, she'd better stop toweling before she rubbed the hair off her head.

Angrily, she flung the towel at the bathroom door.

So it was a good—maybe even spectacular—kiss, but

Trae was no stranger to passion. She might be currently un-attached, but she'd had plenty of boyfriends and even more dates and was acquainted with the excitement such contact provided. Why, then, had she been so unprepared for Rhys's sensual onslaught? And to the point that she'd lost all track of time and place? If someone hadn't coughed discreetly behind them, she might not have had the sense—or even the will—to stop.

Try as she might, she couldn't remember ever being that badly jolted. They could have had an electric current running between them, the way she'd lit up. In fact, her nerves were still humming. Still hoping for more.

Get a grip, she tried to tell herself. Rhys seemed to have suffered no ill effects. As usual, he seemed more concerned with what was going on back home at the office, as evidenced by his preoccupation with the call to his brother the instant they got back to the room. Leaving Rhys arguing over the phone, she'd escaped to the bathroom for a much-needed cold shower.

Unfortunately, she hadn't cooled down one iota, and now she had to go out there and face Rhys. Not to mention the rest of the night. Her, him and that red satin bed.

She wasn't stalling, she told herself as she slipped into a pair of Lucie's black sweats and a bright-yellow tank top. Washing out her bra and panties and hanging them on the door to dry, she knew she couldn't hide out in here forever. Sooner or later, Rhys would want a shower, too.

Snatching up the pink running suit, she took a deep breath as she reached for her friend's sneakers. Lucie. How could she have let herself forget all about her?

Here Trae was obsessing about a brief—not to mention insane—attraction, while her friend remained missing. A friend, by the way, who happened to be engaged to the man in question. If Rhys were right, if Lucie did inevitably mean to marry him, then the current direction of Trae's thoughts couldn't possibly be more inappropriate.

Awash with guilt, she pushed open the bathroom door and entered the bedroom. Trying not to look at Rhys, who was hanging up the phone, she crossed to the closet. Talk about awkward. The kiss they shared might have been phenomenal, but now the aftermath could only be uncomfortable for them both. Where the devil was that cot, anyway? Didn't those people understand what could happen if they forced two able-bodied adults to share a bed?

Her flushed face stared back at her from all six mirrors.

While over by the bed, a perplexed Rhys dominated the background.

"He's done it again," he said to no one in particular. "One simple phone call, is that too much to ask?"

Apparently.

"Jack got 'distracted' and forgot to call Mary," he went on, getting worked up. "That's why there was no reservation. Nor have my cards been reported yet. I'd do it myself but all the numbers are with my PDA, in my missing luggage. I swear, I can't remember when I've ever had so many things over which I had absolutely no control."

He sounded so confused, so frustrated, she spoke without thinking. "Is it such a bad thing to lose control?"

"Of course it is." He frowned at her in the mirror. "Sometimes it can be downright catastrophic." Turning away, he strode to the bathroom and slammed shut the door behind him.

Blushing to the roots of her hair, Trae caught the double entendre. No doubt Rhys was blaming their kiss in the casino on *her* lack of self-discipline. The worst of it was, she had a sneaking suspicion he might be right.

Not about the kiss itself—she knew only too well how it took two to dance that particular tango—but how could she possibly deny how much she'd put into it? One minute she'd been flying high on the excitement of winning, and then there Rhys was, smack dab in her face, and the need to respond had all but overwhelmed her. Telling him no had never even entered into the equation.

Rhys Paxton, for crying out loud. Her best friend's fiancé. Could it get any more out of control than that?

She had to get out of this room, she thought frantically as she finished hanging up the pink running suit. Get some fresh air, clear her head, make sure they delivered that cot. Whatever, as long as she was somewhere else when Paxton got out of the bathroom.

Not that he was about to lose his head again any time soon, but if he did…

Someone had to retrieve their damp clothing, she decided, still in the trunk of the car. They hadn't wanted to drag a trash bag across the lobby, but she couldn't leave Lucie's designer jeans to rot, and his suit must have cost a small fortune. If Trae didn't rescue the clothes now, no doubt they'd be sprouting ten different kinds of mold by morning.

Behind her, the water came on in the bathroom. She had the sudden vision of Rhys stepping into the shower, naked, and lathering up…

Grabbing the car keys, she made her escape.

In some hazy corner of his mind, Rhys heard the door shut, but he was too deeply engrossed in his own concerns for it to properly register. What had he been thinking, kissing Trae Andrelini in the middle of the Snake Pit Casino?

But he hadn't been thinking, of course. Only feeling. Kissing Trae had felt like the most natural thing in the world.

Which was crazy. Sheer insanity. All other considerations aside, the woman was too…too…everything. Including unpredictable. Oh, tonight she might have kissed like an angel possessed, but the next time he was foolish enough to give way to temptation, she was just as liable to slap him hard in the face.

But he wouldn't. Be tempted, that was. He was Rhys Allen Paxton, head of Paxton Corporation. Logic steered his course; this was no time to abandon it.

Hell, he was going to marry her *best friend,* for heaven's sake!

Turning the faucet to cold, he frowned. Maintaining a discreet—and safe—distance would be difficult given their current surroundings. He could only hope that Trae would have the good sense to be tucked in bed.

At the sudden, unbidden vision of her sprawled across the red satin, his entire body went hot with need. So much for the cold shower.

With more force than necessary, he shut off the water and climbed out of the tub. Rasping the towel over his skin, he told himself that it was only natural to feel such urges. He was a healthy male, alone in the room with a beautiful woman. A sexy, vibrant woman. Of course he'd fantasize about jumping her bones.

But that's all it was, fantasy. For a dizzying moment, Trae had shown him an alternate universe, one where he could think and act however and be whatever he wanted. And, yes, he'd enjoyed it immensely.

It did not mean, however, that he could continue to indulge himself. He had responsibilities, an image to protect. At heart, he was just an old-fashioned gentleman with a finely honed sense of honor. He was about to get married, for crying out loud.

Even though his bride had left him at the altar and remained nowhere to be found.

He felt a surge of anger, but strangely enough, the source wasn't Trae this time. Instead it was Lucie. All these years, always expecting him to rush to her rescue, to pick up the pieces, never once stopping to consider that he might have troubles of his own. Needs of his own.

Yet as quickly as it had come, his anger evaporated. That was just vintage Lucie, scatterbrained and careless, oh-so-contrite and eager to make it up to him when he finally found her. He'd known, going in, what life would be like with her, so how could he now justify his sudden resentment?

He glanced up to see his face in the mirror, not at all pleased with what he found in his reflection. His dark hair stood up every which way and his chin now sported a five o'clock shadow. He looked like a bum off the street. An angry, desperate bum, with little hope for the future.

He shook his head. He was frustrated, that's all it was. Lucie's leaving him had thrown his whole world off-kilter and now nothing was going as he had planned. No wonder he was looking for answers in all the wrong corners. Let him get a little control back into his life, and let's see if he'd be kissing Trae Andrelini in the Snake Pit Casino.

Rubbing his hand along his jawline, he decided he needed a razor.

He glanced behind him. Usually, he could find no

purpose for a phone in the bathroom, but it certainly seemed a convenience at the moment. Dialing the front desk, he asked them to send a razor and shaving cream to the room. And while they were at it, maybe a toothbrush and comb.

After he hung up, he realized he should have ordered two of everything. Though Trae probably didn't need any toiletries. The way she kept pulling supplies out of that backpack, she must have packed enough to last a month.

While he had only Josh's baggy shorts and well-used T-shirt. Shrugging into the shorts, he decided he could at least wash the shirt. It should dry by morning, and if not, he could give it a blast with the blow dryer.

Another first, he realized as he wrung out the shirt. Rhys Paxton, doing his own laundry. In a hotel sink, no less. Funny, but he actually felt proud of himself. Now look who could cope with adversity.

Glancing around the bathroom, he tried to figure out where to hang the shirt. The back of the door seemed good, until he discovered he wasn't the only one coping this evening. Two wisps of lace, resembling a bra and panties, hung from the hook.

And there went his pulse again, leaping to all the wrong conclusions.

He had an uneasy moment, concerned with how strongly he'd reacted, but he shook off the worry, as well as his lust, with a healthy dose of self-discipline. Tomorrow he and Trae would find Lucie and that would be that.

He'd pretend Trae wasn't even in the room, he decided as he dried his hands. If they didn't talk, they couldn't get into another heated argument.

To be safe, maybe he shouldn't even look at her, either.

He opened the door, prepared to set the tone for the rest

of their time together. Cool and aloof, he strode across the room, but when he risked a glimpse at Trae, he discovered she wasn't there to witness his performance.

Now, too late, the click of the door registered.

Where had she gone? he thought with a sharp, chill spike of alarm. Who took a walk at two in the morning? Uneasily, he pictured her out there, a lone female wandering around in the dark. She could be mugged. Or worse.

Envisioning all kinds of dangerous scenarios, he hurried back to the bathroom for his shirt. Wet or not, he was putting it on and going after her.

He'd barely gone two steps when he heard the door. He spun around to find Trae shoving into the room, lugging the black plastic bag. Relief swept over him, swiftly replaced by anger when he noticed there was not a single scratch on her.

"Where have you been?" he demanded as he crossed the room to stand in front of her.

She blinked up at him, clearly startled. "Sorry, dad. I lost track of curfew."

"Don't get smart. You have any idea what could have…"

"I rescued your suit," she said, cutting him off before he could get started. She held up the bag as a peace offering. "Another six hours in that trunk and it'd be a goner."

Snatching the bag from her hands and dropping it to the floor, he grabbed her by the arms. "Are you out of your mind, going out at this hour?"

"Jeez, Paxton," she tried to quip. "You missed me that much?"

"I worried that much," he admitted, too rattled to pretend otherwise. "I pictured all sorts of…"

"I'm not an idiot, you know." Green eyes flashing, she

didn't bother to hide her indignation. "I asked the bellhop to get the bag for me. If you must know, I spent the entire time in the lobby, nudging your good pal Lisa to get us a cot."

"You scared the hell out of me, Trae."

As he scowled down at her, Trae lost all ability to argue. He'd surprised her with his anger, but he'd darned near knocked her senseless with his heat. She could feel it in his probing blue gaze, burrowing down into the center of her body. It was there in his firm, strong grasp, in the tiny space between them.

The whole room was too warm, she thought distractedly. Steamy, almost, causing tiny beads of moisture to collect on his bare chest.

Just as in her dream.

As if she'd drifted back to the Amazon, Trae felt again that languid pull between them, an underlying current too strong to resist. She should fight the attraction, she knew it in some hazy part of her mind, but she could not remember how or why.

And then it was too late. Pulling her against him, Rhys took her mouth like a conquering hero, pure onslaught, no mercy, not even remorse. Trae might have whimpered a protest, low in her throat, but neither he nor she paid the least attention. Neither had the slightest doubt about her eventual surrender.

Opening her mouth to him, she could feel a quickening inside her, excitement pooling with need. She reached up for his neck, sliding her fingers into the wet strands of his soft, thick hair, clinging to him as if her very life depended on it.

As he explored her mouth, she could feel his low groan rumble through her. He held her so close she could barely breathe, but she wasn't complaining. She wanted this. Wanted it so much her knees buckled with yearning.

As if her bones were indeed melting, Rhys shifted his arms beneath her knees to lift her up against his chest, never once breaking their kiss. Carrying her to the bed, he pulled away slowly, reluctantly, to place her on the red satin. It was all Trae could do not to reach up and tug his head back down to her own.

But then he, too, was on the bed, kneeling over her, yanking the tank top over her head. As he gazed down at her with fierce concentration, Trae could feel her nipples tighten, the air brushing against them.

Then his hands were on her, his wonderful, incredible, magical hands, trailing up her sides, stroking her breasts, squeezing them, making the nipples go rock hard with desire. Leaning down, he kissed them, devoured them, sending shock waves of pleasure rocketing through her body as his rough chin scraped the tender flesh.

Slipping his fingers under the waistband of the sweats, he slid them down over her thighs, her knees, her feet. Trae could feel her toes wriggling as he tossed the pants to the floor, could sense them curling with pleasure when he turned his attention back to her naked, trembling body.

"No fair," she said, her voice as raspy as his beard. "These have to go." With a flick of the wrist, she yanked down his shorts and flung them to the floor with her own clothing.

Visibly aroused, Rhys took her by the arms with a low, soft moan and rolled her on top of him. Kissing him, exploring every inch of his magnificent body with her hands as he caressed hers, Trae reeled with sensation. She threw back her head, reveling as he brought every nerve ending to sweet, throbbing life. She could feel herself soaring higher and higher with every stroke. Low, soft moans erupted in her throat, increasing with urgency, until with a moan of his own, he rolled her underneath him again and parted her legs.

Breathless with anticipation, eager to feel him inside her, she reached up to encircle his neck. As she did, she was knocked out of orbit by a firm, loud rap on the door.

Attuned to his every breath, she could feel Rhys tense above her, his every last muscle clenching, but it took another rude rap to bring him all the way back to his senses.

She watched it happen. First came denial, as he shook his head and closed his eyes. Next came regret, in the form of a long, slow sigh racking his body. And finally, acceptance, as with a low muttered oath, he leapt off the bed and scrambled into his shorts.

"The damned cot," he muttered by way of explanation.

Halfway to the door, he paused to turn back to her. Still reeling, unable to recover, she waited for him to express his regret.

But all he said was, "I don't suppose you have some small bills for a tip?"

And just like that, Trae came crashing back down to earth.

Gesturing at the bag holding their take from the casino, she watched him stride across the room to open the door. As Rhys calmly directed some guy he called "Juan" to set up the cot in the corner, she marveled at his ability to bounce back so easily. No, she resented it, especially considering she was nowhere near back to normal.

How could she be? She'd been a heartbeat away from giving herself—completely and totally—to Rhys Paxton.

Under the blankets, she wiggled into her clothes. Moments earlier, she'd delighted in her nakedness—reveled in it—but now, she couldn't get dressed fast enough.

Closing the door behind Juan, Rhys turned back to her, holding up a small plastic bag. "Toiletries," he said inanely. "I need to shave."

All Trae could focus on were his hands. Even now, she could feel their magic as if they were still stroking her body. How could he act as if nothing had happened between them?

"What we just did…" she said, pulling her gaze away from his hands. "It was a mistake."

He paused, running a hand through his hair. "You're right, of course."

She was right? Not that she'd expected him to profess an undying devotion, but he didn't have to be so eager to agree with her. Worse yet, did his blasé attitude have to hurt so much?

"A lapse in judgment," she said primly, making a dismissive gesture with her hands. "Understandable, when you think about it, after the excitement of winning all that cash. Just as long as we make sure it never happens again."

He nodded solemnly. "Point made, and point taken. Don't worry, I'll be a perfect gentleman from now on." Placing the bag of toiletries on the desk, he strode to the door and checked the dead bolt. "Mind if I turn off the light?" he asked, flipping the switch before she could offer an objection.

Not that she would—she was just as happy to hide in the dark, thanks all the same—but after such a near miss, you'd think a so-called gentleman should offer a "Wow, that was great." Or at the very least an "I'm sorry."

She could hear him stumbling around in the dark, heard his low, muttered oath as he stubbed his toe on the cot. Serves him right, she thought. Here she lay, her body still quivering, and he thought he could just go to sleep?

"That's it?" she blurted out, unable to stop herself. "We're not even going to talk about what happened?"

"It's late. We need some rest." His sigh sounded heavier than usual. "I can't see any sense in beating ourselves up about it. Like you said, it was a lapse in judgment. Now and then, everybody suffers a lapse."

She was perfectly capable of being inane on her own; she didn't need him parroting her words back to her. "It wasn't just a lapse, it was insanity. I mean, we both know better, right?"

"We didn't do anything, Trae. Nothing happened."

How could he say that when she could still feel his hands on her, taste him on her tongue? "Lucie deserves better," she insisted.

"You think I don't know that?" The cot creaked and the bedcovers rustled as he tossed and turned to get comfortable. "Me, who's spent his entire adult life looking out for what's best for her?"

"Really? And who was looking out for Lucie's interests just now when you were about to sleep with her best friend?"

In the dark, she could hear his sharp intake of breath. "I don't know, Trae. I guess I could ask you the same."

She felt like she'd been slapped. "This is stupid," she said, fighting a sudden need for tears. "If we're just going to argue, maybe we should turn over and get some sleep."

"Isn't that what I suggested?"

With a huff, she turned on her side away from him.

A mistake? she thought angrily. Oh, no, what they'd just done was sheer, unadulterated disaster. Seemed Rhys was right, after all. Losing control *did* lead to catastrophe.

It didn't make sense. On every date, she was the one who controlled the tempo, who chose which base the guy would reach, who never, ever relinquished the decision to anyone. Of all the men in the world, why had she so eagerly handed herself over to Rhys Paxton? What did he have that the others did not?

Those hands, she thought unhappily. She'd always been a sucker for a great pair of hands. Too bad they happened to belong to her best friend's fiancé.

All at once, she wanted to cry. Bad enough that she would have to face Rhys in the morning, but how on earth was she ever going to face Lucie?

"Trae?" Lucie Beckwith frowned, realizing too late that the greeting she'd heard was an automated message, and not her friend's voice. "Oh, Trae, why don't you ever answer your phone any more?"

She waited as Trae went on, her professional tone encouraging Lucie to leave her name and number. But what could she say to the dead air between them? She needed Trae, the real Trae, with her warmth, concern and unique understanding. Not some impersonal machine.

Lucie flinched as another truck whizzed by, the ground beneath her feet vibrating so loud, she never heard the beep signaling the start of her message. She kept talking anyway, the tension of the past few days bubbling out of her. "Knowing you, you've probably been leaving messages, but I lost my cell phone and can't remember how to get to my voice mail. I guess I always relied on Rhys to help me out. Oh, Trae… I really wish you were here. I need to talk to someone. Somebody I can trust. I thought of calling Rhys, but that would be unforgivably selfish. Especially after the way I left him. Oh, Trae, this time I really screwed up."

She stopped, not wanting her friend to guess how close to tears she was.

Today had been awful, with that terrible Lou Carino bellowing at her, and tomorrow didn't offer much improvement. For the first time in her life, Lucie realized, she now had to face her problems alone.

Well, not entirely alone. She had Bobby, lying dead drunk in the back of his van.

"Nothing is turning out like I thought," she went on, thinking longingly of the pretty church, her happy parents, all the startled friends and relatives she'd left behind. "I should never have run away. I mean, Rhys is such a great guy, you know? Looking back, he's given me some of the best times of my life."

She actually did look back, over her shoulder to the van, uncomfortably aware of how recently Bobby had fit that description. "I'm confused, Trae," she added. "And scared. Maybe I don't have what it takes to answer the call to adventure. What if I've messed things up so bad, I can't ever set them right again?"

The question hung there as another ten-wheeler rumbled past the phone booth. In the interval, Lucie imagined her friend's response. *"Buck up,"* she could hear Trae telling her. *"And finish what you started."*

Lucie sighed. If only she was as confident in her own abilities. Sadly enough, she had a long way to go before she could hope to be as strong as Trae, or even half as smart about the ways of the world.

"And what are you waiting for?"

Lucie smiled as she imagined Trae, hands on her hips, asking her the question. She was right, of course. Wasn't that what this journey was supposed to be about?

"Sorry, I don't know why I left this message. You won't be able to reach me anyway. We're driving to Bobby's place—well, looks like I'll be driving while he sleeps it off—and I don't have my cell phone. Don't worry, though. Knowing Rhys, he's probably already on his way to rescue me. He always does, you know."

A thought that both cheered and depressed her. Yes, Lucie liked to imagine Rhys magically erasing the mess she'd made of her life, but she could also see the merit in Quinn's Just-Say-No oath. What kind of wife would she be, what kind of person, if she never learned how to take care of herself?

As much as Lucie wished she could discuss her dilemma with Trae, it was, after all, only voice mail, and the big, drunken cowboy who'd harassed her earlier was now weaving his way toward the phone booth. The last thing she needed was to get involved in another ugly scene, so she said a quick goodbye and bolted for the van.

Cranking the ignition with trembling fingers, Lucie wondered how she was supposed to get them all the way to Louisiana, finding her way all alone in the dark on this never-ending highway. She, who always got in the back and let everyone else do the driving.

Eyeing the backseat, conceding that it was already occupied, she knew that she didn't really have much of a choice. Especially with the big, drunken cowboy still heading in her direction.

I can do this, she told herself as she peeled out of the truck stop.

And if not, there's always Rhys.

Chapter Eight

Vaguely conscious of a door opening, Trae opened her eyes. She worked hard to focus, taking in the green numerals of the bedside clock in front of her. Four-forty-five, it read—a.m., as in morning. Early morning.

Closing her eyes again, she felt the dread rise up in her when she thought of facing her classroom. Lying there, it took a good dozen beats more before it dawned on her that she wasn't at home in her bedroom, gearing herself up for work.

Bit by painful bit, she remembered where she was. In Las Vegas. In this awful room. Alone with Rhys Paxton.

Sitting bolt upright, she felt the blood rush to her head as she clutched the blankets around her.

"Good, you're up," Rhys said with remarkable calm—not to mention annoying alertness—as he set a paper bag on the dresser across the room. "I got coffee. We can be up and on the road within fifteen minutes."

"Fifteen minutes?" Fighting to focus, she watched him pull covered cups out of the first bag. She could see he was in a hurry but darned if she could remember why. On less than two hours sleep, how was a girl supposed to think?

"Oh, that's right," she said, figuring it out at last. "Lucie. You wanted to get to the site early."

He turned with both cups as if he meant to bring hers to the bed, then stopped as he clearly thought better of it. Eyeing the second cup as if it would bite him, he set it back down on the dresser.

Shaking her head, Trae swung her legs to the floor. "I know you want to get there as soon as possible, but must it be at the crack of dawn?" Shuffling over to the window, she pulled aside the drape, only to see nothing in the dark, shadowed alley. "Correction, make that *pre*-crack of dawn."

"Not a morning person, I see."

Normally, she needed a minimum of two coffees and an hour of total silence before she could function. While he…well, obviously he'd been up long enough to shave and comb his hair. The fact that he could stand there acting so in control, so businesslike, so…so cheerful at this hour made her want to throw a pillow at his face.

"You want miracles on two hours sleep? And what about food?"

He gestured at the second bag. "I brought doughnuts."

She must have made a face. "I was in a hurry," he explained curtly. "I thought we were on the same page with this. Isn't haste number one on the agenda?"

"Yeah, okay, so haste I can remember," she grumbled, "but tell me, when did starvation get put on the list?"

"For now, just eat the damned doughnuts." Turning

away, he reached for his coffee. "You can always pick up something more substantial *after* we've found Lucie."

At the mention of her name, the pieces began to fall into place. Lucie. Last night. The resulting awkwardness between them. No wonder he was in such a hurry to go.

She couldn't help but notice that he'd said, *you,* not *we,* implying that once he located his fiancée, Trae would be on her own.

She stole a glimpse at him. He was still looking away, drinking his coffee, both hands grasping the cup as if he hoped to draw warmth from it. Trae had no need for an outside source; heat suffused her entire body as she remembered those hands on her body. Rhys Paxton, the man with the perfect touch.

As if hearing her thoughts, he met her gaze. Something sizzled between them, something almost electric, before he broke away. As his gaze inadvertently fell on the bed, he shuddered.

Oh, yes, she could see the danger in remaining too long in this room with the man.

"I'll give you time to dress," he said stiffly as he hurried to the door. "I'll go check out and wait for you in the lobby."

Disconcerted, she stared at the door he'd slammed behind him. Odd, how quiet the room seemed. How empty.

Get used to it, she told herself firmly. They'd finally be catching up to Lucie in less than an hour, and after that…well, his hasty exit proved how little contact he'd want them to have in the future.

Determined not to waste one more second fretting over that man, she went to the closet and reached for the dreaded pink running suit. The smart thing now would be to hurry up and get dressed, get the whole expedition over with. The sooner they found Lucie, the sooner everyone could get back to his or her own life.

No matter how quiet. Or empty.

Muttering under her breath, she made her way to the bathroom, only to trip over the black plastic trash bag. Cringing, she realized she'd forgotten all about the damp clothes last night. Not good, she thought as she lifted them out of the bag, not if the musty smell was anything to go by. Grabbing the bag hanging in the closet, she decided that somewhere along the way, they had to find a dry cleaner.

Even with the slight delay, she took maybe twenty minutes to shower and collect her meager belongings. The way Rhys was tapping his foot when she met him in the lobby, however, you'd think she'd kept him waiting for hours.

Anxious to prove that "haste" was item number one on her agenda, too, she misread the map and drove off in the wrong direction. Rhys quickly pointed out that he'd be happy to come to her assistance if just once, she'd let him look at Josh's directions. Irritated by his attitude, she tossed the paper in his lap and then had to endure his air of superiority as he guided them back on course.

After forty-five minutes of solid bickering, Trae's last nerves were frayed by the time they reached the film site. She certainly didn't need what her weary eyes were showing her—seven dusty trailers huddled in a circle, like covered wagons that had failed at fending off an attack.

Otherwise, the place was completely deserted. No film crew, no Bobby and certainly no Lucie. Staring out at the bleak desert landscape as the sun crept up over the horizon, she fought an overwhelming urge to weep.

Trust Rhys to voice the obvious. "Now what?"

"How the hell would I know?"

He seemed surprised by her outburst, but then, the man rarely gave rein to his emotions. As he'd undoubtedly put it, *"A Paxton never loses his temper."*

"Apparently, your pal Josh gave us the wrong directions. We'll need an alternate plan of action. I suggest we drive back to that shopping center we passed on the way here and use the pay phone to check our messages. Maybe Lucie will have reported in."

What was he, a robot? How could he continue to act so cool, calm, and oh-so-logical? She had a sudden, strong need to tweak him, goad him into showing some of the less than self-contained being she'd glimpsed last night. "Stop pretending, Paxton."

That got his attention. Stiffening, he turned his head to face her. "I beg your pardon?"

"You heard me. Who do you think you're kidding, acting like this is business as usual? You know as well as I do that last night was anything *but* normal."

The only outward sign that she'd scored a direct hit was the telltale tic above his eyebrow. "I thought we'd agreed to move on."

Move on? How comfortable for him to be able to file it under been-there-done-that, don't-have-to-do-it-again. While for Trae, the memory of their intimacy had become an infection, already throbbing, festering more each moment she left it untreated.

"No, Paxton. *You* made the decision to move on. No doubt you've convinced yourself that you're being a perfect gentleman. Mr. Discretion personified. Know what I think?"

"Haven't a clue but I'm sure you'll enlighten me."

She went on as if he hadn't spoken. "I think you're taking the easy way out. Hiding from the truth. Acting as if you just have to ignore it long enough, and you can believe nothing happened between us."

"Technically, nothing did." He still sounded calm, in total control, but the tic kept pulsing faster.

"You and your technicalities," she said, throwing her hands up in disgust. "Is that how you were able to sleep last night?"

"You think I was able to sleep?" Eyes blazing, he turned to her. She could almost hear the *snap* as he finally lost it. "What do you want from me, Trae? You want me to admit that I'm attracted to you?" Sucking in an angry breath, he leaned closer. "That I'm *very* attracted? That I left the room early this morning because it was the only way I could stop myself from sliding under the covers with you to try it again?"

"Yes." Conscious of his face so close to her own, Trae could only breathe the words. "Yes, actually. I'd love to hear you admit it."

"Then, fine. I am. I did. But that doesn't change much, does it? The fact still remains, I lost control."

He looked so unhappy, she had a sudden urge to reach out and ease the worry lines off his face. "In case you didn't notice," she said instead, "there's a lot of that going around. For the record, I wasn't exactly Miss In Control, either. And let's not forget Lucie, out there running around like some panicked chicken without a head. With all that's happened, why should you be the only one making sense?"

"Because that's how I've always lived my life."

"Well, lucky you." The way he said it, you'd think he expected a medal. "Welcome to the real world. Take a glimpse of how the rest of us have to live."

He tilted his head, studying her, as if her words—or maybe just her—left him bewildered.

"Lucie's running off, your missing wallet, no luggage," she went on. "Everyone else deals with that kind of stuff on a regular basis. You can't always expect life to follow your rules of logic, Paxton. It's full of surprises, and you can't always see them coming. Sometimes, no matter what you try to do, there's no way you can control the situation. Much less the outcome."

"So exactly what are you suggesting? That I give up?"

She shook her head. "No, give *in*. Stop fighting the inevitable. Let it go."

"Let go?" he asked, his gaze narrowing. "Like last night?"

"Yes." Staring into his eyes, distracted by his nearness, she could only breathe the words. "I mean, no. Not that way. Not with Lucie…"

"Yeah." As he gazed into her eyes with unrelenting intensity, she could smell the soap from his shower, could see the nick on his chin from shaving, could feel the warmth of his body mere inches from her own. Lord help her, but she could happily drown in every last detail.

Where had it come from, this sudden need, this overwhelming hunger for him? And how in the world was she supposed to fight it?

Think Lucie, she told herself, breaking their gaze with an inward groan.

His was more audible as he gestured toward the windshield. "We have company."

Following his outstretched arm, Trae saw a large, swirling cloud of dust steadily approaching. As she watched, a convoy of battered pickups emerged out of the cloud, the lead truck holding a dozen or so day workers in its bed. Rattling ominously, it whipped to a stop ten yards in front of them, while one by one, the other trucks parked in front of the varied trailers.

"Maybe they can tell us what happened here," Rhys said, getting out of the car.

Unable to move, Trae watched him walk up to the group now spilling out of a rust-red Silverado. Amazing, how Rhys could so quickly recapture his poise, while here she sat, still weak in the knees, a victim of overloaded senses.

She should have had a second cup of coffee, she decided as she forced herself out of the car. She was never at her best this early in the morning.

Approaching the men, she could hear the driver, a hefty middle-aged man with bad teeth and an accent reminiscent of someone from the Appalachians, explaining that they'd had quite a little brouhaha yesterday. Mr. Boudreaux, the producer, had gotten into it big-time with his financial backer. Seemed the progress of the film, not to mention its quality, wasn't quite up to Mr. Carino's expectations.

Still and all, Boudreaux might have scraped by, if not for the sexy little blonde he'd had with him. The princess, they'd been calling her on the set, but only when the boss wasn't listening. Crazy protective, Boudreaux was. Wouldn't let a sand flea touch his woman's lily-white fingers. Got so he was spending more time in his trailer listening to her than he was out on the set. And apparently, word of this got back to Lou Carino, who pulled the plug and just like that, everybody was out of a job. He and the boys were here today to break down the site and haul away the trailers.

Thanking the driver, Rhys ushered Trae back to the car, obviously lost in thought as he automatically opened the driver-side door for her. Standing so close to him, aware that she might as well be miles away, Trae felt as if each and every one of her nerve endings were on fire. It was all she could do not to reach out and touch his shoulder.

She had to stop reacting to his nearness. It put her at a distinct disadvantage.

Sliding into the driver's seat, she cranked the ignition. "So Bobby got fired," she said, determined to prove she could be as calm and impersonal as he. "No big shock there. He never seems to hold a job for more than a month."

"This is great," he muttered, still ignoring her. "Just great. Now what the hell are we supposed to do?"

Glancing over at him, noticing his stiff posture and clenched fists, she realized how much he'd been counting on this being the end of it.

And given his current temper, he hadn't listened to word one of her little lecture. The man would go to his grave striving to gain control.

"Obviously, we have to follow them," she said tersely, shifting into Reverse with more force than necessary. "Which means figuring out where they'd go next." Whipping the car around, making a dust cloud of her own, she squealed back onto the highway. "I can't imagine Bobby staying here in Las Vegas, and he certainly can't show his face again in Los Angeles."

"That sure narrows it down."

It was her turn to ignore him. In truth, she had her own ideas about their whereabouts but she wasn't ready to share them. Her guess was that Bobby would head home to lick his wounds, dragging Lucie to New Orleans with him.

But before she shared that tidbit with Rhys, and opened herself to further argument, she meant to be sure of her facts. "I think we should do what you suggested earlier," she told him. "Find that shopping center, check our messages. And maybe we can find a bite to eat."

That perked him up a bit. "Food would be good. And I seem to remember a clothing store. I wouldn't mind new pants and maybe a shirt. Something clean, and a little less Beach Boy."

Trae had to laugh at his tone of disgust.

Nor did he get any happier once they reached the shopping center and he discovered his only choice for clothing was a Western-wear store called Dudes R Us. Stalling until after their breakfast of eggs, bacon and mouth-watering biscuits, he finally settled for a pair of jeans, a red plaid flannel shirt and work boots. Leaving him to change into the new outfit, Trae hurried off to find a pay phone.

She had a message from her brother Vinny, warning that the strike was ongoing, and two calls from her mother, demanding she get in touch with them. "Not now, Ma," Trae mumbled into the phone, but she froze once she heard Lucie's tremulous voice, her "Why don't you ever answer your phone?" eerily reminiscent of the previous messages from her mother.

But as Lucie went on, betraying her fear and confusion, Trae felt an uncomfortable tension knot up in her throat. It became painfully clear that Lucie was having second thoughts about running away. And, as usual, was counting on Rhys to come to the rescue.

She's changing her mind again, Trae thought uneasily as she replayed the disjointed message. Picturing Lucie, clinging to the receiver in some dark, deserted roadside pay phone, Trae could see how her friend might lose her resolve. Compared to the none-too-reliable Bobby, of course Rhys would look like a prince. Given the circumstances, it would be easy for any female to convince herself that she did indeed love Rhys enough to get married.

And right now, Lucie was too upset, too vulnerable, to make such a life-altering decision.

Which was why Trae was here, she must never forget, baking under the scorching Nevada sun in this awful pink running suit, after traipsing from coast to coast and all points in between. Her *only* purpose, her only reason for this quest, was to make sure Lucie didn't get railroaded into a marriage she'd regret for the rest of her life.

But did that include developing feelings for the groom-to-be herself?

Trae glanced over her shoulder at Dudes R Us. Rhys would be coming through that door any moment and once he heard this message, Lucie's fate would be sealed. He'd coax and cajole and bully until the poor girl agreed to be his wife.

Just then, a computerized voice came on to describe her options. Replay. Save. Or…

Delete the message, Trae's inner voice told her. If she did, Rhys would never know about it. But as her finger hovered over the number-three button, she could all but hear her mother admonish, "Nice girls don't screen calls."

Just what she needed, another battle with her conscience.

But this wasn't about her, she insisted again. It was about Lucie, and the man's bullying was the last thing her friend needed. Besides, if Lucie wanted Rhys knowing what she was thinking, she'd have dialed his number instead. *Trae* was the one she'd called. *Trae* was the one she trusted, the one who would help her figure this whole marriage business out.

It wouldn't be easy, though, Trae realized as she pressed number three and hung up the receiver. For one thing, it meant keeping secrets, something Trae had never been any good at. All Rhys had to do was take one good look at her face…

She blushed as she remembered how it felt to be under his scrutiny.

Shaking her head, she walked over to the car to wait for him. As she eyed the small interior, it was all she could do not to shudder. That would be the hardest part, being in such close proximity to the man for another few days. Obviously, she'd have to watch herself, make sure there were no slips. She should probably keep the banter going. Keep things light, impersonal and never, ever even think about last night.

Momentary insanity, that's what it had been, and this morning, well, call it residual lust. Nothing she couldn't handle, nothing she couldn't control.

Daunted by how much she suddenly sounded like Paxton, she looked up to see him walking toward her.

He looks good in jeans, she thought inanely. Then again, the man looked good in everything.

She could do this, she insisted. She had to. For Lucie.

"Good news," she announced when he was a few steps away. "I know where they went."

He looked up, smiling, and her heart skipped a beat.

Enough of that, she told herself sternly as she opened the driver's-side door. She had to stay focused on the task ahead of her. It would be no easy feat to convince him to drive to Louisiana.

"I was right," she said over the top of the car. "She took off with Bobby. They're headed back to his place in New Orleans."

"New Orleans?" he faltered a step. "But that's halfway across the country."

"Only half of halfway, actually." With a lame smile, she got behind the wheel, and waited as he took the seat next to her. "Still, it's going to take a couple days to get there. We'll have to take turns driving."

He shook his head in obvious disbelief. "You expect to drive all the way to Louisiana?"

"You see another choice? According to my brother, the airport is a mess. That strike is still on. And other airlines are booked solid because of it. We'll never get a flight."

"But what if we do all that driving and still miss them again?"

She shook her head. "First of all, they're driving, too. Second, they have only a day's head start, if that. If we leave right now and keep a decent pace, we can make up the difference. Who knows, we might even beat them to Bobby's place."

"Hurry? In that car?" He looked appalled at the prospect. "I can't afford another speeding ticket. Two tickets, considering I still don't have my license. Hey, maybe even three, since we'll be violating the lease if we don't take the car back and return it out of state."

"Details." She waved a dismissive hand. "I swear, Paxton, must you be such a stickler for the rules?"

"Try this rule, then. If we don't return it tonight, they're well within their rights to report the car stolen."

"So we call and tell them we've been held up," she told him airily. "Just say you need to keep the car a few more days. It's even the truth, more or less." She stabbed the key in the ignition. "C'mon, it'll be fun," she coaxed as she started the engine. "This can't be the only road trip you've ever been on. I mean, jeez, Paxton, what the heck did you do in college, anyway?"

"I was at Yale, busy getting a business degree. I was told that was the purpose of higher education."

"Silly boy," Trae scoffed. "College is a kid's last chance to find out what he or she is made of. And trust me, nothing tests your inner mettle quite like a road trip."

"Really? And what pearl of wisdom did you glean in Cancun? That you never want to spend another day inside a Mexican prison?"

"If you must know," she told him tightly, "I learned something far more Machiavellian. Watching you in action, I saw how sometimes, the end *does* justify the means."

"Oh, really?"

"Yes, really. Back then, you moved mountains to save Lucie, and as far as I can see, the challenge is no different today. You and/or I have to do whatever it takes to rescue her from Bobby, even if it means driving all the way to New Orleans. I'm certainly up to it. The only real question here is, are you with me or against me?"

He shook his head. "Hey, don't expect any endorsements from me. I'm just going along for the ride."

"In that case," she told him as she backed out onto the road. "Fasten your seat belt, Paxton. You're about to take the ride of your life."

Chapter Nine

So now he was in an amusement park, Rhys thought as they barreled down the highway at ninety-plus miles per hour. Call it Trae's Wild Ride, a roller coaster that took him up, down and every possible which way with no time to draw a decent breath. One minute, she had him so rattled he wanted to wring her lovely neck, and in the next…

He couldn't figure her out. Worse, he was finding it increasingly difficult to figure himself out when he was around her. How had he let himself get convinced to spend another torturous day in this car? This silent-as-a-tomb car, he amended, Trae apparently having opted to ignore his presence for the past few hours.

Trae kept staring ahead, concentrating on her driving, acting as if he wasn't even in the car with her. As if getting too close to him might lead to serious contamination.

He'd been content to let this go on for the first hundred

miles or so, figuring that the less said between them the better, but this was getting ridiculous. Not that he missed her chatter, mind you. He didn't need any more chiding, either, but there were times, like now, when he had to know what was going on in her pretty little head.

For instance, did she keep flashing back, like he did, to the night before?

As if to shake him back to his senses, the car hit another bump in the road. They both winced, though Trae continued to keep her gaze on the road ahead.

"Maybe we should check again on the airline strike. I can get us tickets—"

"With what? You planning on hocking your broken watch?"

He couldn't help but glance at his bare wrist, any more than he could stop himself from correcting her. "Now that I've found my wallet and I no longer have to report my stolen cards…."

"Whoa." That got her attention—and not in a good way. "Back up a minute, Paxton," she said, fixing her piercing green gaze on him. "Josh found your wallet?"

Rhys wished he had kept his mouth shut. "If you must know, I scoured the car again during our last stop. I found it wedged between the seat and middle console. Must have slipped out of my pocket. I don't know how I missed it before," he added sheepishly.

"I knew it!" She pounded a hand on the wheel. "You owe poor Josh an apology."

He might have to endure her I-told-you-so, but he didn't need to add on any more humiliation. "I can't see why *poor* Josh would want anything more to do with me."

She glanced over at him again, tilting her head and frowning. "Wait a minute. When did you find this out?"

"I checked the car while you got gas." He'd also checked his messages, hoping he, too, would have heard from Lucie. He hadn't. The fact that she'd called Trae instead still rankled.

"And when were you planning on telling me? Never?"

A good estimate, actually. "I can't see how it concerns you."

He watched her stiffen. "You're right, of course. Your being solvent again doesn't impact me at all. Unless you were planning on using your resources to try to buy tickets. You do know that it would mean that you're conceding that I won our bet?"

That stupid wager. "A Paxton never concedes," he told her stiffly.

She merely smiled.

"Don't worry," he said, irritated by her smugness. "I can gut it out a few more days. Hey, I've got this great ride, all the fast food I could ever want to eat, and let's not forget the spiffy new outfit."

She laughed. An all-out, throw-back-your-head expression of humor. His mother would call the display unrefined and unladylike, but Rhys found himself smiling. There was something infectious in her laughter, something sexy in the arch of her soft, white throat.

She glanced over and caught him staring at her. Blushing to the roots of her hair, she instantly looked away. Pity, he thought. The color did nice things to her face.

"In a few days those jeans will be fine," she told him just as stiffly. "You just have to break them in."

"They're pants, for crying out loud, not a horse. I thought buying off the rack was ready-to-wear clothing."

"Are you always this hard to please?"

The question caught him off guard, as did her disapproving tone. "Excuse me?"

"Not everyone can afford designer jeans, you know. If you want the truth, despite our winnings, we really can't afford any new clothes at the moment. I just thought, well, you seemed so miserable in Josh's shorts and a new outfit might make your ordeal a bit more bearable. I guess I was wrong. I'm beginning to wonder if anything will make you stop grumbling."

His first reaction was to protest that proper transportation, food and clothing were all he required, but even he could hear how pompous that sounded—"proper" being such a relative term. Given the limited funds, he had to admit that Trae was doing her best to provide all three. Yes, he was accustomed to finer things but his griping made him sound infantile, not to mention ungrateful.

"You're right," he said suddenly. "I have been behaving badly."

That drew her gaze. For the longest moment, she just stared at him with her head tilted slightly to the side. "Hmm," was all she said as she turned back to focus on her driving.

Rhys felt compelled to fill in the silence. "This is all new ground for me. It's not easy to admit, but I'm glad we joined forces. I'm not sure I could have gotten this far without your help."

As painful as his concession speech had been, it was worth every ache to see the slow, budding smile on her face. "Wow."

"I'm not a total jerk, Trae. It's, well, let's just say this business with Lucie has me rattled. I don't understand her lack of communication. I mean, I'm usually the first one she calls."

Trae grimaced but said nothing.

"I'm the one she always contacts when she's in trouble. No offense, but why is she now calling you?"

She shrugged. "You're an intelligent guy, Paxton. You should be able to put it together. She leaves you at the church, runs off with an old boyfriend and then won't talk to you. What do you think?"

Rhys tried hard not to do his own grimacing. "Hey, don't hold back."

"Sorry, that was harsh. I shouldn't have put it so bluntly, but c'mon, hasn't it occurred to you that you might be on a wild goose chase? That I am right, and maybe Lucie doesn't want to get married?"

"She wants this marriage all right." Rhys felt on solid ground with this. "We talked at length about it. She wants nothing more than to settle down and start a family."

"Did she actually come up with this herself, or was it after you and/or her mother suggested it?"

All at once, his ground got shakier. He could remember Mitsy droning on at many a dinner party about how her daughter needed direction in her life, and really, what better purpose could a woman have than being a wife and mother?

"Okay, say you're right," he said, not convinced at all. "Tell me what Lucie does want, then."

"That's obvious. Excitement. Adventure. Fun."

"Did she tell you this, or did she just agree after *you* suggested it?"

That made her pause. "Never mind," she said with a frown. "The fact remains, she called me. Not you. And I'm the one who's been telling her not to marry anyone unless she's madly, deliriously, head-over-heels in love."

Rhys was not convinced. "Lucie must have a logical explanation for why she hasn't called," he insisted. "And I'm certain she expects me to come after her. To bring her back home to be my wife."

She studied him for a moment, then went back to her own reverie, leaving his words to hang between them. Staring out the window, watching the roadside whizzing past, Rhys replayed his last statement. Every syllable he'd uttered had been true, but all he could hear were the words he'd left out. The ones having to do with being madly, deliriously, head-over-heels in love.

Didn't matter, he told himself firmly. He'd made a promise, and a Paxton never went back on his word.

Unlike Lucie....

He shook off the thought.

"Okay," Trae said at last. "Say you're right. Say you do drag her back and nothing I say can talk her out of going through with this marriage. It's a long time between now and death-do-you-part. Unless you change, I can't see how you ever hope to pull it off."

"Beg your pardon?"

"Being the right husband for her. Making her happy. I'm sorry, but Lucie is very special to me. I can't sit back and watch her being miserable for the rest of her life."

"Well thank you very much for the vote of confidence."

"I'm not saying you'd do it intentionally." She nibbled on her lower lip, choosing her words with care. "I know you mean well, Paxton, but you still don't have a clue."

"About what?"

She shook her head, as if he just proved her point. "About what makes Lucie happy. No doubt you can run spreadsheets and balance the books with the best of them, but you can't handle women the way you run your company. If you ask me, you need a crash course on how best to deal with Lucie."

She paused, then brightened considerably. "Hey, that's a good idea. We can call it Lucie 101. I mean, we need a diversion, anyway, don't we? Something to pass the time so we don't…" She hesitated again, her face going pink. "Two more days in this car could be gruesome. This will give us something to do."

"This?"

"Haven't you been listening? I'm going to whip you into shape, mister. When I'm done, you'll be the perfect husband."

She seemed so proud of herself, but Rhys knew he had to nip this in the bud. Trae, turning him into the perfect husband? It sounded like a grade-B version of Franken-stein. "Thanks, but no thanks."

"You don't think Lucie deserves the best life can offer?"

"You know that I do." He met her questioning gaze and was gratified when she looked away first. "Look, Trae, I'm sure you'd like nothing more than to reinvent me, but there's got to be a better way to get through the next two days."

"Such as?"

He shrugged, having no real idea. He had to get her talking about something else. "You must have taken trips as a kid. Played games in the car."

Her grin held a hint of mischief. "Well, there's always punch buggy."

"Punch what?"

"Buggy, as in a VW bug. The grin deepened. "Say you see a Beetle and it's blue. If you're the first one to shout, 'punch buggy blue,' you get to punch the other guy in the arm."

"You're kidding, right?"

"Not one bit. Let me tell you, with five older brothers, I got real quick at spotting those bugs. To make sure I wasn't the one with all the bruises at the end of the trip."

Rhys could picture her as a kid, leaning forward and scanning the horizon, intent upon winning at all costs.

"C'mon, Paxton. You and your brother never played anything like that?"

"My parents split up when Jack was a baby. Jack went with my mother and…" He stopped, realizing he'd been about to discuss his childhood. "Never mind," he said firmly. "Punch buggy is out."

She gave him that look again, the one that showed she was curious, but to his surprise, she didn't pry. "What, afraid you'll lose?"

"Not at all. I just figure you'll need full use of your arms for driving."

"Listen to Mr. Macho. Just like my brothers."

He had to smile at the disgust in her tone. "What, they always get the best of you, too?"

She stuck out her tongue at him. "They tried. Tony, especially. He was only a year older and six inches taller, but in his mind, girls were inferior beings, put on this earth to play run-and-fetch for him."

"Poor Tony."

"Damn straight. By the time I was ten, I figured out that if I didn't soon put a stop to his bullying, Tony would be pushing me around for the rest of my life."

"And how did you manage to stop him?" Rhys chuckled, anxious to hear her story.

"I challenged him to a wrestling match, no holds barred. Of course, being Tony, he just laughed. He never took me seriously. He said he couldn't wrestle a stupid girl, insisted he didn't want to hurt me. I had to kick him in the shins to get his attention."

Rhys pictured them, this big, burly ape of a kid, and tiny little Trae shaking her fist in his face. "So, did you win?"

"Technically, no." She sighed ruefully. "But I could have. I'd watched Tony wrestle our older brothers. I knew his weaknesses, knew all I had to do was trip him and get him on the ground. I almost had him pinned when my dad came along and dragged me off him, kicking and screaming. Had I been one of the boys, he'd have let us fight to the finish, but because I was a girl, the next thing I knew, I was sent off to St. Mary's where the nuns—or so my parents hoped—could teach me to act like a lady."

Rhys laughed. "And how did that work out?"

She shrugged. "I now teach at an exclusive girls' academy. I can act like a lady when I have to."

Yes, he'd seen her in action, at the occasional party at the Beckwith house. The many faces of Trae. "So, I take it there were no more wrestling matches?"

"I don't know, Paxton. You need one?"

She didn't look at him; she didn't have to. Last night had been prelude enough of what could happen between the two of them, her flat on her back, their sweat-soaked bodies entwined…

Obviously, nobody was going to win that match.

"My point is," she went on quickly, as if seeing the pitfall herself, "it's reckless to get too cocky. Just about anybody, any time, can come along and knock you off your perch. Nobody wins all the time, Paxton. Not even you."

"I don't see what this has to do…"

"It's lesson number one." And just like that, she segued back to her original topic. "You know how I feel about this marriage. But you're bound and determined to go through with it. So if you hope to be a good husband for Lucie, you've got to lighten up. Let loose once in a while, and for heaven's sake, stop taking everything so seriously. Especially yourself."

He didn't even bother to hide his irritation. "Forgive me for asking, but what qualifies you to give advice on matrimony? When exactly was the last time you got married? Or for that matter, sustained a long-term relationship?"

She bristled. "This isn't about me."

Watching her profile, Rhys had to wonder why no one had yet laid claim to her heart. With a face like that—and yes, that body—she could have any man she wanted. According to Lucie, she rarely dated anyone more than once. She was too particular and so protective of her independence, she wouldn't know true love if it stepped up and bit her in the face.

Yet clearly, Trae was a passionate woman. Last night was certainly proof enough of that. No one could call him a monk, but Rhys had never before been with anyone so responsive, so attuned to his every touch. Made him wonder what might have happened had they not been interrupted.

He looked away, sternly reminding himself why he was scrunched into this car, chasing across the country with limited funds. Lucie was out there, expecting him to find and rescue her. She needed him.

While Trae, well, obviously the woman could take care of herself.

On the other side of the car, Trae was feeling anything but capable at the moment. Though she stared straight ahead, she could sense him watching her, could feel the heat of his gaze as it burned into her skin.

He was right, of course. She was far from an expert on marriage and probably the last person on earth qualified to dole out advice. She hadn't really wanted to "reinvent" anybody. She'd thrown it out there as a diversion, something to pass the long hours ahead, hoping to avoid awkward moments such as this.

When all the while, she should have been telling him what Lucie had actually said in her message.

Why couldn't she bring herself to tell Rhys that Lucie was waiting for him—no, *expecting* him—to come rescue her? It seemed a stupid thing to keep secret; he was bound to learn of it eventually. And what would Lucie think when she found out Trae hadn't told him? Yet even just now, when the opportunity arose again, she'd opted to keep the truth to herself.

He wasn't going to tell her about finding his wallet, either, she thought defensively, but deep down she knew it wasn't the same. As he'd pointed out, his wallet didn't directly impact her. Lucie's true intentions, however, could make a great deal of difference in what Rhys felt and did next.

Yet Trae still couldn't bring herself to speak.

Fighting not to squirm, she gave him a sidelong glance, avoiding direct eye contact. He was no longer watching her, but his obvious discomfort made her feel even worse. Somewhere along the way, he had stopped being the enemy. She could no longer see him as a monster—he'd become a flesh-and-blood, multidimensional human being instead.

And because of it, tormenting him wasn't half the fun it used to be.

"Listen, I'm going to pull over up here at that rest stop. We can get out, stretch our legs, and maybe you can check your messages. For all we know, Lucie could have called in the meantime."

He merely grunted.

The chances were slim, she conceded, especially considering Lucie's last message, but just in case, Trae decided to check her own messages. Lucie was forever calling with some high drama crisis, only to call back the next day to admit she'd overreacted.

With a silent prayer that this was the case now, Trae pulled into the rest area. There were two banks of phones, so she parked between them. Still not speaking, Rhys marched off to one, while she went to the other.

Trae's sole message was from her mother. A rather long and disjointed lecture, indiscriminately peppered with Spanish, rambling on about some dire emergency requiring immediate attention. Trae caught only two words at the end. The first was *father* and the second was *stroke*.

Heart pounding, she dialed her parent's number. After seven interminable rings, she was startled to hear her father's hoarse growl on the other end of the line.

"Pop?" she asked quickly. "You okay?"

His only answer was a grunt, and a "Here's your mother."

Letting her mom rant, Trae eventually learned that her father had *nearly* had a stroke because his only daughter couldn't take time from her busy life to spend a few hours with her family. Where was Trae last Sunday that she couldn't make it home for dinner? What was so important that she would put her poor parents through untold worry and heartache? Not even a call to let them know she was still alive. They had to find out from Vinny that she'd been off gallivanting halfway across the world.

Hanging on to her patience by the slimmest thread, Trae pointed out that California was hardly the ends of the earth. She could have saved her breath. Apparently, Vinny had mentioned Miami and New Orleans, as well. The fact that Trae couldn't be content with those two cities, that she had strayed all the way to the West Coast and to such a crazy place as Hollywood, was enough to give her poor sainted father palpitations. Listening to her rant, Trae was glad Vinny had had the good sense not to mention Las Vegas.

So when her mother got around to asking where she was calling from, Trae said the first thing that came into her head. "I, uh, I'm visiting an old friend from college." She racked her brains for a name her mother might not remember. "Jo Kerrin. My old roommate. The one that got married. I'm, uh, helping her get settled back in New Orleans." She crossed her fingers behind her back, hoping her mother wouldn't start grilling her for details.

"As long as you're home by Sunday," her mom warned, staying focused on what mattered most to her. "It's CiCi's birthday, don't forget, and she's expecting her favorite aunt to be here. To make it special."

CiCi was about to turn seven, an age when birthdays were monumental occasions. Picturing her niece's beaming face, Trae felt a lump form in the back of her throat.

Staring at the rough desert landscape around her, she did the calculations. Barring any unforeseen difficulties, they should reach New Orleans by Saturday morning. If they located Lucie right away, that should give her ample time to talk with her friend, help her with whatever she decided and still catch a flight home in time for Sunday dinner. Assuming she could afford it and the strike was over. "I'll be there," she said, praying it was true.

"If you're not," her mom pounced, able to catch even the slightest doubt in her daughter's voice, "your brothers will come after you."

No idle threat. A few years ago on Joey's third anniversary, Trae pretended to have the flu so she could go on a much-anticipated skiing weekend with friends. Ever alert, her mom had ferreted out the lie and dispatched Tony, Vic and Mike to the ski lodge. Her brothers had made such a scene, Trae had opted to leave with them to save her friends—and herself—from further embarrassment.

That was her family. Nobody missed a special occasion.

"Dinner will be at four," her mom pronounced. "We'll see you then." And with a quick, sharp click, her mother ended the call.

Frowning, Trae glanced over at Rhys, barking into the phone on the opposite side of the rest area. Still hanging onto the receiver, her mother's words fresh in her mind, Trae was never more aware of how vastly different her world was from the one Rhys inhabited.

Yet the more she thought about it, the more she realized they had one thing in common. Feeling the weight of her mother's expectations, she could sympathize with Paxton's stubborn determination to do the right thing. When the people who loved you counted on you, it was impossible to let them down.

Duty and responsibility might come in many guises, she supposed, but the trap they formed was one and the same. Ironic how Rhys stood in his corner bound by his sense of obligation, while she stood in the opposite corner bogged down by hers.

And in the end it would be their similarities, not differences, that would keep them apart.

Chapter Ten

Rhys listened to his brother describe the crisis brewing in the office. If he had a hundred hours, Rhys could never explain all the pitfalls in the upcoming negotiations, but all he had was a mere five minutes. In all likelihood, the lawyers for Stanton, Inc. would eat Jack alive.

"We have until Monday," his brother offered. "With any luck, you should be back by then."

Rhys clung to that hope. Still, there were preparations to be made. "We need to sit down with the management team. The lawyers."

"I'm on it, Rhys. You can count on me."

"Like with the hotel reservation?"

He could hear Jack sigh on the other end of the line. "Okay, I screwed up. But this time, I won't. No matter what the old man claimed, I'm not an idiot, Rhys. I know how important this is. I swear, I won't let you down."

Rhys could hear the plea in his tone. "Sam Beardsley is still there, isn't he?"

Jack's sigh held a note of exasperation. "Yes, my babysitter is overseeing every move I make. Will you relax? Go find Lucie and bring her home. We can handle things on this end."

With a click, Jack took the decision out of his hands.

Marching to the car, Rhys cursed under his breath. "I'll drive," he announced to Trae when he joined her.

She paused, clearly startled by his crisp tone. "But…"

"You can't drive day and night, Trae. Not if we hope to reach New Orleans in one piece."

He yanked open the driver's-side door, not leaving it up for discussion. She made a huffing sound, as if exasperated, but took her seat on the passenger side tamely enough.

Sliding back the seat and adjusting the mirrors, Rhys pulled out of the gas station in a cloud of dust. He drove with grim determination, chewing up miles and spitting them out.

And with each passing moment, he could feel his muscles loosening, his brain relaxing. What an improvement, being behind the wheel. Not only could he stretch out his legs, but he did some of his best thinking while driving. And let's face it, he had plenty that needed sorting out.

For one thing, he had to ponder the reason why he'd yet to hear word one from Lucie. No plea for help, not even an apology for leaving him at the altar. Granted, she was probably ashamed by her thoughtless behavior, but it had been five days and all he knew—and this from Trae, mind you—was that she'd run off with her old boyfriend without looking back. Maybe Trae was right. Maybe Lucie had decided she didn't want this marriage after all.

And how did he feel about that?

He couldn't afford to feel anything, he told himself

sternly. Until he found Lucie and she told him this herself, the topic was sheer speculation.

No, he might better concentrate on his conversation with Jack and why it had left him feeling off-kilter. The looming acquisition concerned him, yes, but Rhys had adequately dealt with such problems before and would do so again in the future.

No, what disconcerted him most was that talking to Jack had seemed like connecting with another universe. Another lifetime. Here on the road, he no longer had to be Rhys Allen Paxton III, a product of his environment, defined—no, restricted—by his job responsibilities. For once he was free to be an entirely different person.

And how did he feel about that?

Part of him knew he was acting irresponsibly, that he had to put an end to it. The sane, logical, Rhys Allen Paxton insisted he should get back to Manhattan as soon as possible.

But the other Rhys, this new, free-thinking, unrestrained creature he'd discovered, wasn't ready for the adventure to end. Granted, going without money was proving to be more of a challenge than he'd originally anticipated, but hey, nobody could ever call it dull.

And all Trae's accusations aside, he *was* adapting. A road trip to New Orleans might not be his first choice for a vacation, but here he was, driving cross-country, showing that he, too, could laugh and joke and cope as well as the next guy. That he could have fun.

As evidenced by the current smile on his face.

Concerned that Trae might have caught him at it, he sobered instantly. A quick glance in her direction reassured him that she hadn't even noticed. Looking straight ahead, she didn't seem to be focused on anything. Come to think of it, she'd been abnormally quiet for quite some time.

She seemed lost in thoughts of her own. Not good ones, if her tight features and stiff posture were anything to go by. Most telling of all, she was biting her lower lip. Something was bothering her. And for some strange reason, this bothered him, as well.

"What's wrong?" he asked, his voice sounding like a cannon blast in the confines of the car. "Another message from Lucie?"

"What?" She blinked, then recovered. "Oh. No. Just my mother."

"Trouble at home?"

She sighed heavily. "Sometimes I don't know why I return her calls. With Mom, it's always a big emergency."

"Do you need to get back?" he asked.

She shook her head. "She uses my dad's health as emotional blackmail. He's in better shape than the both of us, but she knows I can't take the chance. So I call her back only to find she wants to make sure I'll be home for the family dinner."

"All that for a simple meal?"

"Nothing's simple about Sunday dinner in the Andrelini household." She turned in the seat, facing him, folding a leg beneath her. "You have to understand. For Mom, it's this huge production, the same command performance every week. My parents, my brothers and their wives, all my nieces and nephews. With thirty of us, there's always a special occasion to celebrate. Last Sunday was Little Joey's First Communion. Chasing after Lucie, I forgot all about it."

"Surely, once you explained…"

Trae shook her head vehemently. "You don't get off the

hook that easily with Yolanda Andrelini. All she'll ever see is that I let poor Little Joey down. Even if I show up with the very best gift ever in the world, she'll still make me feel like a worm. And he probably didn't even notice I wasn't there."

"Wow. Put marbles in her mouth, and she'll sound like the Godfather."

That won him the slightest of grins. "She's scarier, trust me. She has her beliefs, and she never backs down. To her, family is everything. Her life, her sacred duty. Do anything to any one of us and she'll rip you apart."

Rhys smiled. "So that's where you get it from."

"Very funny, Paxton." She whacked him gently on the arm. "Sadly enough, though, I'm no match for that woman. She won't let me be. I can get married, have kids and live to be a hundred and still she'll treat me like her little baby."

He was beginning to see why Trae tried to be so fiercely independent.

She sighed again. "Most mothers don't stifle their kids like that. I bet yours didn't."

Rhys thought of his mother, off somewhere on the French Riviera, living far beyond the generous allowance he provided. "Have to admit, it's hard to imagine Deidre fixing any dinner, much less one for a large family."

"Oh, come on. She must have done a holiday or two. Every mother cooks for Thanksgiving."

"Not mine. She never bothered to learn how. Our meals came catered, to be consumed separately in an individual room of choice. I tried the dining room once, but the sound of my silverware echoing off the plate seemed so depressing. Generally, I ate by myself in the kitchen."

"Jeez, Paxton. That sounds like something Dickens would write. Did she make you scrub floors and sleep in the gutter?"

He laughed, the sound dry and mirthless. "As if she'd go to the trouble. She had servants for that and besides, she far preferred to ignore me. Right up until she took off with her lawyer the day before my seventh birthday."

"Your seventh? But you were just a baby."

He liked hearing her concern. Maybe that was why he suddenly felt so expansive. "Jack was only two, which was why Deidre had to take him. She couldn't have people talking about her behind her back, accusing her of abandoning her baby. I'd be fine, she told me before she left. I was self-reliant, I could take care of myself, and besides, I looked too much like my father. Having me around would only upset her. In the same spirit of self-preservation, she's minimized our contact ever since. I've seen her a total of three times—at my father's funeral, the reading of his will and then in court when she tried to contest it."

Trae shook her head, as if she found it hard to believe. "I wondered why she wasn't at the wedding."

"She was invited, but I guess she had to make a statement. My father left control of his estate in my hands, and she's never forgiven me for it. Four divorces can run up a hefty bill."

She was watching him, head tilted to the side. "I'd be devastated if my mother abandoned me. How can you make it sound so...so matter of fact?"

He shrugged, but it wasn't mundane at all. It had taken years to understand that the fault lay with her, and not himself.

"Well," she added with a sigh. "At least you had your father."

"Yeah, that was an upgrade," he told her sarcastically. "Mr. Congeniality himself. His idea of quality family time meant that I never bothered him. Children, he firmly believed, were not to be heard *or* seen."

"But he was your dad," Trae protested, visibly puzzled. "Surely you must have some good memories together. A fishing trip, maybe, or camping in the woods."

He snorted. "Rhys Paxton II, getting his pants dirty? I tried joining the Boy Scouts in grade school, but my father wouldn't participate. He was always out of town on business when the camping trips came up. So, no, we didn't camp and we didn't fish."

"So how did you grow up to be so normal?"

At least they'd progressed to the point where she could consider him normal. "Believe it or not, I adapted. And, yes," he held up a hand as if to stop her, "I did gripe a lot. I guess it's my nature."

She rewarded him with a grin.

"Besides, I wasn't left completely alone," he continued. "Jack visited sometimes, I had friends at school, and then when I was fifteen, Lucie came along."

"I bet she brightened things up."

A picture drifted into his mind, ten-year-old Lucie with her long blond ponytail, perched on the fence as she peppered him with question after question. "She used to follow me everywhere," he said with a smile. "My little shadow, chattering in my ear, describing every thought that ever flitted into her head. I was this hotshot high school freshman, right? Too cool to be bothered by a fourth-grade brat. But there was something about her, something that drew me. Once I met Hal and Mitsy, I saw why Lucie tailed me. Poor kid needed someone to talk to. Someone who would listen and not always judge."

Trae nodded thoughtfully. "Yeah, I know what you

mean. First time I met her, she told me about her mother. Didn't take long before she was telling me every other aspect of her life."

And that must have been when Lucie stopped confiding everything in him. Was that why he'd always resented Trae?

"I always wondered how you two became such good friends," he said, uncomfortable with the realization. "You have to be polar opposites."

"Yeah, I guess." She seemed surprised, as if the thought had never occurred to her. She turned to gaze sightlessly out the windshield, her mind more on the past than the road before them. "I remember the first time I met her. I was so homesick I was literally ill from it. Miles from home for the first time in my life, a nobody from Brooklyn among all those poor-me-I-only-got-one-Porsche-for-Christmas debutantes. It was definitely an adjustment."

Rhys studied her, surprised by her confession. "I have trouble imagining you as a fish out of water. You seem so adaptable."

She shrugged. "What can I say? I'm human. All I know is that I was sitting in the dorm lounge, this close to giving up my scholarship and crawling home in defeat like my parents kept urging, when Lucie strolled up to sit next to me. I can't remember what started our conversation, something silly to do with whatever was on television I imagine, but I can still feel the wonder of discovering somebody who made me feel at home."

Against his will, his heart went out to her. Lately, he'd been finding a lot of vulnerability beneath the brash facade.

With a sigh, she turned back to face him. "I figured it couldn't last," she went on. "I mean, really, Lucie Beck-with, the richest of them all and most qualified for snobbery, giving me her stamp of approval? The next time she was with her friends, who'd only seemed to care about money, she'd have no choice but to snub me."

"We talking about the same girl?"

"I didn't know her then, okay? But, yeah, I soon learned differently. Maybe an hour later, her pals showed up, demanding she leave with them. Lucie told them that she'd talk to whomever she wanted." She paused, smiling inwardly. "I ask you, how can you *not* be best friends with someone who does that for you?"

Rhys felt a rush of pride at the thought of Lucie's coming to Trae's rescue. "She takes friendship seriously. She always says that the best ones are not only a gift, but also a duty."

"Yeah, I got that lecture, too." She shook her head, apparently not comfortable with the memory. "Back when Jo Kerrin got in trouble."

The name rang a bell. Searching his memory, Rhys could remember Lucie talking about one of her roommates. "Jo Kerrin? Isn't that the girl who quit school to marry her high school sweetheart?"

"Right after we decided to leave the dorm and rent a house together. I guess we should have called Jo once in a while after she eloped, but we were annoyed at her for sticking us with the extra rent. If Lucie hadn't tracked her down and kept in touch, we might never have known that Jimmy beat her. Badly enough to put her in a hospital."

Rhys shifted uneasily, wondering why Lucie hadn't mentioned this to him. "She didn't stay with the jerk, I hope."

"Not that time," Trae sighed. "Thanks to Lucie, we were able to get some money together and put her on a bus to a shelter in St. Louis where Jimmy couldn't find her." She shuddered. "I can still see her battered face, what he did to her. It was right after that when we all swore to Just-Say-No."

"To just say what?"

"We swore an oath," Trae explained patiently. "Quinn, Alana, Lucie and I. We all agreed that we wouldn't get married unless we could stand on our own two feet."

That explained a lot. About Lucie, and about the woman beside him. "So that's what you were doing before the wedding? Reminding Lucie of your pact?"

She blushed, admission enough. "More or less. It's also why I'm so desperate to find her. To make sure she doesn't become another Joanna."

"Well, thank you very much."

"I didn't mean it that way," she said quickly. "I know you'd never willfully hurt her. It's the inadvertent stuff that concerns me. Don't you see? Lucie must be absolutely certain she wants this marriage. I don't want her falling back on it because she can't think of anything else to do."

Again, Rhys felt the sting of truth behind her words.

"I know that sounds harsh, and maybe I'm way out of line here, but what if she's doing what Jo did? Going for the tried and true, and not necessarily what's best for her. Or for you, either, Rhys, if you think about it. Every time we thought Jo had it together, that she'd finally learned her lesson, Jimmy would talk her into going back. 'He loves me,' she'd say, then last year she got pregnant and Jimmy proved his love by beating her so badly she almost lost the baby."

"Jeez, why didn't Lucie come to me with this? I could have helped."

"Yes. You and your checkbook."

"No," Rhys argued. "Lucie might enjoy my money and all it can offer, but she has more than enough of her own."

"But your wealth offers a lot of security, Rhys. Not to mention stability."

He couldn't help but notice that she'd called him Rhys, not Paxton. He couldn't help but notice a lot of things—the blazing green eyes, the petal-soft white of her skin, the full red lips drawn in consternation.

"Put that together with all the constant badgering," she added primly, "and it's no wonder Lucie feels compelled to marry you."

"I never badgered her," he protested indignantly. "For the record, Lucie was the one to tell *me* we'd be getting married. So how's that for your theory? She had her china pattern picked out before she'd graduated from high school, for heaven's sake. If she agreed to your pact, I'd bet my last nickel that you girls were the ones who were badgering. I bet she only mouthed the words so you'd all shut up."

He expected a heated denial. To his surprise, she merely laughed. "Touché. I guess we *were* kind of forceful." She shook her head ruefully. "Quinn made us go through this ceremony. We had to tell how we'd achieve success in our chosen careers. When it was Lucie's turn, she mumbled some nonsense about getting her first part in a movie. She, who'd never even considered a career in acting before. I should have known, there and then, that she never took the oath seriously."

Rhys tried to picture Lucie in that circle, but all he could envision was Trae, red hair thrown back and green eyes glittering as she swore off the institution.

"What ever happened to your friend?"

"Last I heard she was moving back in with her parents. That's why she wasn't able to be at the wedding."

"What about you?" he found himself asking aloud,

thinking again about their oath. "Why do you have such a phobia against marriage?"

"I'm not afraid." With a sudden frown, she straightened in the seat. "I just want to get my career going, my future established, before worrying about how to fit a man into my life."

Interesting, how defensive she suddenly sounded. "So the trick," he pressed, "is to make sure no man can get too close?"

"Yes. No. Oh, for heaven's sake, there's no trick, Paxton. I'm simply making sure that I live my life, my way."

Ah, so they were back to calling him Paxton. "And all this time, you've never been tempted to break the pact?" he pressed, needing to know. "Never been in love?"

"I've had a near-miss or two." The speed with which she said it had him suspecting she'd never been tempted at all. "But in each case, we had to break it off. The man involved couldn't accept that my career must come first."

"And which career is that?"

"Don't get snide. You know darned well I'm talking about the writing. I'm not getting involved with a man until my first book is written and sold."

"Even if it takes another twenty years?"

"If this is another crack about my lack of self-discipline..."

"Not at all." He took his gaze off the road to look at her. Sitting ramrod straight, her chin jutted out with defiance, she had all the barriers up. Rhys felt pity for any guy who fell in love with her. It would be no easy trick getting past her defenses.

And damned if that didn't make him want to try. "There's obviously a reason you start books but never finish them. Obviously, you've got the will, heart and talent to accomplish anything you want, and yet *something* keeps holding you back."

"Not everyone agrees that I have talent," she said quietly. "My parents think I'm wasting time with my writing. In their minds, I could better occupy my life with a husband and family."

"So you kill two birds with one stone." She looked over at him, suddenly curious. And vulnerable. "You judge your work with your parent's critical eyes," he explained, choosing his words with care, "and you pick it apart until you can no longer bear it. And then, to compensate for the death of your dream, you refuse to do what they want. Which in this case is to settle down and get married."

"Slick, Paxton. I bet you say that to all the girls."

He could tell by her frown that he'd struck a nerve, but she was right. He had no business analyzing her, however accurate his assessment, not when he was trying to deal with so many issues of his own.

"Sorry, maybe I'm projecting. Let's just say I'm a veteran of parental expectations myself."

"Your father?"

Rhys nodded ruefully. "He had a never-ending list of what his eldest son was supposed to accomplish."

"And you dutifully mastered each and every item. Admirable, Paxton, if a tad obsessive, but c'mon, don't tell me you didn't have dreams of your own."

"Yeah, I did. As a kid, I wanted to design and build boats. I read every book I could find on the subject. I hounded the local boatyards during all my free hours until I became quite the little expert. Then I made the mistake of mentioning my hopes to my father."

He winced, remembering the unpleasantness of that night.

He might have stopped right there, but Trae leaned closer with a concerned expression and he found himself wanting to tell her more. "It was one of those rare nights he was home, and we were sitting in front of the fire. It was warm and cozy and he seemed mellow enough, so I started blurting out my plans for the future. It was the first time I'd ever opened up to him. Come to think of it, it was also the last."

"Oh, no. He shot you down?"

"His exact words were, 'Son, you're a brainless twit.' The fact that I could even consider opening a boatyard in the current economy proved that I didn't have the sense God gave a mule. He wasn't investing in my harebrained scheme, he said. He'd as soon pour his hard-earned money down the drain."

She shook her head sadly. "Talk about harsh. Not to mention shortsighted."

Rhys felt guilty for enjoying her concern. "I'm sure he felt he was acting in my best interests. In his mind, we had a business to run. There was no room for dreaming."

"No offense, but did the man have a heart? He was your father, not your business advisor. His job was to support you, whatever your dream."

"Like your family?" he asked wryly.

For an instant, he wondered how different his youth might have been if he'd had someone like Trae for a champion.

"Well, he isn't here to stop you anymore," she went on, ignoring his comment. "With all that money at your disposal, what's stopping you from building your boats now?"

"I'm head of a major corporation. Too many people depend on me."

She swiveled in the seat, leaning toward him. "And that means you're not entitled to happiness, to fulfillment? Your boatyard might be a risk, but so was the first magazine your dad acquired. And what about the sports team he had to sell because it was losing so much money?"

For someone who'd always been so disdainful of his company, she sure seemed to know a lot about it. About him.

Uncomfortable with her questions, he tried to change the subject. "So, what do you think of the scenery? Nice place, huh?"

She ignored him, well aware that the landscape hadn't changed much in the past several hours. "We're talking about your dream, here," she pressed, her voice ringing with urgency. "Your vision."

"Not me. I'm talking about the scenery."

"Stop hiding from the truth, Paxton," she pressed, stubborn to the core. "And start listening to what your heart's trying to tell you. No more quibbling over the dollars and cents, and for heaven's sake, no more parroting your father. Or the next thing you know, you'll be passing the same sterile legacy down to your own children."

Rhys had the sudden uncomfortable memory of Jack accusing him of sounding too much like their old man. Was that what he'd left them? A sterile legacy? And was Rhys that close to following in his footsteps?

"Let's just drop the subject, shall we?" he said, not happy about where his thoughts were leading him.

"Listen to you." Green eyes flashing, she faced him squarely, her entire posture a challenge. "What a hypocrite. You sit there berating me for not following my dream, while making lame excuses for not pursuing your own. What is this, do as I say, not as I do?"

She was right. He could come up with a thousand reasons for not building those boats, most inherited from his father, but the bottom line was, the only real limitations were the ones he put on himself.

Fulfillment, Trae had said. Something to do himself, for himself. He didn't have to build the *Queen Mary,* for crying out loud. He could start small, start slow and see how it went.

"Tell you what," he said after a long pause. "You sell your first book and I'll invest in my boatyard."

"And aren't you the clever businessman? You figure you're safe, that I'll never finish a manuscript."

He shook his head "On the contrary, I *know* you'll finish that book."

"Is this where you go all 'one for the Gipper' on me, giving me the rah-rah speech about my talent and potential?"

No, this was where he dared her, knowing Trae Andrelini never backed down from a challenge. "I doubt you need a speech. All I'm suggesting is a bet. Your completed manuscript versus my first seaworthy vessel. Let's see who gets there first."

"Another bet, Paxton? Didn't you learn your lesson the first time?"

"I haven't lost yet. The fact that I'm still wearing these jeans is living proof of that. C'mon Trae, what's with the hesitation? You chicken?" He made the same clucking sounds that she had used on him.

"In your dreams." She leaned over the seat, reaching for Lucie's backpack. "I just so happen to have a notebook. Maybe I'll get started right now. If I were you, Paxton, I might want to find a name for my boatyard."

Trust Trae to meet his challenge, to challenge him back.

And in the process, forcing him out of his comfort zone, pushing him to think and say and do things he'd never before imagined, leading him to a world in which he had no prior experience and no hope of control. She infuriated him, yet she invigorated him and left him eager to go at it again. All too easily, all too enjoyably, he could envision a life of one confrontation after another.

He frowned. Unfortunately, he'd be marrying someone else.

Chapter Eleven

Scribbling in the notebook, Trae marveled at how quickly words and ideas were coming to her. She'd been at it for hours now and still had plenty more. She had Rhys to thank for her sudden burst of creativity. Talking with him—really talking—she'd realized what she wanted to write about. The story of two very dissimilar people, off on a quest, learning about each other bit by bit along the way.

She paused, glancing over at him, struck by how he'd become an entirely different person than the one she'd known last week. Listening as he'd told her about growing up in such a sterile environment, she'd understood so much about him. All too easily, she'd pictured that younger Rhys, sitting all alone in his big, empty kitchen. Broke her heart, made her wish there was something she could have done, could do now, to keep that lonely note out of his voice.

Yet comparing his childhood to her own, she could see

why they always came at a problem from different directions. And how sometimes it wasn't such a bad thing to have different perspectives. Take what he'd said about her writing. Being around her parents all the time, she'd never thought she might be blocked by their blatant disapproval. It took someone from the outside to pick up on that possibility.

His suggestion had planted a seed, and when he'd issued his challenge, none-too-subtly egging her on to finish her novel, inspiration had blossomed. She needed a new approach, her own approach. In the past, she'd been laden with literary aspirations, which in her mind meant wringing every last ounce of angst out of the situation. But listening to Rhys tell her about his life, hearing the pain beneath his words, she'd realized it wasn't enough to merely tell a story. She had to *feel* it. A little bit of Trae Andrelini had to be there on every page.

So no more indulging in literary pretense, she decided. She found it too constricting. In writing, as in life, she was better off just being herself.

And on that thought, the car made an ominous coughing sound. Rhys muttered an oath. Focused on his scowl, she didn't realize that he was pulling off the road until the car chugged to a stop.

"What's wrong?" she asked, sitting bolt upright, blinking as she glanced around her. All she could see were the low, rolling hills of sand and brush, and in the distance, a glowing orange sun rapidly sinking below the horizon. "Why did you stop the car?"

"I didn't." Rhys seemed as confused as her. "It stopped itself."

"We must have run out of gas."

"I don't think so." He pointed at the dashboard. "Unless

that gauge is broken, we still have half a tank. I'm guessing it's something with the engine, the way it sounded there at the end."

"Okay, then let's pop the hood."

He eyed her as if she'd just suggested flying to Saturn. "I don't know what each part is, much less how to repair it. You know anything about the inner workings of the automobile?"

"I always let my brothers fix my car."

"So there you have it." He pulled on the emergency brake, cursing when it didn't engage. "Useless piece of…"

Shoving open the door, he got out of the car. "Grab your stuff, we're going for a walk. I noticed a truck stop about a mile or so back."

Trae eyed the dark, dusty road behind them. Now, more than ever, she missed her cell phone. "I don't know. Maybe I should stay with the car."

He leaned in, scowling. "I'm not about to leave you out here in the middle of nowhere. Come on, Trae. While they fix the engine, we can get something to eat." Leaving no room for argument, he slammed the door shut.

Trae stuffed her notes in the backpack and joined him on the side of the road. He'd had her the moment he mentioned eating. She was ravenous.

As they started off, Rhys put himself between her and the highway. A few days ago, she might have scoffed at the gesture. Talk about hopelessly heroic—as if he could absorb the impact of a megaton truck before it could crash into her. Tonight, though, she merely felt warmed, knowing it was just part and parcel of the man Rhys was. One of the last genuine good guys.

As if to prove this, he put his arm around her and

eased her off the shoulder, shielding her with his body as another ten-wheeler barreled by. He didn't even realize he was doing it, she realized. Being protective came naturally to him.

She felt a sudden urge to lean into him, to absorb his strength and warmth, but once the truck whizzed past, he promptly let her go, leaving Trae feeling desolate, and more chilled than the warm night air would warrant.

This was bad, very bad. She'd promised herself she could handle being around the man, that she wouldn't let errant thoughts get the best of her, yet here they were— she, Rhys and the soft, sultry breeze—and all she could think about was snuggling closer.

"Look," he said suddenly, gesturing ahead at the welcoming lights of the truck stop. "We're almost there."

Almost being a relative term. Trudging into the area a good fifteen minutes later, they paused for a moment to scope the place out under a huge neon sign urging motorists to Come Fill-Er-Up, whether it be with food, drink or gasoline.

"Oh, good, they have a diner," Trae remarked. "I was afraid we might have to make do with that prepackaged mini-mart stuff."

"It's crowded. That's usually a good sign. Though out here in the middle of nowhere, I guess there's not much of choice for dining. Even the mini-mart is bustling."

The truck stop did seem to be a popular spot. The gas station was three cars deep at the pumps and two in the bays, while another vehicle was waiting outside the garage with its engine idling. Inside the mini-mart, a good half-dozen people waited at the counter, with at least that many more milling about the aisles. The diner had them lined up at the door, while music blared from the bar on the right.

Only one area appeared to be deserted. The dingy motel on the left, advertising cheap rooms for the night.

Following her stare, Rhys shook his head. "No sense worrying about that unless we have to. Let's go talk to the mechanic first, and then we'll get something to eat."

The mechanic was far from encouraging. He estimated it would take an hour before he could tow the car, and even then it might be ten or eleven o'clock before he got the chance to look it over. Of course, if the problem required a part and he didn't have it in stock…

He let the words trail off with a shrug, his message clear. Miles from anywhere, they were at his mercy. They'd find no public transportation, no car-rental agency, not even another garage to render a second opinion.

If they needed a place to sleep tonight, the mechanic suggested with a brief nod behind him, they could try his brother's motel. Not much to look at, maybe, but Irv kept the place clean and the price was nothing to gripe about. When it came to overnight lodgings, they could do a lot worse.

"Thanks," Rhys said quickly, "but we'll take our chances that you can fix the car." Informing the mechanic that they'd check back with him in an hour, Rhys took Trae by the elbow to steer her toward the diner.

"What, we're not going to have a chat with Irv?" Trae asked all too sweetly. "I thought you liked to plan ahead."

"I do. Just call me optimistic."

"Okay, Mr. Sunshine, got any positive thoughts for that?" she asked, pointing ahead at the line gathered in front of the diner.

Rhys groaned. The crowd seemed to consist mainly of truck drivers, all cranky from the road and in no better mood to be waiting than they were. Twenty glares followed them as they pushed inside to ask how long the wait would be. Making it plain that his woes were not her own, the beefy waitress imagined it could easily be an hour.

Though if they didn't mind sandwiches and were okay with the two-drink minimum, they could get served a lot quicker over at the bar.

"What do you think?" Rhys asked Trae.

"Correct me if I'm wrong, but our choices are waiting here for half the night, dining alfresco with a plastic hot dog from the mini-mart or belting down a beer and a hot pastrami? Me, I'd say it's a no brainer."

"Yeah, but the bar seems dark. And loud."

"Spontaneity, Paxton. Trying new things, remember? We can at least check it out. If it's truly awful, we can always come back here and get in line."

The bar *was* dark, and the jukebox by the door could probably blast out their eardrums, but since the only other patrons were a young couple in the corner and a lone man in a Stetson nursing a bottle at a dimly lit booth in the back, they decided to give it a try.

Seeing no hostess to seat them, they went to the bar. Built completely of oak, which had darkened with age, it dominated the large room. A mirror covered the back wall, with bottles lined up in front of it, while a series of ladder-back swivel stools sat waiting for customers.

The bartender was a solidly built man, his thinning salt-and-pepper hair pulled back in a ponytail. He introduced himself as Max, eldest of the three brothers who ran the rest area. Used to be a biker bar, he told them—which explained the black clothes and tattoos on his arms—but nowadays it catered mostly to truckers.

While Rhys ordered beers, Trae took in their surroundings. To the left of the bar, the room held a small stage and an empty area no doubt meant for dancing. On the right, lining the walls, sat a series of padded booths, each with its own window. Add in the scuffed pine floorboards covered with sawdust and the round wooden tables that could easily seat ten, and the place looked like a Hollywood rendition of an Old West saloon. All that was missing was the swinging double doors at the entrance.

"Let's sit there," she told Rhys, pointing at the first booth. "Then we can watch and see when the car is towed in."

Fifteen minutes later, seated on the bench across from Rhys with her iced mug of beer and a slab of pastrami piled high on rye, Trae felt as if she'd died and gone to heaven. She noticed that Rhys had no trouble in wolfing down his cheeseburger and fries, either.

"Not bad, huh?" she asked as she watched him drain his beer. "Admit it, Paxton, you're glad we tried this."

He shrugged. "Except that now we'll never know how the blue plate special tasted. For all we know, we could have missed something special."

"Try this," she said, offering him her sandwich. "This will help you forget about the diner."

He leaned across the table to take a bite. Suddenly aware of how close her fingers were to his lips, Trae felt a stirring deep within her. As her eyes met his, a jolt of desire rocketed through her body. It was all she could do not to drop the sandwich on the table.

"Hmm, you're right." Smiling as he chewed, Rhys sat back, completely oblivious to her reaction. "Want to try mine?"

Aware of the double entendre—though he apparently

was not—Trae shook her head. What was wrong with her? Who got turned on while eating a sandwich?

It was all his fault, she decided. Did he have to look so rugged and appealing? The sleeves of his flannel shirt were rolled up to his elbows, revealing his strong, capable forearms. Couple that with his windblown hair and five o'clock shadow, and he looked like he'd just felled a tree somewhere. Or something just as physically demanding.

Certainly a far cry from the "surfer dude" of last night, or the annoyed executive she'd originally hooked up with. How was she supposed to regain her equilibrium when he was never the same man twice?

Finding his gaze on her, she realized she must have sighed out loud. Flustered, she looked away.

"How about another beer?" Not waiting for an answer, Rhys signaled Max with two fingers.

"But who's going to drive?" she asked, anxious to focus her attention on anywhere else but his face.

He raised an eyebrow. "What's this? Trae Andrelini, recommending caution? What happened to living life on the edge?"

"I'm just pointing out that two beers, on top of so little sleep, will make me worse than useless in the driving department."

"Don't worry, I'm fine. Besides, they haven't even gone to tow the car yet. The two beers will have more than worn off by the time we get back on the road."

He nodded out the window where the bright-red tow truck still sat beneath the huge sign. To the right, she could see the mechanic, still working on the car he'd been repairing when they had talked to him.

Grabbing the ketchup bottle, she slathered some on her

fries. "So we'll have to kill some time. Ready to get back to your training?"

"For crying out loud," he growled, not bothering to mask his irritation. "Does it amuse you that much to point out how bad I am at relationships? You can't find anything positive I could possibly bring to the marriage?"

Startled, she glanced up to meet his gaze. She saw anger there and maybe even a little hurt, and she felt instant regret. She sounded like his parents, harping on his faults, withholding their approval. Rhys deserved better.

"I'm sorry, okay? I meant it as a joke, something to lighten the mood, but you're right. You have a bunch of great things to bring to the table."

"Such as?"

Big mistake, she thought as she stopped to consider his assets. She could think of a good twenty without even trying. She seized on the first. "Well, for one thing, your hands."

Splaying his fingers, he studied them in confusion.

"I have a thing about hands," she confessed. "Someone once told me they revealed a great deal about a person's character."

"And mine tell you what?"

"Well, they're strong and firm, yet warm and gentle at the same time." She blushed as she realized what she'd admitted. As they both stared at his hands, she wondered if he, too, was remembering how deftly he'd used them on her the night before.

"There's also the way you shielded me out there on the highway," she said quickly to change the subject. "You never once paused to consider your own safety. That's some good stuff, Paxton. I think we can put being the perfect gentleman on the pro side of your list."

He looked up, tilting his head as he studied her. "Really? And here I thought that always annoyed you."

Flushing to the roots of her hair, she wished he wouldn't stare at her so intently. "Back then, everything about you annoyed me."

"And now?"

"You're not so bad now that I got to know you, okay?"

"Okay." He gave a half grin, as if recognizing how much the confession had cost her. In truth, "not so bad" didn't begin to express her opinion. Nor explain the sudden yearning welling up in her chest.

Stop it! she told herself. This was supposed to be a safe topic. How had it strayed onto such perilous ground?

Not that Rhys seemed aware of any danger. "But enough about me," he said, pushing his plate to the side and leaning forward. "It's your turn. Let's analyze *your* good and bad points to death."

"I'm not the one getting married."

"Fine, we'll start with that, then. Let's figure out why you're so dead set against marriage."

"I'm not." She meant to sound flippant but it came out sounding defensive instead. Knowing better than to look at him, she pushed her fries around her plate. "I happen to find it a perfectly admirable institution. Provided people enter into it for the right reasons."

"Meaning, there has to be love."

"No!" she protested without thinking. She couldn't think straight, not with him staring her in the face. "I mean, sometimes love makes you too crazy. You don't think right, you act like an idiot. You're so busy convincing yourself you're in heaven, you totally overlook the possible hell."

"Jeez, Trae, never knew you were such a romantic."

Stabbing a fry with her fork, she held it up, waving it as she stressed her point. "Go ahead, laugh, but deep down, you know I'm right. How many times have you seen it happen? Love strikes—or, more accurately, lust strikes—and just like that, life's a mess. Two otherwise intelligent adults get the hots for each other, and every sane, rational thought goes out of their heads." She paused, painfully aware of how she could put herself into that category.

Setting the fork back down on her plate, she tried an example. "Look at my mom. She wanted to be a dancer, dreamed of seeing the world. But then she meets my father at a high school dance, and all of a sudden she can't think of anything else. Married at seventeen, with two kids by twenty and one on the way. Her bright, shining future narrowed down to a brownstone in Brooklyn, filled to the brim with children whose needs will always supercede her own."

"But they're still happily married, right?"

How could he so stubbornly miss the point? "I won't end up like her, Rhys. And I sure as hell won't become another Joanna."

He frowned. "Despite popular belief, not all men are pigs, you know."

"I know that. But when those hormones start buzzing, everything gets hopelessly messed up."

She looked out the window, sipping her beer, trying to hide the sudden color in her cheeks. All too vividly, she remembered the quagmire of sensation when lust had flared between them last night. Maybe that was because it was still flaring on her part.

And maybe his, too. He certainly seemed in a hurry to make his own protest. "In case you're interested, hormones didn't dictate my reasons for getting married. Lucie and I based our decision purely on compatibility, our shared vision for the future."

"Wow, that sure sounds hot. I bet poor old Lucie goes all quivery inside at the mere mention of your honeymoon. Tell me, Paxton, have you ever given her more than that quick, brotherly peck on the cheek?"

"You're contradicting yourself," he said impatiently. "In one breath you tell me that marriage can't be based on lust, and in the next you're nailing me for not being horny enough. Make up your mind, Trae. You can't have it both ways."

"Yeah, well, neither can you. How can you expect to make Lucie happy if you treat her like a little sister? A girl needs more than an occasional arm draped on her shoulder, or a quick squeeze of the hand. When was the last time you backed her up against the wall and kissed her until her knees went weak?"

She regretted the outburst the instant it left her mouth. She imagined they were both only too aware of how her knees had buckled last night.

"Okay," he said with an edge to his tone. "When we find Lucie, I swear I'll sweep her off her feet and declare my undying devotion. Will that make you happy?"

"Yes," she said emphatically, but, mesmerized by his gaze, she realized the prospect didn't please her at all. For the first time in their friendship, she found herself envying Lucie.

And resenting her friend for taking Rhys for granted.

Watching Trae's expressive face, Rhys knew she was right. Lucie did deserve passion from the man she married, but over the years, he'd fallen into the habit of acting more like her older brother, and in truth, he couldn't remember the last time he'd kissed her.

Fine, he'd take care of it. The instant they found her, he'd knock her little designer socks off. He knew damned well how to effectively kiss a woman. Forgive him for boasting, but he'd pretty much proved that to everyone's satisfaction last night.

Against his better judgment, his gaze went to Trae's lips. As if aware of his thoughts, she looked down, blushing profusely.

Case closed.

Or was it? Yes, he'd given her a good kiss, a great kiss, but if he stopped to think about it, what had he accomplished besides proving her theory? Guess who had let lust get the best of him? Talk about acting crazy.

And here he was, unable to take his gaze from her, waiting for any opportunity to go crazy again.

He felt a sudden need to get out of there, put distance between them.

"It's been a while," he said abruptly, gesturing out the window as he rose to his feet. "I think I'll go out and ask Jerry what's holding things up."

"Jerry?" She looked up, startled.

"The mechanic," he explained. "That's what it said on his shirt. You'll be okay here while I go try to move things along?"

"Yeah, sure—" she made a shooing motion with her hands "—take your time."

She seemed anxious for him to go, which, irrationally, annoyed him. What did he hope, that she'd make a grab for him, cling to him, make it impossible for him to leave?

Yes, that was exactly what he wanted, he realized as he strode to the door. She'd been smart not to comply. Even now, his blood was pulsing double-time. Had he stayed with her, had he gazed one minute more into her deep, emerald eyes…

.For an instant, he let himself imagine the possibilities. Touching Trae, holding her, tasting her—would that be so great a crime? Lucie had run out on *him,* after all, and it wasn't as if she'd made any attempt to make amends.

But do you love her?

Realizing that he could no longer determine which one was the "her" in that question, he shook his head and shoved through the door. Only one thing was clear. Love— no, make that lust—really did screw up everything.

If he couldn't trust himself in a bar, with people around them, he had better avoid her. Maybe he'd just take his time, chatting with Jerry.

So the mechanic's name was Jerry, Trae thought in be- musement as she watched Rhys walk to the gas station. Of course he'd notice the name tag. That was Rhys, always good with details. No doubt he was in there charming Jerry now, urging him to fix their car, convincing the poor mechanic that it would be in his own best interests to see them swiftly on their way.

She certainly hoped so. Out on the. road, one or the other of them was always too busy driving. But here, well, who knew what would happen….

Funny, how weird it seemed without Rhys there. You'd think she'd breathe easier with him gone, but she kept glancing out the window, hoping he'd return. How could she feel so lonely already?

Then again, maybe she just felt alone. With the young couple leaving and a group of truckers coming in, the atmosphere in the bar had shifted noticeably. Armed with beers, the newcomers had taken the stools at the bar, calling out jovially to the man who'd been drinking alone in the corner. "Yo, Clay, you buying again tonight?"

Picking up his bottle of tequila, the man they'd called Clay wove toward the bar, listing seriously to the left. She couldn't help but notice how little was left in the bottle. "Sure, why not," he slurred in a slow, Texas drawl.

She realized she was staring, and worse, Clay was staring back. She smiled faintly, half in apology and half as a polite, impersonal greeting, but his answering wink glittered with lascivious intent.

Trae was no stranger to horny lotharios, but this one was huge, and he'd had far too much to drink. Sitting unsteadily, Clay saluted her with a tug on the brim of his Stetson. He elbowed the trucker next to him and they both began to laugh.

Aware of their continued scrutiny, Trae shifted uncomfortably on the bench as she repeatedly consulted her watch, then the window. Where was Rhys, anyway? How much longer could she sit here with that cowboy watching her every move?

She decided this was as good a time as any to pay a visit to the restroom.

She picked up her backpack and followed Max's directions to a narrow, dimly lit hallway, littered with discarded furniture. Turning sideways to squeeze past a broken table, she found two doors, one predictably labeled Gals and the other Gents.

After washing her hands, she dug into the backpack for a comb. While she was at it, she might as well brush her teeth, check her makeup, file the chipped nail. Essential tasks, she tried to tell herself, but deep down she knew she was hiding.

Eventually, she ran out of things to do and could stall no more. Crossing her fingers that Rhys would have returned by now, she ventured into the hallway.

"Hey there, pretty lady."

Leaning against the wall as if it propped him up, Clay seemed to fill the narrow, dingy space. He'd spilled tequila on his jeans, she noticed. And she didn't even want to guess the source of the stain on his blue striped shirt.

Peeling himself off the wall, he teetered toward her, his unfocused leer all the more threatening in the confined area. Huge? The man was monstrous, and he was coming her way.

"Been watching you all night, sugar. You're one hot little mama."

Hot little mama? "No, I'm not," Trae said firmly, stepping forward. "What I am, actually, is tired. Beat. And in absolutely no mood for this. So please, do us both a favor and move out of my way."

Planting his feet firmly, looming larger and a good deal steadier than he'd seemed earlier, Clay shook his head. "C'mon, you know you want it," he said with another leer. "You want it bad."

"Not that bad." Trae tried to push past him, but she might as well have tried to move the wall.

"That guy you're with," he wheezed, leaning closer. "Ain't never gonna get it up for you, sugar. You're wasting your time on him."

Had she been that transparent? Embarrassed, and annoyed at Clay for catching her in an unguarded moment, she pushed harder.

And bounced back like a ping-pong ball, which seemed to amuse him further. "Now, now, where ya going in such a hurry? Stay here with good ole Clay and let him show you how a real man appreciates a woman."

She was supposed to trust a guy who spoke of himself in the third person?

Thanks to her older brothers, Trae generally knew how to handle lecherous drunks, but as they'd so often cautioned, some jerks never listen to reason. When you run up against one of those, they insisted, your first best option is to run away.

Excellent advice, except she was in a dead-end hallway with Clay blocking the exit. Glancing quickly behind her, seeing the door to the ladies room, Trae decided to duck inside and pray for the lock to hold.

Unfortunately, Clay noticed her backward glance. Clamping down on her wrist, he held her in place. "Whoa, sugar. Where ya think you're going?"

Second course of action, she remembered, was to kick and scratch and bite, but Clay must have read the same manual as her brothers. Before she could act, he spun her around and clasped her in a viselike grip against his chest.

Heart pounding, she tried to remember her self-defense classes. What had the instructor said to do in this situation? Right, stomp down on the perp's foot.

Stomp hard.

But again, Clay proved remarkably agile. Not to mention one step ahead. Lifting her off the ground before her heel could do much damage, he brought his face close to hers for a sloppy kiss. "Relax," he hissed in her ear. "We ain't near to finished yet."

"I beg to differ," said a deep voice behind her. "This is where a wise man knows to cut his losses and run."

Chapter Twelve

Rhys had often heard the term *seeing red,* but until that precise moment, he'd had no idea what it meant. The instant he saw that Neanderthal pawing Trae, every ounce of blood he had went rushing into his head, clouding his vision—and his other senses—with a definite reddish hue.

All his instincts screamed at him to attack, but he forced himself to ignore them. The issue here was control. The one who maintained it would retain the advantage. "Let her go," he said, his calm tone liberally laced with menace as he slowly, steadily approached. "None of us wants any trouble."

The words got him little more than a bark of derision, but Rhys hadn't expected the man to respond with anything close to reason. According to Max, this guy had been drinking all day, and even at the best of times, was not what you'd call a rational fellow. The main objective, Rhys decided, was to divert the drunk's attention from Trae, and to himself. And, with any luck, get them all out of this hurdle-strewn hallway before the punches started.

"You should know…" Rhys went on in the same even tone "…I'm well trained in three different disciplines—boxing, wrestling and martial arts."

"Well, ain't you a regular James Bond. Go away, fancy man, or I'll knock you three ways from Sunday."

"You could try. But here's the thing. If I'm not back at the bar in three minutes, Max plans to call the state marshals. And from what he tells me, you don't want to be talking with those people again."

As hoped, this got Clay to relax his grip. Seizing the opportunity, Trae pushed away, catching her captor off balance, sending them both staggering backward. Since there wasn't a lot of wiggle room behind him, Clay crashed into the wall with a loud, reverberating thud.

His cowboy hat went flying, revealing a shiny, prematurely balding head.

Surprised, he bounced back off the wall to grab his quarry. Twisting and turning, Trae squirmed to get free, but Clay maintained a death grip on her arm. Intent on reeling her back in, he never noticed Rhys easing closer. He did, however, notice the quick right jab to his chin.

Howling, Clay let go of Trae to cover his lower face with both hands.

Frustratingly enough, his solid bulk was planted with Trae trapped behind him. "Why'd you go and do that for?" Clay whined, eyeing Rhys with a perplexed expression.

"I warned you to release the lady."

"That ain't no lady." Clay glared at Trae. "She's a cold, nasty bi—"

Rhys stopped him with a solid punch to the gut.

Dropping his hands to his midsection, Clay doubled over. Trae picked up her backpack and raised it over her shoulder.

Rhys shook his head in warning. The last thing he wanted was Clay turning on her while she was still on the other side of him. "What's the matter, Clay?" he taunted. He had to keep the man coming at him, toward the open barroom where no one would be impaled on broken furniture. "Can't handle a little jab in the belly?"

Growling, Clay charged, an oversized fullback lowering his shoulder. With no room to maneuver, Rhys had to take the full brunt of his attack. Reeling backward, he crashed into the table. It broke apart beneath him, sending him toppling to the floor.

Staring up at the brute towering over him, Rhys mentally assessed the damage. No broken bones, though he'd hurt like hell in the morning. The most serious bruise, he figured, had to be to his ego.

Scrambling to his feet, he stumbled backward again, his goal still the open barroom. Clay followed, victory gleaming in his eyes. In his smugness, he failed to notice Trae swinging her backpack behind him.

Not until she caught Clay on the top of his shiny head.

Rhys braced himself. Not one to be publicly humiliated by a female, Clay grabbed a broken table leg and spun to face Trae. Backing away slowly, her face pale with fright, she seemed painfully aware that she was no match for the beast now looming over her.

Not waiting to see what Clay might do next, Rhys charged.

Hitting the man was like banging into the proverbial brick wall. No more seeing red; all Rhys could see now were stars. Staggering, he shook his head in an attempt to clear his vision.

"Rhys," Trae screamed. "Watch out!"

Ducking instinctively, he took a glancing blow above his right eye. Not much impact, but it broke the skin, causing it to bleed profusely. Blinking away the dripping blood, he jabbed upward with his left and caught Clay under the cheek. This sent the drunk stumbling over a chair and banging into the wall.

Reaching out, Rhys seized Trae's arm and pulled her to him. By the time Clay could recover enough to focus, Rhys had her safely behind him.

"Why, you little…" Clay snarled as he came at Rhys, murder in his eyes. "I'll show you what's what."

Rhys merely smiled, his fists poised and ready, his legs planted firmly. "You're welcome to try."

Before either man could land a punch, a gruff voice called out from the doorway.

"That's enough, fellas," boomed Max. "I suggest you both move it along if you don't want any trouble. The law is on the way."

The words had more power to stop the drunk than any punch Rhys could have landed. With a look of abject horror, Clay stopped in his tracks. "What'd you go and do that for, Max? You know they're gonna lock me up this time."

"Can't have you busting up the place, Clay. Bad for business."

Muttering curses, Clay pushed past them in his haste to get out of the bar. Rhys turned instantly to Trae. "Are you all right?"

"I'm fine." Her low, raspy tone belied the assurance. "I'm more worried about your eye."

"It's just a simple cut." Rhys reached up to his forehead,

applying pressure to the wound to stop it from bleeding. "You should see the other guy."

"It's no joking matter. You could have been badly hurt."

"So could you. Sorry, Trae, I don't know what I could have been thinking, leaving you alone in a place like this."

He expected her to argue, to protest that she was a big girl and could take care of herself, but the incident with Clay must have shaken her considerably. Laying her head against his chest, she let him wrap his arms around her. "Yeah," she said quietly. "But there you were when I needed you most."

His chest tightened, as did his grasp. Trae "I-can-take-care-of-myself" Andrelini had just said she needed him, a prospect that both soothed and exhilarated him. It felt right, somehow, as if it were always meant to be. Breathing in the sweet scent of her, he lost himself in the moment.

Until Max spoke out behind them. "Sorry about that, folks. Clay gets carried away sometimes."

They broke apart, like kids caught making out in the basement. "What's with that guy?" Rhys asked, trying to sound normal, while inside he felt shaken to the core.

Max looked over his shoulder, as if half expecting Clay to be eavesdropping. "Let's just say things haven't been going so well for him lately. Second time this week he went on the prowl. Been having troubles with the little woman at home."

"Go figure," Trae said quietly beside him.

"Yeah, well, he'll sleep it off and not remember half of it in the morning. Though he'll probably be taking his nap in the county lockup."

"So you did call the police?"

"Hell, yeah. Business comes first. Speaking of which, you folks about ready to settle up?"

More than ready, Rhys thought. With all that had happened, he couldn't get out of the bar fast enough.

Insisting on carrying the backpack after they'd paid their bill, Rhys led Trae outside, his arm wrapped protectively around her shoulders. Once outside, he noticed with relief that the big red truck no longer sat under the Fill-Er-Up sign.

Looking up, he spotted the tow truck on the highway, their rental car attached to the back of it, making a hard right turn into the truck stop.

"Finally," Trae said, echoing his relief aloud.

"I suggest we go over to the garage and light another fire under Jerry. Apparently, that's the only way things get done around here."

"While we're there, let's see if he's got a first-aid kit." She reached up to gently brush the hair off his forehead. "If we don't do something to stop the bleeding, this 'simple cut' is liable to drain you dry."

Hers was a simple gesture, one of caring and concern, but that didn't stop the hot flash of desire. Gazing down at her, aware of how she continued to tremble, he marveled at how Trae needed him now. Far more than Lucie. All this time, not one cry for help from his fiancée, while here stood Trae, shaking like a leaf, trying to reassure him with false bravado. Overwhelmed by emotion, he reached out to shelter her in his arms.

"No," she said suddenly, taking a step backward.

At the same time, a loud siren pierced his eardrums. Following where she pointed, seeing the flashing lights of the approaching police car, he realized Trae hadn't been rejecting his gesture but rather reacting to the situation unfolding before them.

As the troopers wailed into the truck stop, a battered

green pickup wove toward the same exit. Rhys didn't need to see Clay's angry face through the windshield to know it was the drunk. The zigzag pattern told it all.

Though there was sufficient space for the pickup and the police car to pass without incident, Jerry, who'd stopped under the sign, chose that moment to release the rental from its moorings.

The emergency brake isn't up, Rhys thought in alarm, even as the rental car began to bounce into the path of the approaching squad car. Though the police swerved at the very last minute, Clay delayed his reaction by too wide a margin. Ramming into the car with a resounding crash, he sandwiched it between the front of his truck and the now blinking Fill-Er-Up sign.

"No," Rhys echoed Trae's protest aloud.

But, of course, it was already too late.

"It's late," Rhys was saying dully as Trae dug through the first-aid kit they'd gotten from Jerry. "I should be going."

Sitting on the bed in front of her, staring off into space, he made no real effort to stand, much less move to his own room, three doors down. Once they'd realized they were stuck for the night, they'd agreed to stay at the hotel but opted for separate accommodations. Irv made it easy, offering two rooms for half the price of Chad's tacky love nest.

"Stay where you are," Trae told him firmly, looking up from the night table, where she'd set up the ointment and bandages. "We need to clean that wound and dress it with a butterfly bandage. We don't want it opening up and bleeding all night. Need I point out how little I need you dying of blood loss and leaving me alone in this place?"

She couldn't control a shiver as she looked around her.

She was referring to the truck stop, not the room itself. As Jerry had promised, Irv did keep the place clean, if a tad quaint. Gazing at the water bed, multicolored beads and tie-dyed fabrics, she decided he'd last redecorated late in the sixties. She could almost hear the strains of a sitar and smell patchouli incense. No wonder her head was spinning.

Then again, maybe her sudden inability to focus could be attributed to tonight's series of improbable events.

"I feel like I'm in the middle of some fever dream." Reaching up, she swabbed his forehead with the damp cloth. "What a night. I can't believe the Neon is gone. You're sure it's totaled?" Silly question. She'd been there, felt the impact, witnessed the tangled remains of the poor car.

"Dead and buried. They'll be holding a memorial service in the morning," Rhys sighed. "And there goes our road trip. Hard to tour about the country without wheels."

He winced as she dabbed at his cut, and she winced at the finality in his statement. Applying the antiseptic ointment to his bruised skull, she felt a sudden need to grab hold of him and not let go.

"Clay sure left us one fine mess to clean up," Rhys went on, oblivious. "I'm not looking forward to calling the rental car company."

Rhys winced again as she applied the bandage to his head. "We should have pressed charges. If you ask me, that table leg qualified for assault with a deadly weapon. And I hate to think of what he might have done to you had I not shown up when I did."

"Clay's in lots of trouble." All too vividly she could picture him, hands cuffed behind his back as he was shoved into the police car. "And really, all he did was kiss me.

Besides, it would mean coming back here to testify. You think I want to face that man again?"

Turning at the sudden break in her voice, he reached up for her hand. "You're trembling."

Her hand, her voice, her entire being shook. She couldn't seem to stop. "I—I've never felt so powerless," she blurted out. "I took all those defense classes. I couldn't have been better trained. Yet when my moment of truth came, I couldn't do anything."

Rising, he took her in his arms, cradling her against his chest. "The man was twice your size and you had no room to maneuver in that hallway. I don't see who could have stopped him."

She pulled back a bit to look up at him. "You did."

"I wasn't alone," he said with a rueful grin. "Someone was swinging a pretty hefty backpack, as I remember. It took two of us to bring that jerk down."

"Still, if you hadn't shown up…"

"But I did." Staring into her eyes, his expression went grave. "You're safe now," he said quietly, his hand gently brushing her cheek. "And I'm here to keep you that way."

She felt his words as much as heard them, down deep inside the core of her being, and all at once it was as if the rest of the world no longer existed. All she could see, hear or feel was this man before her, bruised and battered from the battle on her behalf. How beautiful he seemed to her, how precious, from the cut on his forehead to the bruises forming on his knuckles.

"Your poor hands," she said softly, bringing the injured one to her lips.

She'd meant it as a "here, let me kiss it and make it feel better" gesture, but the instant her lips touched his skin, a fire was lit within her. With her last coherent thought, she heard his sharp intake of breath, saw the answering spark ignite in his eyes. He, too, felt the pull, saw the futility in resisting it.

With a low groan deep in his throat, he took her head in his hands. Sliding his fingers into her hair, he covered her mouth with his own.

She moaned as their lips met, her body acknowledging how deeply she'd craved this. Craved him. Opening her mouth, she welcomed him in, going weak with sensation as he used his strong, warm hands on her body. Sliding his fingers down her neck, along her sides, he touched her like a blind man, taking his time, savoring every inch. Through it all, he kept seducing her mouth, his tongue encircling hers in a dance as slow and as sensual as a moonlit tango. Dazed by longing, Trae could only follow where he led.

Until he drew back, his lips clinging to hers until the last possible second. In some scattered part of her mind, she understood that this was it, that he was pulling away and breaking all contact, but all she knew for certain was that she couldn't allow it. Not now, not yet. Not ever.

Moaning in protest, she reached for him, exerting her will, pressing her body up against his as she deepened their kiss. Rhys no longer fought her. Grasping her tighter, he acknowledged the urgency, the inevitability of their coming together.

And as if a switch had been flipped, their kiss came alive, became frantic. Their hands moved everywhere in a desperate need to pop open buttons, undo zippers, remove whatever stood between them. In a flurry of movement, shoes were kicked across the room, socks flew in the air, pants and shirts landed helter-skelter in piles about the floor.

Trae barely noticed the flurry of activity, focusing on the hard, virile chest in front of her. Running her hands across the muscled expanse, rasping her palms across his bare nipples, she knew she could never get enough of this. Of him.

"My turn," Rhys said huskily, sliding his large, capable hands across her breasts. Cupping them, he circled his thumbs over the swelling nipples. As he leaned down to take her breast in his mouth, a pure, white heat exploded inside her. And in that instant, her knees gave out on her.

Rhys was ready for her, sweeping her up into his arms to lay her down on the bed. The mattress rippled as the warm water ebbed and flowed beneath her. She found it an unbelievably erotic sensation, floating on the shifting mattress while Rhys stared down at her naked body, devouring her with his gaze.

She held out her arms to him, and with a groan, he joined her on the bed, rolling them back and forth on the mattress as he continued to kiss her. Helpless under the renewed onslaught of his tongue, Trae clung to him, drowning in sheer pleasure as he again kissed her breasts, his tongue performing the same magic it had unleashed in her mouth. As he alternately sucked, then twirled his tongue around them, Trae could feel her nipples reaching out for him, growing tight with need.

Mindless with desire, she ran her tongue over his ears, his neck, his chest. Her hands went everywhere, her fingers tracing the tight, hard lines of his arms and legs, the swell of his buttocks, the slick warmth of his groin. As her hands closed around his stiff, swollen shaft, he moaned again, a guttural sound this time.

As if yet another switch had been flipped, a new current flowed between them, a new urgency fueled their actions.

Water sloshed around them as they writhed on the mattress, limbs tangled, tongues entwined. She continued to stroke and fondle with a frenzied motion, the need to have him inside building to a fever pitch. She could feel his hands on her waist, her hips, sliding between her legs, his fingers dipping into her hot, wet core. She arched her back, offering herself to him.

"I want you so bad," she whimpered into his ear.

For Rhys, the words were like a siren's call, a lure he couldn't imagine resisting. Gazing down at Trae's naked, writhing body, he was completely captivated. She seemed so beautiful to him, so precious. He had to have her. "Me, too," he rasped, the need rising up and tightening in his throat. In truth, he couldn't remember ever wanting anything this badly. "I want to touch, taste and feel every inch of you."

Proving this, he trailed his tongue along her throat, over her breasts, down her belly, between her thighs. She called out his name as he delved into her, but if she meant it as a protest, it was a feeble one. He thrilled at the sound of her moans, the feel of her body arching into him. He heard his name once more, deep, hoarse and urgent, as she began to spasm with pleasure.

For Rhys, all that existed was this warm, vibrant woman beneath him. He felt consumed by her heat, engulfed by her maddeningly indefinable scent, ensnared by her very essence. He had to have her. Had to make her his own.

Unable to hold off any longer, he knelt between her legs, sliding into her hot, wet body with an all-consuming fervor. They gasped in unison as they came together, moving with one rhythm as nature took over. Being inside Trae felt so good, so right, as if he'd belonged there forever. As if everything in his life had been leading up to this moment.

Wrapping her arms and legs around him, she clung fiercely to his back as he rapidly lost control, driving into her faster and harder, each stroke probing deeper, reaching, straining, climbing until Trae cried out, "Oh, Rhys!" and sheer, unadulterated pleasure exploded inside him.

He buried his face in her hair, taking a deep, cleansing breath. Even now that they were done, now that he was tired and spent and aching in every muscle, he still couldn't bear the thought of breaking away from her.

Still clinging to Rhys, Trae could feel a thousand sensations engulfing her body, but she could think of only one word to describe them. *Perfect.* She could weep with the overpowering beauty of it all. She knew she could make love a million times, a billion, but no other man could ever make her feel this deep, soul-shattering sense of rightness.

Sighing with happiness, she looked up into his beautiful face. Rhys smiled, one of those heartbreakingly genuine smiles, and darned if the tears didn't start dripping down her cheeks.

His expression clouded. With a long, drawn-out sigh of his own, Rhys slowly withdrew, rolling over to lie on his back on the bed beside her. Afraid to speak, Trae listened to his breathing as the rolling motion of the water slowly subsided beneath them. Bit by bit, the sense of enchantment drifted away.

"Sorry," he said tightly, taking the last fragment of illusion away.

Trae didn't trust herself to speak. After what they'd just shared, all he could say was *"Sorry?"* And what was wrong with her, that she still wanted to hold onto him, cling to him, beg him to give her yet another chance? Had she no pride? She had to know that in the end, he'd always go back to Lucie.

She flinched, feeling ugly inside, as she remembered her friend for the first time. "Yeah, me, too."

He said nothing, remaining stiff and silent and so out of reach. Unable to bear it an instant longer, Trae got out of the bed, holding the tie-dyed spread against her. "What was I thinking? But I wasn't, of course. Thinking, I mean. I was feeling. Feeling way too much."

"A lot of that going around."

Shoulders drooping, she stood at the side of the bed, looking down at him. "Oh, Rhys, how could we do this to Lucie?"

"Do what, Trae? He sat up, his expression pained. "She left me at the altar, remember, and then went traipsing around the country with her old boyfriend."

"Yeah, but…"

"It's not as if she's sitting around, waiting for me to show up," he interrupted. "She hasn't even once thought to call me."

Wincing again, Trae knew she could no longer keep the truth from him. "Yes, she has," she told him, her voice as small as she now felt. "She wanted to call, but she felt bad after what she did to you. And just for the record, she *is* expecting you to show up."

Resting his head against the wall behind him, he closed his eyes. "And you're telling me this now because…?"

She wanted to cry. She wanted to go back in time and erase the whole evening. But most of all, she wanted to climb back into bed and snuggle up against him.

"I screwed up, okay?" she said, turning away before she could commit further lunacy. "I swore up and down I'd never let this happen, but somewhere between Clay and the car, and then this—" she gestured around the room "—this throwback to Timothy Leary, I must have lost touch with reality."

Behind her, Rhys sighed. The bed made a sloshing sound as he rose to his feet and started rooting around on the floor for his clothes. Turning back to watch him, Trae could see his anger, could feel him slipping further and further away from her.

"Fine," he said tersely. Shrugging into his pants, he turned to her. "Should we call it a mistake and be done with it?"

"Mistake?" she asked, feeling as if she'd just been slapped in the face. "Is that what it feels like to you?"

They stared at each other, the vast expanse of the water bed yawning between them. Looking away first, Rhys stabbed his arms into his shirt. "Give me another word, then. I'm going to need something that makes sense when it comes time to tell Lucie."

Trae felt chilled, inside and out. "She'll be so hurt," she said in a choked voice, imagining that confession.

"She probably will." He buttoned the shirt, his movements as clipped as his tone. "But to lie to her, on top of this…I won't do it. I won't start my marriage that way."

"Of course." Trae was proud of how calm she sounded, how matter-of-fact, when inside, she felt as if she were dying. He was determined to marry Lucie. A brief little roll in the hay wasn't about to alter his plans.

He studied the floor, intent upon finding his shoes. "Don't worry," he told her as he picked them up and slipped them onto his feet. "I'll take full responsibility. I'll explain it in a way that Lucie won't blame you."

"And how do you expect to pull that off?" Not liking how shrewish she sounded, she lowered her tone. "In her place, I'd never forgive me. If you were mine, I'd tear out the throat of any woman who came near you."

He glanced up from tying his shoes, giving her a funny look. Trae waited for him to state the obvious. That he wasn't hers, not by a long shot.

"Yeah, I bet you would," he said instead as he rose to his feet. "But let's face it, you're not Lucie."

That felt worse, so much worse. "Right," she said stiffly. "Lucie's the kind of girl a guy marries. Me, I'm just a party animal. A let's-have-fun-and-not-bother-with-any-commitments kind of gal." After a moment, she added, "A mistake."

"C'mon, Trae, that's not…"

"No, it's true. Every word of it. Which makes my behavior tonight doubly reprehensible." Biting her lip, she clutched the bedspread to her chest. "A quick, impulsive biological urge and ten years of friendship go out the window."

"Biological urge?"

She waved a hand in the air. "You know what I mean. And so will Lucie. She'll know, Rhys, no matter how you try to sugarcoat it. And I don't see how she'll ever be able to get past it."

"Biological urge?" he repeated, towering over her. "Is that what just happened between us?"

All at once, she got angry. "You tell me. You see us going anywhere with this?"

"How can it? I'm getting married."

The words shouldn't have hurt—she knew they were coming—but it was all she could do not to flinch as he flung them at her face.

"Then I rest my case," she told him, hoping to sound flippant but tending more toward petulance instead.

An uneasy silence filled the room. They faced each other, suddenly strangers, the stark, brutal truth driving a wedge between them. He belonged to Lucie, and that, folks, would always be that.

"As you said, it's late," she blurted out, unable to bear the strain a second longer. "We've got a lot to deal with in the morning so maybe it's best that we both get to sleep."

"Trae, I never meant…"

She waved her hand to stop him from saying more. The last thing she wanted was his version of her own usual exit line. None of those poor guys in her past had cared what her true intentions were, she now realized. All they'd known, all she now knew, was that it hurt like hell when you weren't the one leaving.

"Good night, Rhys. It's been a blast, really, but I'm about to drop from exhaustion."

He raised a hand as if to reach for her, but just as quickly lowered it. He had to agree, didn't he, that there was no sense in pursuing this? That nothing he could say or do now could ever make anything better?

But he was Rhys Paxton. And a Paxton would go to his grave trying.

"Good night, Trae," he said gruffly as he headed for the door. "I'm sure things will seem less…complicated in the morning."

Lame, Paxton, she wanted to shout at him, but how could she trust her voice?

Instead, she let him go, listening for the click of the lock before facing the awful emptiness he'd left behind.

Emotionally drained, she sat on the edge of the bed, marveling that she'd managed to remain upright this long. Was it true, what she'd told him? Had making love to Rhys been merely a biological urge that she could easily forget and move on from?

Without Rhys there, getting in her face and disturbing her equilibrium, she should be able to think straight. She should be able to get back to her own love-'em-and-leave-'em self, the Trae Andrelini she'd been before she'd ever met him.

Trouble was, she could still feel the rasp of his beard on her cheek. Bringing her hands to her face, she traced her fingers up her chin to her mouth. His scent lingered, haunting her with the memory of all they had done.

Lord help her, she was in trouble.

Forcing her hands to her sides, she marched to the window. She knew it was sad, pathetic really, but she had to catch one last glimpse of Rhys before he vanished into his room.

She found him standing in front of his door, staring at his key, the flickering light from the Fill-Er-Up sign lending a surreal note to his hesitation. Watching him, Trae felt a spurt of hope. Was he, too, regretting the words they'd exchanged, wishing for the chance to do it all over?

"Come back to me," she heard herself whisper, knowing it would be oh-so-wrong, yet praying he'd do it, anyway.

As if he heard, he turned to glance at her window. She ducked back out of sight, not wanting to be caught mooning after him. From a safe distance, she watched him look first at his door, then hers. Everything seemed to stop—even Trae's breathing—as he cupped the key in his hand and headed in her direction.

She had thirty glorious seconds of hope, but at the last moment, he veered to the right, striding with a visible sense of purpose into Irv's office. Through the big window, she watched him hand over the key, then march in the same determined manner toward the huge trucks parked in the distance.

He's leaving, she thought in a daze. And chances were good that she'd never see him again.

All in all, it was a hell of a time to discover she loved him.

Chapter Thirteen

Rhys stopped beneath the Fill-Er-Up sign, its flickering neon putting a cap on what had to have been the most bizarre evening of his life. Remembering the unwelcome altercation with Clay, he reached up to touch his forehead. Funny how it throbbed, now that he had time to think about it. In the heat of the battle, he'd been more concerned about Trae. And afterward…

He'd been overly concerned with her then, too.

He winced, but not from the pain in his forehead. One of the hardest things he'd ever done was walking out of that room and leaving her behind. But, really, what choice did he have? Lucie was waiting for him to come rescue her.

At first, he'd been angry at Trae for not telling him sooner, but deep down, in that place where he could still be honest with himself, Rhys doubted the knowledge would have made much difference. Could anything have given him the good sense, much less the strength of will, to keep from tumbling into bed with Trae?

Even now, he burned with an overwhelming need to go back to her.

Which was crazy, he told himself, pointedly turning away from her door. Not to mention irresponsible. Lucie was his future, part of his Grand Plan. You didn't throw away nearly twenty years of dedication to someone because of some...some *biological urge.*

All at once, he felt empty inside. Had he been so wrong, thinking that what they'd shared was something special? Something less lust and more...

It didn't matter, he told himself firmly. All that should concern him was the fact that Lucie still needed him. The honorable thing, the *only* thing to do was to get to New Orleans as soon as humanly possible. He had to find transportation out of here, and Max should know the best way to arrange it.

Determinedly turning away from Trae's door, he squared his shoulders and marched to the bar.

Trae opened her eyes, amazed that she'd fallen asleep. Still in a groggy state, she was vaguely aware of a word being repeated over and over, but it was drowned out by a loud, incessant pounding and a rhythmic rumbling in the distance.

She blinked, trying to focus. It was still dark outside; it couldn't be more than an hour since she'd fallen asleep. Was she dreaming? Or could that really be Rhys, calling her name?

She tumbled out of the bed, wrapping the sheet around her as she crossed the room. Sucking in a breath to steady herself, she opened the door.

Rhys stood before her, six full feet of walking, talking impatience in a black leather jacket. Behind him, idling loudly and just as impatiently, stood a huge, vintage Harley.

"What's going on?" she asked, clutching the sheet tighter as she gaped at the motorcycle. "I thought you'd left."

He grimaced. "I couldn't. We have an agreement, remember? We stick together until we find Lucie. Now get dressed before I change my mind. You've got five minutes."

He eyed the sheet, but quickly looked away, shaking his head. "Here," he said, thrusting a second leather jacket in her hands. "Compliments of Max. He says you'll be glad to have it out there on the road."

Trae could already feel the predawn chill on her bare shoulders; she imagined it would be twice as cold on the bike. "Thanks," she said in a daze, hugging the jacket. She remembered the bartender telling them that the truck stop had once been a biker hangout. "That from Max, too?" she added, pointing at the Harley.

Rhys nodded. "Used to be Clay's, though. Max got it from him to pay off his bar bill. And all the broken furniture."

"He must have run up quite a tab. I remember Max said it was Clay's second incident this week."

"Funny thing about that. Turns out Clay was pestering a cute little blonde while her boyfriend was passed out in the back of his truck. From the description, sounds like he must have gone after Lucie, as well."

She'd been calling from *this* truck stop? No wonder she'd sounded so frightened.

"All things considered," Rhys went on, "Max figured it was only fitting that Clay should help us out. However indirectly."

Never having ridden on a motorcycle before, she felt

suddenly uneasy about the prospect. "That bike looks awful big, Paxton. You sure you know how to drive it?"

"You think I'd risk our lives? Trust me, I know what I'm doing."

She did trust him. Enough to get on that monster behind him and drive off to whatever further mishaps might come their way.

"Get moving," Rhys pronounced, giving her no time to reconsider her impulsive decision. "As I said, five minutes."

He got on the bike, straddling it to wait the obligatory five minutes. Seeing that she hadn't yet moved, he pointed at his wrist, then cursed as he no doubt remembered he no longer had a watch.

It was enough to get her moving, though. Shutting the door behind her, she raced around the room, gathering her belongings. *He didn't leave,* her mind kept chanting. Only a fool would read too much into it, she knew, but even so, she couldn't help but be elated. She felt like she'd just been given a reprieve.

Outside the door, the Harley gave a sudden roar, both bike and driver displaying their eagerness to get out on the road. Stuffing things into the backpack, she told herself she could straighten everything out later. Right now, she couldn't take the chance that Rhys would leave her behind.

Heart racing, she was out the door in under the allotted five minutes. Not that Rhys acknowledged this or complimented her for the effort. "Put this on," he growled, thrusting a helmet into her hands. He'd already donned his own helmet, shiny black with a tinted visor. He seemed mysterious, dangerous, now that she couldn't see his features.

"What did you say?" she asked, putting a hand to her

ear. She'd heard him fine, but before she got on that monster of a bike with him, she needed to see his face.

As she'd hoped, he flipped up the visor. "You need to wear a helmet," he repeated slowly, as though conversing with the village idiot.

Oddly enough, his irritation reassured her. Smiling sweetly, she took the helmet from his hands. "Gotta say, this is certainly a new wrinkle. You've taken this road trip thing to a new level, Paxton. Talk about born to be wild."

"That was my brother. Jack used to race motorcycles before he blew out his shoulder, but my bike was solely for transportation. We used to drive all over the place together when he came to visit in the summers."

She liked the way his voice softened when he mentioned his brother. But then it did the same thing whenever Lucie's name entered the conversation. Lucie and Jack, the two people he loved most in the world.

A timely reminder, she thought grimly, slipping the helmet onto her head.

"Give me the backpack." Taking it from her, Rhys stowed it under the seat behind him. As he did, Trae did a mental inventory to make sure she'd left nothing behind. "Your clothes," she said suddenly, turning back to look at Jerry's garage. "They're still in the plastic bag in the rental."

He, too, glanced back at Jerry's. "Forget it. I never liked that suit, anyway."

Trae could only hope that Lucie felt the same about her jeans.

"Hop on, Trae. Time to hit the road."

She didn't actually gulp, but her throat tightened as she faced the immediate reality of being so up close and personal on the bike. She'd have to touch Rhys, lean against him, wrap her arms around his waist.

"What are you waiting for? Times a'wasting. We've got to leave right now if we hope to catch up to Lucie."

That helps, Trae thought as she slid onto the seat behind him. As long as she stayed focused on her friend, on getting to Lucie and making amends, Trae should be able to get through the uncomfortable hours ahead.

To stay on the safe side, she gripped the backrest rather than Rhys's waist, doing her best to avoid unnecessary contact with the man. But when he roared out of the truck stop, kicking up gravel in their wake, she had to cling to him for dear life.

They went a mile before she caught her first decent breath, and it was a good ten more before her breathing returned to anything near normal. As she settled into the motion, growing accustomed to the vibrating power beneath her, she found a certain exhilaration in riding with Rhys on the bike. Chalk it up to one more adventure for the record books.

Unlike in the car, they couldn't talk as they rode, not with the engine roaring and the wind whipping past. For once Trae didn't mind the lack of conversation. What could they possibly say to each other, anyway? No sense rehashing what they'd said and done last night.

Instead, knowing the unlikelihood that she'd ever experience this again, she reveled in the sensation of leaning against Rhys, feeling the warm, solid strength of him with her arms around his waist. Breathing in his scent—did the man always have to smell so terrific?—she realized that this was how it could have been if Lucie weren't between them.

A stolen moment, that was all she had, but who would it hurt if she made the most of it? Truth be told, it was sheer heaven.

This is pure and utter hell, Rhys thought hours later. Bad enough the relentless sun had to beat down on his black leather jacket, but each time Trae shifted her position, his mind flashed back to the night before, and his body overreacted.

And they still had another twelve hours before they reached New Orleans.

But he'd convinced himself it would be fine. He was a master of self-control, and besides, what could happen on a Harley?

As if to prove the idiocy of that statement, Trae shifted again.

He wouldn't make it. He was a determined man, more stubborn than most, but not even a superhero could drive a Harley cross-country on so little sleep. And with a beautiful woman—check that, an off-limits beautiful woman—snuggled up to his back. He might have good intentions, honorable ones, but he wasn't going to keep them if they continued like this.

Soon, they should reach Dallas. He had business associates there who would be only too happy to help him. Forget the stupid bet. It would be foolish—no, make that irresponsible—not to take advantage of any available assistance.

He should call ahead, though, to alert them that he was coming so they could start the ball rolling. Spotting a gas station up the road, he decided to pull into it.

"What's going on?" Trae asked groggily, sitting up straight and looking around her when the Harley rumbled to a stop.

"Getting gas." Hopping off the bike, Rhys shrugged out

of his jacket. The temperature had to be close to one hundred. "Don't know about you, but I think I might use the restroom. Maybe splash some cold water on my face."

As she studied his face, taking in his features, Rhys felt suddenly self-conscious of his day-old beard. "Guess I could use a shave, too," he said, reaching up to rasp a hand across his chin. "Getting kind of scruffy."

She shook her head. "I like it. Makes you look... rugged."

Rhys had been called many things in his life, but rugged had never been one of them. He found he liked it.

And there Trae went again, getting through his defenses, finding things in him that nobody else ever noticed. He had to fight the sudden urge to reach out for her and hold her against his chest.

"The restrooms are over there," he said, nodding at the building.

"Oh, yeah," she said distractedly, pulling her gaze to the building. "Thanks."

Watching her wander off, he realized he'd failed to mention the main reason he'd stopped. No big deal, he thought with a shrug. She'd learn soon enough.

What are we doing here? Trae wondered, gazing around her at the posh surroundings of Petermann, Beckley, Inc. Disappearing behind the large, brass doors at the end of the hallway, Rhys had promised to be back to explain in a minute.

Not that it was a hardship, sitting on the cushioned leather chair with a view of Dallas stretching out before her many stories below, but his so-called minute had stretched into five, then ten and fifteen, and here she sat no closer to an explanation. If Rhys didn't show his face soon, she was going to...

The sad fact was, there was little she could do but sit and wait.

"Ms. Andrelini?" said a soft voice behind her. Swiveling in her chair, Trae faced a middle-aged brunette, dressed in a crisp navy suit. "I'm Ellen Smith, Mr. Petermann's assistant. Mr. Paxton asked me to inform you that he's been unavoidably detained. If you'll follow me, I'll escort you to our executive suite. He feels you'll be more comfortable waiting for him there."

Popping up from the seat, Trae fell into step beside her. "How long is this going to take?"

Ellen shook her head. "Sorry, I have no idea." Pushing open a door at the other end of the hallway, she ushered Trae into a room done in dark wood and several shades of green. Like the waiting room she'd just left, it had floor-to-ceiling windows and a plush leather sofa. A mahogany bar stood in one corner, a plasma TV in the other, yet the overall effect was of peace and relaxation. Even the forest-green carpet looked soft enough to sleep on.

"Mr. Paxton thought you might want to shower, perhaps take a nap," Ellen went on as she crossed the room and opened a door on the right. "Here is the bedroom, and the bath is behind it. You'll find towels and a robe laid out for you."

"Wow," was all Trae could think of to say. "Thanks a lot."

Having done her job, Ellen walked back to the door. "If you'll excuse me, I'll leave you to it, then. If you need anything else, don't hesitate to call. You'll find my extension number next to the phone in the bedroom."

"A phone?" Trae asked, perking up as she thought of checking her messages. "Can I dial out?"

"Of course. Just dial the number nine, then the phone number."

With a soft, gracious smile, the woman eased out of the room as gracefully as she'd entered it.

Left alone in the sudden quiet, Trae felt unbelievably tired. A shower should help wake her up, she told herself as she headed into the bedroom. But first, she should check if she'd heard anything more from Lucie. She still hadn't given up hope that her friend might have had yet another change of heart.

No such luck. Trae's only message was from her mother, her voice increasingly shrill as she fretted over why Trae wasn't answering her phone. Her mom rang off, reminding her daughter about the importance of being home for Sunday dinner, threatening that if she didn't hear from Trae soon, she'd be sending her brothers to come get her.

Appalled by the prospect, Trae started to dial home, then thought better of it. Her mother wanted results, not explanations. Besides, if they were in Dallas now, they'd be in New Orleans by tomorrow, which was Saturday. All she had to do was stop at Bobby's, collect Lucie and make sure she was okay. With any luck, Trae could be home by late tomorrow evening.

Plenty of time to listen to her mother's ranting and raving then.

She opted to call Vinny instead. Good news, he told her. The Worldways strike was all but over. Warning him that she'd need a standby ticket tomorrow, she promised to call with the where and when in the morning. When Vinny tried to grill her about her whereabouts, she told him her ride was leaving and she had to go. "Tell Mom not to worry," she added before hanging up. "I'll be home by Sunday."

She was only half-conscious of crossing her fingers behind her back.

Remembering her promise to keep her friends up dated, she tried calling Quinn next. "Ms. Reynolds is in court," the voice mail message told her, but if she'd like to leave a message…

Alana answered on the second ring, sounding harried explaining that she was in the midst of putting together project. Apologizing for seeming so scattered, Alana asked what was going on. Had Trae heard anything from Lucie

Trae confessed that she'd hoped their friend might have called there. Alana regretted having to answer in the negative.

Interestingly enough, though, Alana had heard from Jo Kerrin. She and her little girl were all settled in with her parents in New Orleans. Jo had left a voice mail on Lucie's phone, too, so if Lucie checked her messages she'd have heard the news. Trae might want to try calling Jo. Knowing Lucie, she'd make time to stop by for a visit.

An excellent idea, Trae thought. Using the number Alana gave her, she next tried the Kerrins.

Jo was delighted to hear from her but dismayed to hear about Lucie's disappearance. If Lucie called, Jo promised she'd be sure to call Trae the minute she got off the phone

Trae tried to think of who else she should call, only to realize that the one person she truly wanted to talk to was Rhys.

Where was he? she wondered, glancing at the clock on the bedside table. By now, he'd been gone for nearly an hour. He must have encountered some sort of business emergency—she'd noticed him on the phone at the gas station—but she wished he'd hurry up and take care of it so they could get back on the road.

Speaking of which, she should probably take a shower

er, in case Rhys suddenly appeared with another five-minute ultimatum.

The toiletries in the bathroom were worth a king's ransom, and the warm water, washing away the heat and dust of the road, was beyond price. Too bad neither did anything to revive her.

Bundling up in the soft, terry robe, she felt pampered and relaxed, a dangerous combo in her sleep-deprived state. Drifting through the bedroom, her gaze focused on the soft goose down comforter and mountain of pillows on the bed. What could it hurt, she told herself as she plopped down on the mattress. She'd just rest her eyes for a couple of minutes...

"Ms. Andrelini?"

Trae popped up, embarrassed to be caught nodding off. She could hear Ellen Smith in the other room, talking through the door as she waited for Trae to make an appearance. Scrambling out of bed, securing the sash on the robe, Trae tried to make sense of her damp, tangled hair. A quick glance out the window showed that it was just starting to get dark. Just how long had she been on that bed, anyway?

Hurrying to the living room, she found Ms. Smith holding a shopping bag. "Sorry to wake you," she said in her calm, no-nonsense tone, "but Mr. Paxton is ready to leave." Smiling warmly, she held out the bag. "He asked us to purchase a new outfit for you. He imagined you'd enjoy something new and fresh to wear. He's waiting downstairs," she added when Trae took the bag from her hands. "When you're ready, I'll take you to him."

"But I can't wear this on a motorcycle," Trae protested as she held up the cute flowered sundress, leaving the silk underwear and white leather sandals in the bag.

"No, I wouldn't think so." Shaking her head, Ellen Smith smiled knowingly as she left the suite. "But I'm sure Mr. Paxton will explain the change in plans."

Change in plans? Could the woman make it sound any more ominous? Slipping into the clothes he'd bought her, Trae fretted over what she could have meant.

Rhys had been gone for hours; he could have planned a major battle in less time. Had he arranged to pack her off on a bus while he flew back to the office? Businessman that he was, he'd have assessed the facts, coming to the inevitable conclusion that she was a liability. This little respite, her sojourn into the lap of luxury, could be his way of letting her go nicely.

Increasingly depressed, Trae followed Ellen Smith to the elevators. As they took the long ride down to the ground floor, she couldn't help but wonder if Rhys would be standing there as the doors opened, his handsome face grave as he waited to hand Trae her walking papers.

She couldn't find it in her heart to blame him. Their adventure had to end sometime, and after the way she'd clung to him last night, only an irresponsible fool would prolong it. Something Rhys most definitely was not.

However, nobody stood in the elevator banks, nor could Trae find Rhys anywhere in the empty lobby. Not faltering a step, Ellen Smith marched to the revolving door at the entrance, her heels clicking loudly on the polished marble floor.

It wasn't until they were out the door that Trae spied him, chatting with a liveried limousine driver on the curb. Gone was the black leather jacket, the jeans and flannel shirt, the rumpled hair and scruffy beard. Even the bandage was missing, his forehead now dressed with a small, nearly invisible Band-Aid. Dressed in a sharp navy suit that put his gray one to shame, he seemed almost a stranger.

So it was back to the old Rhys Paxton, she thought in dismay. The brisk, no-nonsense business executive who'd always looked down his nose at her.

She felt suddenly as if she'd just lost a good friend.

"Here she is now," he said to the driver, turning to Trae. "Ready to roll?"

"In this?" She eyed the sleek black limo with something close to aversion.

"I was going to rent a car, but this way we can both catch up on some sleep. I don't know about you, but I'm in no condition to be rescuing anyone at the moment."

There were probably a thousand questions she should ask him, but all she could wrap her thoughts around was her relief. For now, it was enough that he'd waited for her, that he'd included her in his plans.

Enough that they'd keep looking for Lucie together.

Swatting at yet another mosquito, Lucie Beckwith thought seriously about calling home. Not that she could actually call her parents, there being no phone within a ten-mile radius, but even listening to her mother rant about her irresponsible behavior had to be better than sitting through another day on this rickety porch with a dead-drunk Bobby sleeping it off inside his awful, musty cabin.

This was not what Lucie had envisioned when she had run away from the altar.

Staring at her hands, she nearly cried when she noticed another broken nail. She desperately needed a manicure, but there were no salons in the swamp. No health spas or five-star restaurants, not even a mall. Just miles and miles of muddy water and swarms of pesky mosquitoes.

She was so disappointed, she could have stomped her foot—if she thought the porch floor could take it. What had happened to her grand adventure?

Back in Los Angeles, Bobby had been every bit as exciting as she'd remembered. Heartthrob handsome and oozing with Southern charm, strutting like a king among those wannabe actors and fame-starved agents, he'd promised to make her a star. Awestruck by the future he'd painted, Lucie had been only too happy to follow him to Las Vegas.

But then Lou Carino had shown up, and the Bobby she'd admired had vanished. Scared of the man's power and connections, knowing he could never repay the fortune Lou had invested in him, Bobby had run like a frightened little boy to hide here in the swamp. Hard to remain a king with your tail between your legs, she supposed, and your palace being this ramshackle hunting shack deep in the bayou.

She hated it here. She even hated Bobby here. No doubt he'd expect her to get her own dinner again, and clean up the place after. Look at the way he'd made her drive the whole distance, being too drunk to get behind the wheel half the time, and too hungover the rest of the time.

And all the way here, she couldn't help but compare him to Rhys. Rhys never made her cook and clean or even drive, for that matter. He never drank in excess, never even let a single hair stray out of place. Always presentable, always in control. Ever dependable Rhys, who'd never once dreamed of failing her.

Yet...

She paused, realizing that this was how the old Lucie would have thought, the pre-run-away-from-the-altar

Lucie. Thanks to her grand adventure, she wasn't that girl anymore, and she really had to stop acting like her. Deep down, she knew she didn't want to spend the rest of her life relying on Rhys to rescue her.

Why blame Bobby for all her troubles? If not for him, she'd never have remembered how much she enjoyed acting—if only for a day—and how good she actually was at it. Or how she could do so many more things than she'd believed possible. She, who'd never driven very much, had managed to make her way halfway across the country. Okay, so maybe she still wasn't a big fan of getting behind the wheel, but hey, she'd proved to herself she could do it. And she was pretty darned proud of her achievement.

Trae would be proud of her, too, she realized. She and Quinn and Alana would encourage Lucie to continue.

Just say no.

Looking up, she saw Crazy Elmer slowly poling his pirogue in her direction. An elderly Cajun who lived at the other end of the bayou, Crazy Elmer seemed to feel obligated to stop by every evening to see if Bobby needed anything in town. Most times, Crazy Elmer wasn't even close to sober by the time he returned each night, but then, Lucie wouldn't need to come back with him, anyway.

And just like that, she realized what she had to do. She had to get out, get away, and really, when she thought about it, was there any better time than the present?

Hurrying inside, she gathered up her few belongings and scribbled off a note. In it, she told Bobby she was sorry but she just couldn't sit around anymore and watch him drink himself into a stupor.

Then she went back outside and got into the pirogue with Crazy Elmer. As they poled off, she glanced back at the cabin with a sigh. Bobby would be hurt, she knew, but there was little she could do about it. Lord help her, she still loved that boy, and probably always would, but there came a time in every girl's life when she had to make a decision. She had a life to live, things to accomplish, and she'd never get anything done by hiding out here in the swamp.

As her friends would say, when it came to Bobby Boudreaux, it was time to "Just say no."

Chapter Fourteen

"So, what's the plan?"

Settling into the right-hand seat as the limo took off from the curb, Rhys looked up to meet Trae's sharp, probing gaze. "Finding Lucie. What else?"

She frowned, sitting ramrod straight in the seat opposite. "You tell me. One minute I'm bumping down the highway on a Harley and the next thing I know, I'm gliding off in luxury. What's next? The company jet?"

"It wasn't available." He started to grin but thought better of it when he saw her frown. "Seriously, Trae, I'm not that rich. Don't you think if I had a plane, I'd have used it long before now?"

"Instead, you call on the old company limo."

Was she actually complaining about riding in luxury? "Don't knock it. With Leroy driving, I can send e-mails, set up appointments, maybe even fit in a nap. All of which I could never do on a Harley."

"Yeah, but I miss that motorcycle," she said wistfully as she gazed out the window.

So do I, he almost told her, but all good things must come to an end. Living life on the edge had been an exhilarating experience but Rhys could no longer ignore the fact that while he'd been chasing Lucie, his other world—the *real* world—had been coming apart at the seams.

Still frowning, she nodded at the laptop and briefcase on the seat beside him. "So that's why you have the office equipment? Couldn't go this long without checking in to the office?"

He hesitated, wondering what to tell her. "There's trouble with our new acquisition," he said, opting for the truth. "Stanton, Inc. has hired new lawyers, greedy ones. Jack swears that he's got things handled, but…"

"You've never been one for standing on the sidelines," she finished off for him.

He couldn't have explained it better. "Yes, I'm used to being in charge. It doesn't feel right, being so far away at such a crucial moment." He knew he had no one but himself to blame for his predicament. Traipsing around, pretending he had no responsibilities to anyone but himself—what did he think would happen?

"People are depending on me," he insisted. "Not least of all my brother. Jack was just starting to come around, to show some responsibility, but these negotiations might be more than he can handle."

"Must be tough, Atlas, having to bear the whole weight of the world on your shoulders."

"And what is that supposed to mean?"

"C'mon, Rhys, nobody should ever be that indispensable. Give poor Jack a chance to prove himself. He's never going to know what he's capable of if you're forever bailing him out of trouble."

"But what if he screws up?" Rhys said, shaking his head. "It could cost the company a great deal of money."

She frowned. "And what's more important? Money, or your brother's self-esteem? And before you answer, feel what's in here…" She leaned over and laid her hand over his heart. "Don't just parrot some nonsense your father put in your head."

Rhys felt suddenly unable to move, caught by the earnest intensity in her gaze. She was doing it again, making him feel things, want things…

He looked away, knowing he couldn't let himself get drawn back into that fantasy. "It's all a moot point. We should be catching up to Lucie soon, anyway, and I will go back to the office. And before I forget…" Sighing, he reached into the briefcase and pulled out a banker's check. "Here's what I owe you."

"What's this?" She looked concerned—no, worried— as she studied the numbers on the check.

"I'm paying up. Clearly, you won our bet."

He braced himself, waiting for her to start berating him for giving up, but she merely dropped the check on the seat as she gazed listlessly out the window.

"I also took care of the rental company." He sighed again. "That was fun," he added, sarcastically.

Studying his face, she seemed upset. "My, my, weren't you the busy little beaver? While I was so blissfully napping, there you were, solving all the world's problems by writing your checks."

"This annoys you? I thought you'd be relieved."

She looked as confused as he felt. "I am. I only wish it didn't make me feel as if I've just been paid off."

It was his turn to be annoyed. "You and your stubborn pride. I should have known you'd react like this. Especially after Cancun."

"What is it with you and Cancun?" She sat forward, her green eyes flashing sparks. "The way you talk about it, you'd think I'd committed some major crime there. For the record, it was Quinn's idea to go to Mexico, and I sure wasn't the one dancing on the table. Why are you always singling me out for all the blame?"

Good question. Maybe because even back then, she'd represented danger. Not just for Lucie, but also himself. From the start, he'd sensed how a man could get lost in her deep, fathomless gaze.

"No one is singling you out," he told her brusquely. "And I wasn't paying anyone off. I'm merely trying to tie up lose ends."

"So now I'm a loose end. What comes next? You toss me, with your stupid guilt check, out on the next corner?"

"Cut it out, Trae. I already told you we can devote one more day to this."

"And then what?" She glared at him from the opposite seat. "I'm supposed to slink off into the sunset?"

"What the hell do you want from me? I thought we both agreed that last night was a mistake?"

She looked away first, but not before he saw her wounded expression.

"I didn't mean…"

"I know what you meant," she said dully. "And don't worry. I, of all people, know better than to make more out of last night than was actually there. We had a thing. It's done. Time to move on."

"Trae…"

"No, it's okay, really. I…I guess I got caught a little unprepared." Refusing to look at him, she played with the hem of her skirt. "I knew our little adventure couldn't continue forever, especially not after what we did last night, but I guess I didn't expect it all to end so abruptly. Look at you in your suit and tie, surrounded by your equipment, landing smack dab back in the middle of square one. Call me rigid, if you must, but I need some time to adjust. Another day or so, and maybe I, too, can go on as if this whole week never happened."

"That's not what I…"

"Who am I kidding?" she interrupted, squeezing the hem in her fingers. "I doubt I'll ever get to that stage. I'm afraid I'm going to remember this week for the rest of my life."

Rhys closed his eyes, not knowing what he could possibly say to her. He wanted to tell her that she was not alone, that he'd probably be doing the "what ifs" to his grave, but how would that help either of them? "I'm sorry, Trae," he said stiffly instead. "If things were different…"

He trailed off, realizing that it, too, was a fantasy going nowhere. "But they're not," he went on firmly. "I made a promise to Lucie. I have to keep it. Even if… Even if Lucie is having trouble holding up her end of the bargain." Seeing Trae form a response, he quickly added, "And, yes. It's that important to me."

"I know. A Paxton never goes back on his word."

"No, you don't know. Not all of it."

"Then tell me." She leaned forward. "I'm listening."

Trae always listened, he realized. Which was probably

why he kept telling her things he'd never admitted to anyone else.

And maybe he owed her this. More than anybody, Trae deserved to know why last night, no matter how incredible, could never be repeated.

"You need to understand what an impact Lucie made on my life," he began. "It was awful after my mother left with Jack. That big, rambling house, dozens of empty rooms all silent as a tomb, and me the only sign of life in them. Everything seemed bleak and black. Then Lucie came along and suddenly there was light. Laughter. I loved to hear her giggle. I was fascinated by the lilt in her voice."

He paused, caught up in the memory. "I remember the day I first brought Lucie into my father's house. Her voice didn't just echo through the halls. It resonated, like it belonged there. I knew then that her laughter, and that of our children, was meant to fill up the empty rooms of the house."

"It's okay, Rhys," Trae said tightly. "You don't have to…"

He held up a hand. "Let me finish. I made a commitment to her. To myself. We had a pact, nothing as formal as yours and your roommates', maybe, but I made it clear that I'd always look out for her. That I'd always be there if she needed me."

Trae sighed heavily. "Until death do you part."

He felt compelled to explain. "I do love her, Trae. Maybe not with the wild, untamed passion you talk about, but it will suffice. In my own plodding way, I swear I'll be a good husband to her."

She looked away, her voice low and nearly inaudible. "What about her? After the way she ran out on you, aren't you worried that she might not be the best wife?"

For the first time in his life, Rhys was speechless, Trae's

words hanging between them like an accusation. It struck him that he'd been so busy playing Lucie's rescuer, he'd never stopped to consider if she could ever be the wife he needed. And after this past week with Trae...

Filled with a sudden longing, he fought the urge to reach out to her. He was a Paxton, he'd given his word and, ideal situation or not, he was honor bound to find some way to make this marriage work. "Right now, Lucie might be desperate for adventure," he explained with a sigh, "but when all is said and done, she'll expect me to be there. She needs me, Trae. I can't turn my back on that."

He didn't know who he hoped to convince, her or himself. Trae nodded slowly. "I know," she repeated softly as she leaned back against the window. "One last piece of advice, Paxton, and I swear you'll never hear another word about it. If you want to be a good husband, then you'll have to show Lucie she's more important to you than your money, your business or *anything* else. That's all any woman wants from her man. To know that she always comes first."

Her words hovered between them in the ensuing silence. True to her word, Trae turned away in silence, curling up on the opposite cushions as if meaning to go to sleep.

Rhys tried to concentrate on the figures on the computer, but his gaze kept drifting to her. Amazing, how much pleasure he derived from just looking at Trae. How peaceful she seemed, yet sexy as hell at the same time. It took every last shred of his willpower not to go over there and take her in his arms.

He wished he were a different kind of man. He wished he could forget his promise, could ignore his obligations, could pretend that only he and Trae existed. But he wasn't, and he couldn't and that was the end of it.

Or it should be. The trouble was, ever since he'd hooked up with Trae, logic kept getting tangled up in emotion. She was right—Lucie deserved to know he loved her, but how was he supposed to show adoration when deep down he feared he'd never feel the kind of love Trae was talking about? All he could feel, all he knew, was this bone-deep longing for the wrong woman. Lucie might have brought light into his life, but Trae had filled it with color. One moment in her arms and he'd known more passion than he'd felt in all the years of loving Lucie.

And tomorrow, he'd relinquish it forever.

He slammed shut the laptop, knowing he'd never get anything done. He might have replaced the bike with the air-conditioned limo, but he was still in hell.

And it didn't look like he'd be leaving anytime soon.

"She's not here."

Staring at the bleary-eyed Bobby Boudreaux, squinting at them from inside his decrepit cabin, Trae felt too stunned to speak. All this time, she'd been gearing herself up for facing her friend, only to learn at the moment of truth that her confession would be delayed.

Rhys seemed likewise afflicted. Standing beside her on the rickety porch, he opened his mouth, then promptly shut it again when nothing came out.

Ironically enough, given the strength of his obvious hangover, only Bobby seemed capable of coherent speech. "Took off last night," he mumbled, gesturing vaguely down the bayou. "And she ain't comin' back."

"Did she say where she was going?" Rhys asked, recovering first.

"Try to think, Bobby," Trae pleaded when he shrugged

off the question. "You must have some idea where Lucie went."

Bobby shook his head. "I'd be the last one she'd tell. She's like a dream, you know? The harder you try to hold onto her, the more she slips away."

Yeah, Trae thought. She'd been noticing that about her friend.

Bobby seemed lost in the past, his red-rimmed eyes seeing beyond the dreary cabin. "She damned near took my breath away, showing up like that in Los Angeles. I mean, how many guys get a second chance? Said she wanted to be an actress, hoped I could make her a star. I tried, but Lou keeps a tight clasp on his wallet. Lucie thinks I've been moping about losing my movie deal, but hell, I saw the writing on the wall. I knew once she saw I had nothing to offer, she'd take off without looking back."

He held up a hand, clutching a rumpled piece of paper. "This is it, all I have left of her. Just this dumb note hoping we still can be friends. Friends," he snorted. "All this time, and she still has no clue how much I love her." He shook his head, sighing. "Then again, until she left, I really didn't get it myself."

He sounded so sad, so defeated, Trae had to resist the urge to reach out to him. He was right, though. He'd blown it, and wasn't likely to get a third chance.

"The note," Rhys said sharply, proving he had little time and even less patience to listen to anyone singing the blues. "Did it give any hint where she might have gone?"

Again, Bobby shook his head. "You know Lucie. That girl can rattle on forever without reaching any real point. Though she did get a call from Jo Kerrin. Maybe she went there."

"Thanks for the suggestion," Trae said, "but Jo promised to call the instant she heard from Lucie."

Rhys thrust his new cell phone in her face. "You haven't checked your messages this morning."

No, she hadn't. Taking the phone, she punched in the number. Hurrying through the five increasingly threatening calls from home, she hit pay dirt. "Lucie's here," Jo's breathless voice told her. "And she'll be staying overnight."

Replaying the message for Rhys, she watched a grim determination take over his features. "Let's go," he announced, snapping the phone shut and turning back to the sleek powerboat he'd rented.

Trae hesitated, feeling a sudden strange kinship with Bobby, wishing there was something she could to do help the man feel better. But all that came to mind was the old adage about it being better to have loved and lost, and she just couldn't see how that would provide comfort to him. Or herself, for that matter.

So all she could do was shrug and leave him standing alone in the door.

"Good luck finding Lucie," Bobby called out. "And when you do, tell her I miss her like hell already."

His words followed her through the bayou. Maybe she and Bobby had more in common than she'd thought. From the start, she'd known it couldn't last with Rhys—at first she hadn't wanted it to last—but somewhere between here and the Bahamas, she'd let herself grow accustomed to having the guy around. What was she supposed to do, come tomorrow, with no one to argue with, no one to ask for advice?

Watching Rhys maneuver the boat through the hauntingly beautiful swamp, she understood how poor Cinderella must have felt, approaching the midnight hour, knowing everything magical in her life was about to instantly vanish.

She'd never see him again, she realized. Certainly not like this, not like they'd been. It wouldn't be fair to Lucie. It wouldn't be fair to herself. Each time she faced him, each time she had to walk away, a little part of her would die inside.

Studying his profile, drinking him in, it was all Trae could do to stop herself from weeping.

Rhys followed Trae into the Kerrins' old-fashioned parlor, part of his mind admiring the fine antiques and polished oak molding, another part wondering what on earth he was going to say to Lucie. All that came to mind at the moment was, "So sorry, dear, but I've slept with your best friend and I don't think I'll ever be the able to forget the experience."

He knew he had to be honest with Lucie, but how did he accomplish that without hurting her or letting her down?

"Trae!" Lucie squealed, running across the room to hug her friend.

Standing alone in the doorway, Rhys felt a bit irked. All the time, effort and emotion he'd put into this and Lucie was more concerned with greeting Trae than her jilted fiancé?

"What are you doing here?" Lucie asked, pulling back to study her friend's face. "No, let me guess. Quinn sent you, didn't she? She wants to make sure I keep saying no."

"More or less. Listen, Luce, there's…"

"I can't. Say no, I mean. I'm meant to marry Rhys. Eventually. It's expected."

Hard not to flinch as Lucie parroted the words he'd so recently uttered. He wondered if his voice had betrayed the same lack of enthusiasm.

"Luce, I need you to focus," Trae went on firmly. "There's something Rhys and I have to tell…"

"Rhys is here?"

Rather telling, when he thought about it, that she'd failed to notice that he was in the room. Glancing around, she finally spotted him in the doorway. Her pretty face broke into another dazzling smile.

"You came to rescue me," she said with a happy sigh. "Just like always."

Funny how this time her gratitude felt like a prison sentence. "Lucie, we have to talk," he announced crisply, striding to where the two girls were standing. "Trae, will you excuse us?"

"But you promised…"

He held up a hand to stop her. Yes, he had agreed to let her talk to Lucie first, but he'd also promised to shield her when confessing to Lucie, and, in his mind, that took precedence.

Protecting Trae, he realized with a start, had become more important than saving Lucie.

"Please," he told Trae, making it clear he wouldn't take no for an answer. "Lucie and I have a lot we need to discuss. Alone."

"Oh." She looked from one to the other, her green eyes wide and vulnerable. "Oh, of course. I—I guess I can wait for you out in the hall."

Blinking rapidly, she darted from the room, closing the door behind her. It was all Rhys could do not to chase after her and take her in his arms.

But he had a responsibility here and it just wasn't in him to shirk it. "Okay, Luce," he said to the woman before him, "you and I need to do a lot of catching up."

* * *

Trae stood in the hallway, trying not to tremble, trying not to cry. No matter what lies she might try to tell herself, she'd seen the way her friend's face lit up when she spotted Rhys, how his softened in return as he approached Lucie. Clearly, Trae's glimpse into the future.

"Trae?"

Coming down the stairs behind her, Jo Kerrin could be the Madonna, serenely carrying her eleven-month-old baby like the treasure she was. "It's been so long. I can't tell you how happy I am to see you."

Stepping up to Trae, Jo wrapped her free arm around her shoulder, including the baby in her embrace. As the child gurgled, Trae caught a whiff of talcum powder and the fragrance of baby shampoo.

"And this is Jill," Jo said, holding the baby out. "Say hi to Aunt Trae, sweetie."

Trae felt herself melt as she took the baby into her arms. For the first time, she could imagine herself being the proud mama. The sudden yearning nearly buckled her knees.

Especially when she realized who she wanted the proud papa to be.

"She's absolutely beautiful, Jo," she said, handing Jill back to her mother. "Then, so are you. You look fantastic. Motherhood agrees with you."

"It does." Jo's slow smile seemed old and wise and perhaps a bit wistful. "In more ways than one. Thanks to Jill, I've finally broken free of Jimmy."

"Oh, Jo, that's great news."

She beamed. "Ten months now and I'm not ever going back. Having Jill has taught me so much." Hugging the baby, she smiled with heartbreaking tenderness. "It took me a long time but I've finally learned that real love isn't selfish. If you really care about another person, you don't make demands, don't ask them to change who they are. Jimmy and I started out loving each other, but we got so caught up in wanting the other to change that we were destroying the very thing that brought us together. After all this time, it finally dawned on me that if I really loved Jimmy, I'd just have to let him go."

"Wow."

"Yeah." Jo nodded at the parlor door. "Speaking of love, Rhys is in there with Lucie?"

A simple question, so why did it bring tears to Trae's eyes and make her suddenly unable to speak?

"Oh," Jo said at her stiff nod, her soft brown eyes going from Trae to the closed door and back to Trae again. "Oh, Trae, I'm so sorry."

"Am I that transparent?"

"Other than that heart on your sleeve, I wouldn't be able to guess anything at all."

Trae managed a rueful grin. "A mistake. We both agreed it was. In fact, I was getting ready to leave. Lucie might be the one with acting aspirations, but even I can recognize the cue for my exit."

Jo placed a comforting hand on her shoulder. "I'm hardly the expert on affairs of the heart," she said gently, "but I'm here for you if you want to talk about it."

"Thanks, but you've already put it quite succinctly." With a heavy sigh, Trae nodded at the front door. "If you love someone, sometimes you just have to let him go."

"What happened to your head?" Lucie asked, pointing to the bandage on his forehead.

"It's nothing." Rhys shrugged. "I got in a fight."

"You?" She tilted her head, clearly confused. "I've never even seen you argue."

"There's a lot about me you've never seen." Before being plunged into this madcap adventure, he'd been too intent on bottling up his emotions, sacrificing his own needs and wishes for the good of his family and business. Amazing how much his life had changed in the space of a mere week.

"Rhys, what's going on? You're starting to worry me."

"Am I?" All at once, her inability to see past her own worries was too much for him. "Don't you think it's a bit overdue? Couldn't you have shown a bit of concern when you left me at the altar?"

She winced, but it wasn't enough for Rhys. "Bad enough to leave me alone to face all those people, but you let me chase you cross-country and back, sick with worry, not knowing if you were dead in a ditch somewhere. Not a call, not an e-mail, nothing." He knew he was ranting now, but it felt good—no, necessary—to get it all off his chest. "If you must know, I'm fed up to here with being the good guy, Luce. I no longer have it in me to be calm and rational and understanding. What you did to me was wrong."

"I know," she said, biting her lip and looking away. "I'm sorry, Rhys, truly I am, but I was scared and confused and so full of doubts."

"And you think I wasn't?"

"You're never confused or doubtful," she said, sounding almost indignant. "Everything you do is according to plan."

He remembered Trae making the same accusation. For some reason, it merely made him angrier. "Yeah?" he said, for once speaking before carefully weighing each word. "You really think I *planned* to sleep with your best friend?"

Clearly stunned, she backed into the nearest chair and plopped down into it. "You…and Trae?"

Damn, this was a far cry from how he'd wanted to break it to her. Gazing down at her shocked features, a wave of tenderness overtook him. How many times had he cradled her, murmuring assurances, his mind racing with the ways he could make things right?

This time, there would be no fixing things. Whether she realized it or not, they'd both reached a fork in the road and were now headed in different directions.

Lovely little Lucie, the girl next door. But looking at her now, he realized that he'd loved her more like a sister than the woman he wanted to make his wife.

He squatted down in front of her, taking her hand, touching the engagement ring on her finger. He remembered them picking it out, he with cold, practical efficiency, Lucie distracted by a pair of pearl earrings. An expression of their love, the jeweler had called it, but eyeing the diamond, Rhys still could find nothing warm on its hard, reflective surface. "Ah, Luce, what are we doing here?"

She blinked at him, more bewildered than ever. "I—I don't know anymore. I mean, I've spent most of my life knowing we'd get married someday. Now it doesn't seem likely, does it?"

"No," he said, feeling both sad and free at the same time. "No, it doesn't. Let's face it, Luce, we don't love each other enough. Not in the way it counts to make such a long-term commitment."

She started to protest, but he put a finger on her lips. "You made a pretty clear statement when you fled from the altar. You felt trapped, you had to escape, and that's no way to start a marriage. I'm sorry, Luce, but I don't want to end up like my parents. When I get married, I want to be madly, deliriously, head-over-heels in love."

Nodding with a tearful smile, she slipped the ring from her finger and placed it in his palm. "You sound like Trae," she said with a sniff. "Did you really sleep with her?"

"It just happened, Luce. One minute we were…"

It was her turn to put a finger on his lips. "It's okay, Rhys. You don't have to explain. Actually, I'm rather happy it's Trae. I always said you two should like each other."

"Really? How could you come to that conclusion when we were barely civil to each other?"

Taking his hand, she closed his fist over the ring. "I guess even back then you two had more chemistry between you than we ever had. I can't say I'm not going to miss you, but you're right. It would never work out between us. I love you, Rhys, I always will, but it's more like the way I'd feel about a big brother. I was wrong to insist we get married. I should have released you from your promise a long time ago."

Rising to his feet, Rhys gazed down at the woman he'd almost married. For all his adult life, his every plan had centered on Lucie. She'd been his focus, the anchor of his existence, and just like that, it was over.

Funny thing, though. You'd think he'd feel lost and adrift, but all he felt was a profound sense of relief. And he understood how Lucie must have felt, running away from their wedding.

"You sure you're okay with this?" he asked her.

Smiling broadly, she stood up to kiss his cheek. "I want you to be happy. But you know," she prodded gently, "you've neglected to mention the most important thing of all. Tell me, Rhys, do you love her?"

He found himself grinning. "Madly. Deliriously. Head over heels."

"Then what are you doing wasting your time here with me?" She pushed him gently on the shoulder. "Go get her."

Chapter Fifteen

Trae stared at her computer with a sigh of satisfaction. Fifteen solid pages of her new novel. A good start, despite the interruptions, including a mandatory visit to the Andrelini household.

She smiled ruefully. Riding home on the plane, she'd come to the conclusion that if she wanted anyone to take her writing seriously, she'd have to show—not tell—them how important it was to her. So she'd gone to her parents' house, armed with her gift for CiCi, but she'd refused to stay for dinner. She had a book to write, she'd announced to her stunned family, and she meant to finish it before the end of summer vacation.

Her mother had protested—and called three times since—but Trae remained firm. Nobody said anything when Vinny had to go work at the airport, she'd insisted, or Eddie got called to a fire. Writing was her work, her calling, and if it took up her every free hour, they'd just have to learn to accept it.

Her mom had tried her usual, "But when is my only daughter ever going to get married?" Throat going tight, Trae warned her that there might never be a wedding.

How could there be? The only man Trae wanted was already taken.

Pushing away from the desk, she'd refused to get maudlin. It wasn't all bad. She was a better person for the week she'd spent with Rhys and hopefully, a better writer. And how could she begrudge him his happiness with Lucie, now that he'd finally have all that laughter to fill up the empty rooms of his house?

She wanted the man she loved to have everything he'd dreamed of—even if it was with someone else.

She had to be strong, she wanted to be brave, but darned if her eyes didn't start filling up again. Crying had become a familiar hazard in the day-and-a-half since she'd last seen him.

Dabbing at her eyes, she went into the kitchen alcove to make a bracing pot of coffee. Might as well keep working, pull an all-nighter. Wasn't as if she was looking forward to climbing into her big, empty bed alone.

"I'm sure gonna miss you, Paxton," she whispered to the wall.

As if in answer, there was a loud knock at the door.

Ripping off a paper towel, she wiped her face dry as she strode to the door. No doubt her mom had given up on the phone campaign and had sent one—or all—of her brothers to come get her. The last thing Trae wanted was their teasing, or their third degree, if they came here and caught her crying.

"It won't work anymore," she said angrily as she undid the chain, lock and two dead bolts her parents had insisted on installing. "You can march right back home and tell her I'm not going anywhere with you."

But as luck would have it, it wasn't her brothers she faced when she flung open the door. Standing on the other side was a stunned and blatantly concerned Rhys Paxton. "Lucie called you?"

"Lucie?" Rather startled herself, Trae struggled to grasp what he could mean. "Uh, no, not Lucie. I was talking about my mom. I thought she'd sent my brothers." Shaking her head to clear it, she gestured back at her computer. "I skipped Sunday dinner. I told them I had to write."

His sudden smile could have lit up the room. "Then in that case, mind if I come in?"

This did nothing to help her regain her composure. "The place is a mess," she tried to protest, but he'd already marched past her and into the living room area.

"Looks great," he said, but he wasn't looking at her tiny studio apartment.

Which, of course, flustered her more than ever. Trae was well aware of how she must appear, in her baggy sweat pants and ragged tank top, her hair haphazardly piled on her head and her eyes all puffy and red.

Then again, he seemed a little worse for wear, himself. He wore the navy suit, but it looked as if he'd slept in it. Several times. His hair had that I-just-woke-up confusion, his eyes barely focused. And his beard hadn't seen a razor in some time. Gazing at him, Trae barely refrained from blurting out, "What happened to you?"

Instead she asked the second most obvious question, "What are you doing here?"

He smiled again, lighting up the place, dwarfing it with his presence. Yeah, he might look like something the cat dragged in, but Trae had never seen anything more beautiful in her life.

"I'm here," he explained patiently, "because you left without saying goodbye and we happen to have several unresolved issues." He reached into the inside pocket of his jacket. "Number one is the check. You left it on the seat of the limo."

Angry with herself for hoping he'd come to do more than settle old debts, she took the check from him and promptly ripped it up. "Our bet might mean I have to take your money," she told him haughtily. "But nothing says I have to keep it."

"Vintage Trae." He shook his head. "Guess I'll have to find some other, more devious way to pay off that bet."

"Give it up, Paxton. I won't take your money. Let's just call it even and leave it at that."

He glanced down at the paper scattered at her feet. "That's another issue, by the way. My money. It's not who I am, Trae. I need to make that distinction."

She must have shown her confusion. Taking a step closer, he went on to explain. "You asked why I keep harping on Cancun. I thought about it long and hard the whole way here. I kept picturing us in that Mexican airport, you glaring at me like I was the enemy. The Establishment. Not a person with hopes and fears and goals of my own. Dammit, Trae, I didn't rush down there to flaunt my wealth, to lord it over you. Believe it or not, I was only trying to help."

Thinking back, Trae could see how hers might have been a bit of reverse snobbery.

"Maybe I have put too much emphasis on that incident," Rhys went on, "but let's face it, so have you. You're still defining me by my money. After this past week, I'd have hoped you could see the man I am inside."

If he only knew what she could see. Even back in college, she conceded, she'd seen enough to be afraid. From the very beginning, he'd had a strong effect on her.

"Take my money, Trae," he said, stepping up to her and pulling a second check out of his pocket. "Prove that this never again has to be an issue between us."

She stared at the check for a long, painful moment, all too aware of the finality of the moment. Once she took it from his hands, he'd be out the door and out of her life forever. Yet she also knew what it meant to him for her to accept it.

"Thanks," she said simply, putting the check on the table beside her.

"You'll cash it?"

"Yes, Paxton. I'll deposit it in my account first thing in the morning."

"Good," he said, looking relieved. "You'll need to get a dress for the wedding."

Could he be any more insensitive? He had to know how this was killing her. "I doubt I'll be going this time. Pretty tacky, really, to show up after what I did to Lucie."

"Lucie wasn't at all upset by it. She said she'll never be able to feel that way about me. To her, I'll never be more than an adored older brother."

"And you're going to marry her, anyway?"

"No, I'm not. And even if she hadn't admitted her true feelings to me, I was going to admit my true feelings to her. So, no, I wasn't talking about Lucie's wedding, I meant ours." Going serious all of a sudden, he took her by the arms and gazed deeply into her eyes. "I love you, Trae. I need to have you in my life."

Her throat felt so tight, all she could do was gape at him. "But Lucie…"

"…is determined to make her own way in life—without me."

"But the office…"

"…can do just fine. I canceled some of the meetings and left Jack to handle the rest. As you said, he needs me to be a little more trusting."

"But your business…"

"…can wait while I take care of what truly matters. I'm told that's all any woman wants from her man," he added, his gaze searching hers. "To know that she always comes first."

Trae could feel the moisture well up in her eyes. "I can't believe this."

"You'd better believe it. I just spent the most torturous eighteen hours of my life trying to get to here. Turning around, finding you gone, I've never felt so devastated. It was as if all that meant anything had suddenly gone missing."

"But we were together only a week."

"But in that time, you became my world. You made me laugh, coaxed me into taking chances, showed me how life has so many more colors than black and white. I never realized how contained I'd been, how stifled, until you showed me passion."

His words resonated in her heart. He was right; they'd packed more into seven days than some people managed in a lifetime.

"I know it sounds corny, but you really do complete me." Smiling tenderly, he wiped the tears from her cheeks. "Isn't it ironic? I'm more accustomed to being needed by everyone in my life. It's not easy coping with the fact that I need someone else. I can't make it without you. Please say you'll marry me."

Trae's head was spinning. "I love you, Rhys, more than I thought possible, but how can it last? My haphazard way of doing things is bound to drive you crazy, and we both know I'll never back down from your ultimatums."

"We'll compromise. We don't have to get married right away if your pact is so important to you. We can live here, or at my place, or even both until you're ready. Whatever you want, as long as we're together."

It seemed too good to be true. Rhys, here before her, saying all the things she'd dreamed of and more. No wonder she couldn't trust her emotions. "I just don't think…"

"No more thinking," he said firmly, putting his arms around her and pulling her closer. "Start feeling instead. I'm willing to bet we can find some way we'll both be happy."

"Another bet?" she asked, snuggling closer, feeling as if her heart had just taken flight. "You got anything to offer as collateral?"

Taking her hand, he laid it on his chest. "My heart," he told her tenderly, then proceeded to prove that this time, he was going to win the wager.

"Give it up, Trae," he said after kissing her thoroughly. "Just say yes."

And six months later, after finally selling her first book… Trae did just that.

* * * * *

Silhouette®

Desire

When Kimberley Blackstone's father is presumed dead, Kimberley is required to take over the helm of Blackstone Diamonds. She has to work closely with her ex, Ric Perrini, to battle not only the press, but also the fierce attraction still sizzling between them. Does Ric feel the same...or is it the power her share of Blackstone Diamonds will provide him as he battles for boardroom supremacy.

Look for

VOWS &
A VENGEFUL GROOM

by

BRONWYN
JAMESON

Available January wherever you buy books

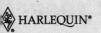

REQUEST YOUR FREE BOOKS!
2 FREE NOVELS PLUS 2 FREE GIFTS!

SPECIAL EDITION®
Life, Love and Family!

YES! Please send me 2 FREE Silhouette Special Edition® novels and my 2 FREE gifts. After receiving them, if I don't wish to receive any more books, I can return the shipping statement marked "cancel." If I don't cancel, I will receive 6 brand-new novels every month and be billed just $4.24 per book in the U.S., or $4.99 per book in Canada, plus 25¢ shipping and handling per book and applicable taxes, if any*. That's a savings of at least 15% off the cover price! I understand that accepting the 2 free books and gifts places me under no obligation to buy anything. I can always return a shipment and cancel at any time. Even if I never buy another book from Silhouette, the two free books and gifts are mine to keep forever.

235 SDN EEYU 335 SDN EEY6

Name	(PLEASE PRINT)	
Address		Apt.
City	State/Prov.	Zip/Postal Code

Signature (if under 18, a parent or guardian must sign)

Mail to the Silhouette Reader Service™:
IN U.S.A.: P.O. Box 1867, Buffalo, NY 14240-1867
IN CANADA: P.O. Box 609, Fort Erie, Ontario L2A 5X3

Not valid to current Silhouette Special Edition subscribers.

Want to try two free books from another line?
Call 1-800-873-8635 or visit www.morefreebooks.com.

* Terms and prices subject to change without notice. NY residents add applicable sales tax. Canadian residents will be charged applicable provincial taxes and GST. This offer is limited to one order per household. All orders subject to approval. Credit or debit balances in a customer's account(s) may be offset by any other outstanding balance owed by or to the customer. Please allow 4 to 6 weeks for delivery.

Your Privacy: Silhouette is committed to protecting your privacy. Our Privacy Policy is available online at www.eHarlequin.com or upon request from the Reader Service. From time to time we make our lists of customers available to reputable firms who may have a product or service of interest to you. If you would prefer we not share your name and address, please check here. ☐

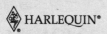

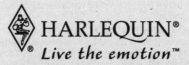

COMING NEXT MONTH

SSECNM1207